CONFEDERATE CAVALRYMAN
Nick Hardeman

A novel

Nick Hardeman

CONFEDERATE CAVALRYMAN

A Novel

by

Major Benjamin Hord, CSA

HERITAGE BOOKS
2019

HERITAGE BOOKS

AN IMPRINT OF HERITAGE BOOKS, INC.

Books, CDs, and more—Worldwide

For our listing of thousands of titles see our website
at
www.HeritageBooks.com

Published 2019 by
HERITAGE BOOKS, INC.
Publishing Division
5810 Ruatan Street
Berwyn Heights, Md. 20740

*By arrangement with the estate of
Benjamin Hord.*

Cover design created using a photo by
David Mark from Pixabay and a silhouette image by
OpenClipart-Vectors from Pixabay

International Standard Book Number
Paperbound: 978-0-7884-5898-9

FOREWORD

Major Benjamin Hord, CSA wrote this novel sometime between 1865 and 1922 when he died. Since then his manuscript lay unpublished among his family's records until this year of publication.

In it, he develops a fascinating and curious tale of a young cavalryman's service during the Civil War, mostly in Missouri. It is an eyewitness depiction of the battles and skirmishes in which he fought. Hord uses his family's experiences during the war and those of his friend Nick Hardeman, as the setting for the story. Because he wrote his book over one hundred and twenty years ago, his engaging Victorian style lends unusual authenticity to the cavalry actions, as it does to the whole tale.

Benjamin Hord began his freshman year at the University of North Carolina at Chapel Hill in 1860. He met Nick Hardeman, an upper classman, who became his friend and protector during the hazing endured by most freshman. When war broke out a year later, they volunteered to join the First North Carolina Regiment and served in an early battle at Big Bethel below Yorktown, Virginia; then they were sent west to different armies.

Long after the war ended, the University of North Carolina presented diplomas to thirteen surviving students who failed to graduate because they had left to join the Confederate army. Major Hord was seventy years old by then, and had written this newly discovered novel.

Frank Boensch, MD, *great grandson of Benjamin Hord*
2019

CHAPTER I

I ENTER COLLEGE.

Walker DeJean Hardeman was his name. There could be no mistake about this. It was so recorded in the Family Bible - not one of those old family bibles covered with mould and mystery that we so often read of, but a fresh new volume stoutly bound in calfskin suggestive of a newly married couple, and the stout binding of long service in holding birth records of a numerous family - but at the time of which I write "WALKER DEJEAN HARDEMAN, October 4th, 1837," was the only name recorded in it.

In addition to this evidence as to his name, this same chubby black-eyed baby, some five or six months after the above date, was christened in the old ivy clad Cathedral that in those days stood fronting Jackson Square. When the venerable Bishop, richly clad in his official robes, asked, "Who gives this child to God and by what name?" Colonel Lewis Hardeman and his beautiful creole wife, Catherine DeJean, replied, "We, his parents, and his name is Walker DeJean Hardeman." When the holy man asked, "Who stands as Godfather for the babe?" A tall young man between 25 and 30 years of age, whose broad shoulders and erect figure gave him a military air, and whose handsome face bore a striking resemblance to the young mother, stepped from behind the couple, and lifting the little bundle of humanity enveloped in lace and embroidery from the arms of the negro nurse answered, "I, Walker DeJean, am Godfather for the babe."

I am particular in giving these details as to the name of Hardeman, because at the time this story opens in September 1859, there were not fifty out of the five hundred students then attending the University of North Carolina at Chapel Hill who either knew or called him by this proper name, not withstanding he was the most popular man at the University, for "Nick" Hardeman, as he was called, had as many friends and admirers amongst the freshmen and lower classes as with the seniors, of which he was at that time a member.

Although christened in the old cathedral at New Orleans, Nick was a Texan by birth and residence. His eyes first opened to the light of day in the pretty old town of San Antonio and almost in the shadow of the walls of the historic Alamo. As a sturdy little barefooted urchin he had played hide-and-seek amid the rubbish and ruins of the old fort. When he had grown old enough to understand, his father told him not only the history of the ruins, the heroic deaths of Travis, Bowie, Crockett and its glorious other defenders, most of whom he knew personally, but also the history of his state. He recounted her brave struggle with Mexico in which he had borne a conspicuous part, and the great achievements of her little army under Houston, until the lad's heart glowed with love and pride for his state and her gallant defenders.

It was at the University of North Carolina I first met Hardeman. I was not only a freshman, but a very fresh specimen of that proscribed set. Born and reared on a farm in Tennessee. I had never more than a half dozen times been outside of my county and never beyond the limits of my state until I went to Chapel Hill. I was fairly well advanced in my studies, having attended a good military school in my county town with a view of entering West Point. At the last moment, however, my dear maternal Grandmother, who had exercised a mother's care over my sisters and myself after the death of our mother, changed her mind. Instead it was decided to send me to the University of North Carolina. I well remember the evening this decision was reached. My father and grandmother were sitting on the front porch, he with his pipe smoking and she with some light needle work in her lap rocking to and fro, occasionally letting her beautiful brown eyes, still bright as a girl's, despite her seventy years, rest thoughtfully on me and then turn to watch the expression on my father's face.

"So you have at the last moment changed your mind, Madam, and don't want him to enter West Point", he said, resuming a conversation my appearance had evidently interrupted.

"Yes, I think, all things considered, it will be best to send him to Chapel Hill."

There was a moment's pause, and then turning his head so as to conceal a slight smile that for an instant lit up his usually stern face said, "I am sure, Madam, it is not that you fear he has no material in him to make a good soldier that influenced your decision in this matter."

He had intentionally touched a sensitive spot of the dear old lady's heart, and from his quiet smile evidently knew what was coming.

Her brown eyes opened wide and sparkled with mingled pride and indignation.

"I am surprised, Sir, knowing the history of my family as you do that you should even intimate that any one who carries one drop of my father's blood in their veins should fail to make a gallant soldier or -"

"My father, Sir, as you well know -"

"Yes, Madam, "interrupted my father, knowing he had opened up the strong suit of the old lady and that she would most likely go on for hours giving the history and genealogy of her family, "I know your distinguished father, Captain William Lytle, was on the staff in the field directly under the eyes of General Washington, and that his beautiful and accomplished daughter when she was a little miss," bowing to her again most courteously, "danced a cotillion with the 'Father of his country:' therefore I am perfectly willing for her to decide as to where her grandson shall get the most of his education."

"Thank you," she said, wonderfully softened at the compliment paid her, for a women never gets so old but that well turned compliment on her youthful beauty is appreciated.

"One reason I am so anxious he should go to Chapel Hill is to have him get acquainted with some of my husband's family, his McCulloch kin-"

"Yes I know the, Madam," interrupted my father, "Wealthy, influential and all that, but nothing of this kind will help the boy in his studies."

"But, Sir, you must consider the social advantages."

"You do not apprehend any danger to his health I hope from over application to his books while taking a social course of study at the same time." The irony with which he spoke and the downward curve of his mouth escaped the attention of my little grandmother.

"Oh, I hope not; he must guard against that; although he told me that by hard work and close application he stood first in two of his classes at the Military Academy." I could feel the blood surge to my face as my father gave a quick, sharp glance at me, then at my grandmother.

"So I have heard, Madam,," he replied, "and if you intend him for a soldier he might on certain occasions find one of his accomplishments - fast running - quite as useful as the other would be if he should turn his attention to prize-fighting. But I leave the matter entirely with you. Make such arrangement for his departure as your think necessary."

Rising from his chair, and knocking the ashes from his pipe, he turned into the house, remarking more to himself than to her, "I fear the boy will find in the near future more need for a military education than he will for either a social or literary one for we are fast approaching a crisis on the slavery question - God grant it be a bloodless one!"

"Your father is in one of his despondent moods this evening," she said as we listened to his receding footsteps in the hall.

"He has been so for several days, grandmother," I replied. I was glad to divert her attention from my "accomplishments" he had referred to for in truth I was not specially fond of my books, and at the close of our session at the Academy, when the dear lady had asked me how I stood, I told her I was first in two of my classes, but was careful not to say what classes they were. I had the medal of my class as the best sprinter for a hundred and fifty yards and stood No. 1 in the boxing class, much to the gratification of old Doyle, our professor, who said I only needed a little more "reach in the arm" to make me an expert.

How clear was my father's vision concerning the coming strife, and how distinctly his words were recalled to my memory only a few years later when a soldier I was following the starry crossed battle flag of the Confederacy.

Thus it was that at the age of 16 I went to Chapel Hill, a very fresh Freshman, and sadly deficient in worldly knowledge.

Much to my secret delight, my tailor was instructed by my grandmother to add an evening dress coat to my wardrobe. "You need not mention this to your father. He has some peculiar ideas about such things for young gentlemen of your age. I will explain it when the bills are sent in after your have left," she said in a confidential tone as we left the shop. This arrangement met my unqualified approval.

Knowing something of the "peculiar ideas" referred to, it is not necessary to say that this cherished article of dress after leaving the hands of the tailor was never exposed to the light of day except to my own and to my grandmother's admiring eyes, until I was comfortably established in my rooms in the little village of Chapel Hill, when my opinion of her wisdom and forethought in the matter was at once confirmed by seeing it was a part of the everyday wearing apparel of a majority of the students, but I was soon to learn why the silent minority, the Freshmen, did not indulge in this costume.

At the time of which I write the fashion of wearing dress coats, or "spikes" as the students called them, prevailed with all professional men and largely in commercial circles. The students of course were by no means slow in following that fashion, but it was an unwritten law of the sophomore class at Chapel Hill that no student while a member of the freshman class should be allowed to wear a "spike" on the University grounds. Hazing was never carried to the extent in any southern university that it was, and is yet in the North, but there were certain rules a freshman dare not transgress. Liberties the higher classes could indulge in, but which under no circumstances could he presume to take without being made to pay the penalty in some way most mortifying and humiliating to his pride.

CHAPTER II

I AM INTRODUCED TO NICK HARDEMAN.

The circumstances under which I first became acquainted with Hardeman were not altogether marked by the pleasant courtesies usual in forming new acquaintances, but what they lacked in this respect was more than made up for by this lively - I might say marked impression - made on both my mind and body on that occasion.

It was a bright afternoon in the latter part of September, some two or three weeks after I had entered the University. The bell on the old chapel was calling the various classes to their 3 o'clock recitations. Owing to the large number of students and the insufficiency of room in the college buildings, many of them like myself had secured lodgings in the village. All the walks leading up through the college grounds to the recitation rooms were thickly sprinkled with students, singly and in groups, hurrying to their respective classes. I was a little late, having paid more than usual attention to dressing, as I had decided to appear for the first time in my evening coat, and was hurrying up the walk alone when I heard a shrill cry behind me of "Fresh with a spike on," which was echoed and re-echoed from all parts of the grounds. Neither had I ever heard the term "spike" applied to this article of dress and consequently paid no attention to the cries, but hurried on to my recitation room which I reached just in time to avoid a rush, which I did not understand, from a half dozen or more Sophomores.

My classmates were all seated when I entered, and had I appeared divested of half my clothing I could not have caused greater surprise or consternation, mingled with surpressed laughter. Looking around for an explanation I even detected a smile lurking around the mouth of our tutor as he bade me take a seat. I was not left long in ignorance of the gravity of the offense I had committed against the customs of the University, or the yells of the Sophomores that had greeted me as I was walking trough the grounds. A number of my classmates found opportunity during our recitation hour to inform me fully on the matter, each one intimating with a broad grin as to what humiliation I would be subjected to at the hands of the sophomores as soon as I appeared outside of the room. So when the bell tapped announcing all recitations over, I was undecided whether to trust to my accomplishment as a "sprinter" and make a break for my rooms in the village, or to assume a lofty air and treat any undue familiarity or rudeness with dignified contempt. The question was decided for me in a few moments. I had not taken a dozen steps from the door before again the cries of "Fresh with a spike on" filled the air from half a hundred throats, and the next moment I was surrounded by as dense a crowd of hooting, yelling, laughing young devils as ever made a freshman heart-sick for home. No band of wild Indians ever exhibited more fiendish delight over a captive, and no captive ever felt more helpless.

"Out of that coat, Fresh," shouted a half dozen.

"Yes, and out of it quick; 'Baby-Buntin and we'll set a rabbit skin to wrap the baby up in'" sang out another. There was nothing left for me now but to try the dignified dodge, so folding my arms and drawing myself up, I began -

"Gentlemen -"

"Oh hear! hear! they shouted, "Listen to the mocking-bird."

"Shut up your fly-trap and haul off your spike - we are going to make you take it out of this grounds on a pole," said a big red-headed fellow.

"But gentlemen -" I began.

"Butt your brains out if you like, but off with the spike."

"And be quick about it, my little dandy, or we will make you take off your pants also," said my red-headed friend.

Just then some one crushed my hat down over my eyes. Wheeling around to see who it was, my arms flew out and were instantly seized by two of the boys who tried to strip off the offending coat. I succeeded in shaking them off, but the next instant two others, one on either side, had caught the tails and pulled them over my head and shoulders. In my efforts to free myself my beloved spike was split up the back to the collar. I heard the rip and knew what had happened.

Blind with rage, as well as by the tails of my coat which were drawn over my face, I struck out viciously and hit some one - I could not see who, for at that instant my feet were knocked from under me and with a boy holding each leg they were dragging me on my back at a lively trot down the gravel walk surrounded by the crowd cheering lustily and to their immense satisfaction and pleasure, judging from the roars of laughter, when they suddenly came to a halt and I heard someone say, "Hold on boys, you are most too rough with him."

"Get out of the way, Nick, he is our meat," a half dozen shouted.

"That's all right boys, you know I am with you" replied the first speaker, "but you are carrying this a little too far, - don't you think so?"

"No, no, we are going to cart him and his spike off the grounds as he refused to carry it out on a pole. Get out of the way!"

While this conversation was going on I made repeated efforts to regain my feet only to be again whirled over on my back.

"Let's talk a little about it first," said the one they call Nick, and without waiting for a reply he pressed in between the boys holding my ankles and caught the wrist of each, evidently with a grip like an iron vise, for the fingers of each flew open as if they had been holding live coals. In an instant I was on my feet and without ceremony hit the nearest man to me. In turn I received a stinging blow on the side of my head from someone and another in my ribs from a different source. I shot out my fist again at a chubby little fellow I suspected had hit me, but quick as a flash Nick caught the blow on his arm, grasped me firmly by the wrist with one hand, at the same time skillfully warding off with his other arm in the blows aimed at me.

"Stop boys! Stop! Just for a moment. Fair play, you know, is a jewel. You certainly are not all going to pounce on this poor little devil at once," he said, as they paused to hear what he had to say. "Why there is not a man in your class but that can do him up. He's not as big as a pound of soap and is half dead with fright already - Just look at him!"

As he said this he held me out at arm's length from him as easily as if I had been a child, not withstanding my efforts to get loose. The sight certainly was ludicrous - my coat was in shreds - my long hair, which was strictly the style in those days, was standing up on the back of my head, which in scraping along the ground had accumulated a liberal supply of sand and trash in addition to a number of sharp gravel that were sticking in my scalp. My hands were bleeding from cuts received from stones and shrubs that I had clutched at frantically while they were carting me along on my back, my face also was slightly scratched in one or two places, and a very perceptible bump was beginning to show itself on the side of my head that had caught the blow someone had dealt me. The sight I presented seemed to make a complete change in the feelings of my tormentors from anger to mirth, and Nick himself could not refrain from joining in the laugh at my appearance as he still help me off at arm's length in his iron grasp. The ridicule was worse than their anger and increased my wrath tenfold.

"I can whip your whole damn class and two at a time," I shouted, shaking my loose fist under the nose of my big red-headed friend who was nearest to me and seemed almost convulsed with laughter.

"It's a go. Start in on me," he answered as soon as he could stop laughing.

"Turn him loose, Nick," said a half dozen at once. "He shall have a fair chance."

"Freshy," said Nick, addressing me while still holding my wrist, "you had better put the coat on a pole and carry it out of the campus as they tell you to. It is customary here if a Freshman presumes to wear a spike on the college grounds for the Sophs to make him do this.

"I'll die first," I answered.

"All right, Freshy, but I warn you in advance that you have undertaken a big contract and are going to get a terrible beating. Give him room boys and a fair chance."

If I had not been enraged beyond all reason I might have listened to Nick's advice, but being free and on my feet again a bit more of heart came into me. I held back my arms and the fragments of my spike fell off. As I stood in my shirtsleeves I felt something of the old confidence that I had when, thus stripped, I stood in the boxing room of our old Military Academy. My antagonist stood laughing at the wreck of my coat.

"Save your mirth for another time," I said, "Are you ready?"

"Yes, in a moment. Here, Tom, hold my books a second. We will wrap this little fellow up in the tails of his spike and carry him out in a wheelbarrow."

I threw up my guard as he stepped forward and waited a move on his part that would give me some idea as to his skill. The first pass he made told me as plainly as if he had spoken the words that he knew nothing of the sport, so it was only a question with me where and when to hit him - the opportunity came inside of ten seconds. I made a feint with my left hand. He threw up his arm to ward the blow and I drove my right fist under it, straight from my shoulder, and landed full on his cheek bone. Had there been room he would have fallen to the ground, but was caught by one of the boys standing in the close ring around us.

"By Jove! Did you see that? Bully for the Freshy!" I heard a voice behind me exclaim that I recognized as Nick's. It was the only word of encouragement that had a touch of sympathy in it that had I heard and it was like a stimulant to me. My blood was up and I was playing at my own game, and on the impulse of the moment I shouted out, "Pass me up another, and try to pick me out a better one this time."

Let me at him," exclaimed a tall thin visaged fellow elbowing his way up.

"No, no, me, me," exclaimed a half dozen others as they pressed up close around me. It looked as if I was going to have decidedly more than I could conveniently attend to when the strong arm of Nick Hardeman was again thrust in front of me pressing back the crowd.

"Hold up, boys, hold up - remember you promised him a fair chance>'

"Then I'm the man for him! Out of the way boys." The speaker pushed his way through the crowd and stood in the little ring before me. He was a good looking, trimly built youngster about my size and weight, but his bright handsome face was disfigured by a badly swollen mouth from which the blood was still trickling, showing the hurt had just been received.

"Ah," thought I, as he pressed his handkerchief to his lips to staunch the blood, "You are the duck that caught my unexpected blow on your mouth when you had the tails of my coat over my head so I could not see - Very well, now I will give you another with my eyes open - if I can," I mentally added, for he had thrown down his handkerchief, divested himself of this coat and cuffs and while turning back his shirtsleeves stood eyeing me from head to foot in a way that satisfied me he knew what he was about.

"Better let some one else try him, Dick," said Hardeman laughing, it seems he already left his mark on you."

"That's just the reason I am going to leave mine on him and it won't be an accident like this was," pointing to his swollen mouth.

"All right, my boy, but I'll tell you beforehand he may be a freshman in his books, but he is in your class when it comes to boxing, judging from the way he punched Doss just now, and you know I am something of a judge in such matters."

"Thank you for your caution, Nick, but if he knows more about the game than I do, let him take the trick. Get out of the way, boys, and give me room," he answered without once taking his eyes off of me.

"Ready?"

The word had scarcely passed his lips when he attacked me fast and furious. Hedged in as I was in a close little ring it required all my skill to protect myself from his quick and vicious leads. We had been a minute or perhaps a little more and he had not succeeded in landing a blow of any consequence; having baffled every effort he made to get inside my guard gave me confidence. I had been acting entirely on the defensive but now began to force the fight and look for an opening myself, when some one shouted;

"Old Tigs! Look out boys, here comes old Tigs!"

The cry evidently startled and disconcerted my antagonist. For an instant only his eyes wavered from mine, but it was long enough for us to thrust out my left arm and land a light blow on his chin. To my great astonishment he jumped back, stooped down, picked up his coat and cuffs and hat, and saying "another time" darted away as fast as his legs could carry him.

For this first time since I had been surrounded by my tormentors I had leisure to look around me. To say I was amazed at the sight but mildly expresses it. The boys had scattered and were running at top speed in all directions, some down the walks towards the village, some across the grounds, others disappearing around the building, while a few were dodging and hiding in the shrubbery.

There is not feeling that can be communicated quicker, either in man or beast, than fear. I have seen a thousand cattle lying down at night perfectly quiet and apparently asleep, stampeded instantly by the popping of a match struck by the herdsman to light his pipe, go tearing across the prairie trampling to death anything in the way of their wild rush. And I've seen a brigade of as good soldiers as ever stood the shock of battle thrown into a panic by the galloping of a horse and the accidental discharge of a gun.

As I looked at the crowd of boys fleeing in every direction as if their lives depended on their escape, I knew something dreadful had happened or was about to happen, and that indescribable feeling of fear began to take possession of me. I had heard the cry "Old Tige! Look out boys, here comes old Tige" and in an instant it flashed through my mind that there must be a "zoo" connected with the University and that the tiger had escaped or that a dangerous, vicious dog called "Tige" had broken from his kennel and was ready to pounce upon any one in sight. All of this flashed on my mind in an instant and I was about to follow the crowd at my best sprinting speed when, glancing over my shoulder to see how near the thing, whatever it might be, was to me, I saw Hardeman standing close by convulsed with laughter.

"What is it? Where is it? I asked hurriedly, but feeling somewhat assured by his presence. Before he would answer I heard some one say in a loud and rather harsh tone;

"Mr. Hardeman, I am surprised, I am astonished sir. Is it possible that I find you, a member of the Senior Class, engaged in a fight and within the limits of the University grounds?"

I turned and saw approaching us a well formed man about 40 or 45 years of age, with a strong stern face covered with a closely trimmed beard, and holding by the hand a lad 7 or 6 years old. Having come out of one of the walks concealed by shrubbery he was quite near us before he was discovered. As soon as he could suppress his laughter, Hardeman bowed respectfully to him.

"Pardon me, Professor, but you are mistaken - I've not been engaged in fighting. On the contrary I have been acting the part of peacemaker and the good Samaritan to this freshman, whom I do not even know, by taking him out of the hands of the Philistines."

"Ah, then he has been fighting, has he?"

"I did not say that, sir. Some of the boys were having a little sport at his expense. I happened to be passing by and thought they were most too rough and was trying to persuade them to stop, but the sight of you had more influence than my than my presence or persuasion."

"Why do you call such rowdies my boys, Mr. Hardeman? Am I responsible for every rough character in the school!" - and the old fellow's checks flushed with anger.

"Not at all, sir, I did not mean that, but my impression is these were sophomores and I believe you have that class in French, and at the same time you try to teach them good behavior. They evidently appreciate your efforts in this direction for they fled as from the wrath to come as soon as they caught sight of you."

"Since you are so well informed concerning these young men I will ask you to give me the names of those engaged in this rough sport that you speak of," and taking a little notebook and pencil out of his pocket he prepared to write them down.

"You will have to excuse me there, Professor," said Hardeman smiling pleasantly. "While I know a great many of the Sophomore Class by sight my memory is very defective as to names."

"At times no doubt," said the old gentleman with the least bit of sarcasm.

"At times undoubtedly," replied Hardeman in the same tone.

The two stood looking squarely into each other's eyes. There was a gleam of anger in the professor's. He knew from Hardeman's evasive answer and the steady look in his black eyes that be intended to protect the boys from punishment by not giving in their names.

"You can at least tell me what you saw of this rough sport as you call it. Perhaps your memory is better on that than it is on names."

"Very much better, Professor, and I will tell you with pleasure," said Hardeman.

"After recitation I saw a crowd of boys over here who appeared to be having a good deal of fun over something. I walked over to see what is was and found they had this freshman by the heels dragging him down the walk. The freshy did not seem to be enjoying it as much as the others, so I prevailed upon them to stop and we were just settling the matter in a most satisfactory manner in all parties, especially to the Fresh, when you made your appearance, and the boys, from some cause, scattered and disappeared like a covey of birds when a hawk is around."

"What is your name, sir?" asked the old gentleman turning to me.

"Hord, sir, "Where are you from, Hord, and how long have you been here?"

"I came about three weeks ago, I live in Tennessee."

"Freshman Class, I suppose."

"Yes, sir."

"Why were they dragging you down the walk?"

"Because I refused to pull off my coat and carry it off the college grounds on a pole."

I thought I could detect the faintest glimmer of a smile in the deep set bluish gray eyes of the professor as I made this reply. I might however have been mistaken in this, but there was no mistake in the audible snicker of this little chap he was holding by the hand.

"Where is your coat, sir," he asked.

I looked around but could not see it.

"Here it is sir, or what is left of it," said Hardeman stepping to one side and picking up what looked to be a bundle of rags, and holding it up so as to show the wreck to the greatest disadvantage. In the melee it had been trampled upon so that the tailor who had made it could scarcely tell what it had been.

"Shameful, disgraceful, outrageous," said the old fellow as Hardeman held the garment up before him.

"This conduct shall be stopped if we have to expel the entire Sophomore Class. Give me the names of the students who committed this outrage," he said as he prepared to write them down in the little book he still held in his hand.

There are times when one can feel the object of the closest scrutiny without being able to explain why. When the professor asked me for the names of the students I could feel that Hardeman was looking at me intently. My first angry impulse was to give the names of the three or four I happened to know in the crowd, but my instinct said "no" - and having just heard Hardeman evade this question I determined to follow his lead, so I promptly answered.

"I've only been in college a short time and know but very few member os the sophomore class. I do not know who tore my coat or who was dragging me." This was literally true, fro the tails of my coat were drawn over my face when it was torn, and I was in such a position when they were carting me along that I could not see who was holding my legs. I did happen to know the names of the two boys I had fought, but as he had been thrown clear off the track concerning this fights by the evasions of Hardeman, he made no inquiry about fighting, After having me account for my cut hands and scratched face he made me give him my full name and location in the village, and bowing stiffly to Hardeman gave me a slight nod, and taking the hand of the lad he continued his walk.

"Who is that?" I asked my companion as my eyes followed the erect figure of the old gentleman.

"Why, Freshy, don't you know? Is it possible you have been here three weeks and don't know "Old Tige'?"

I confessed my ignorance but remarked that I was very much relieved when I discovered "Old Tige" was a man and not a vicious beast of some kind as I was led to believe from the way the boys had scattered. I explained to Hardeman that I was about to follow them when I discovered that he was still with me.

"Why, Freshy, that is Professor Smith, a member of the faculty, a man of the most irascible temper on the top side of the earth, and knowing this the Sophomores, who recite French to him, make his life a burden. He is a thorough gentleman however, straight as a post in every respect, and, outside of his duties as a member of the faculty, a genial old fellow as you ever met; but he is radical in his views and when he takes up an idea there is no wavering in him. His latest fad is to stop hazing, and he will sit up a week without a wink of sleep to catch some poor soph indulging in this time honored custom. That little tot you see trotting by his side is his son Hoke and as full of devilment as a young mule. He and I are great chums."

Neither Hardeman or I ever dreamed that his chum, the "little tot" as he called him would in future years be an important Cabinet officer to a President of the United States.

But which way are you going, and what about this coat?" he asked.

The mention of my coat caused my wrath to kindle anew but as I looked at Hardeman, standing with his arms outstretched, a tattered tail in either hand, the mirth that twinkled in his black eyes and handsome face was so contagious that in spite of myself I could not help but join in.

It was the first opportunity that I had of taking more than a hurried glance at my new acquaintance. A half century has passed since then, and time has silvered my head with gray, yet in the twilight of life I love to look back and see Nick Hardeman as I saw him that bright September evening. I can see a young man 22 years old, dark skin, but so clear and fine in texture you could almost see the rich blood coursing beneath it in his cheeks; a straight nose and nostrils as thin and delicately cut as a woman's. A light jet black moustache that shaded his upper lip made his fine even teeth, when he smiled, look whiter by the contrast. It was a bright, brave, handsome face, one that would inspire confidence in a child, respect in a man, and admiration in a woman. But handsome as it was, to one drilled in the athletic department of a military school as I had been - form and figure - man and muscle - were first in my thoughts, and never had I looked upon a more perfect specimen of physical manhood than now stood before me. He was very near six feet in height, but owing to his symmetrical proportions, scarcely looked so tall. Contrary to the prevailing custom he did not have on the conventional spike, but was clad in a suit of light gray flannel cut close to his figure, as was the custom in those days. His hands were large and strong but as shapely and looked as well kept as woman's. The only defect my critical eyes could find in his make up was the slender feet with their arched instep - they looked too small for a man of his size.

For a moment we stood silently looking at each other, he with an amused expression on his face and I with open admiration in mine. As I looked up he said, smiling pleasantly and extending his hand,

"So your name is Hord and you are from Tennessee. Our names are something alike, mine is Hardeman, and as my grandfather came from Tennessee, we might claim acquaintance, although I am from Texas."

"I am glad to know you, Mr. Hardeman, and thank you for interposing just now in my behalf."

"I know how to sympathize with you from the fact that I had some experience very much like it myself when I cam here a freshman three years ago, but not quite so expensive in wearing apparel. This coat looks as if it was new."

I had never worn it before."

However, you might keep it as a souvenir," he said laughingly as he handed me the bundle. "If you are going down to your rooms and do not object, I will walk with you." My quarters are just beyond yours."

Throwing the remnants to my beloved spike across my arm and remarking to my companion it was at least more satisfactory to carry it that way than on a pole, we started for the village. For a moment or two we walked along in silence. I could feel that my companion was again scrutinizing me closely. Presently he asked,

"Did you know the name of any of those Soph that were hazing you?"

"Yes, several of them," I replied.

"Then why didn't you give them to old Tige when he asked you?"

"Why didn't you when he asked you?:

"Oh, I'm a member of the Senior Class and it would not have been proper in me."

And I did not think it would be proper in a Freshman."

"Why not?" he asked.

"Because a Freshman, even if he is not allowed to wear a coat like a Senior, can at least have some of his instincts."

"Well answered, Freshy, and I like you all the better for not giving the boys away. But where did you learn to box?"

He gave a merry laugh. I looked up inquiringly.

"I cannot help laughing when I think of how you surprised Dick Blanchard. Dick was the chap before you when old Tige came on the scene. He was just confident of pounding you in a half minute from the time he threw off his coat as he ever was of anything earthly, and so was I, for he is by far the best man in his class and one of the best in the University with gloves."

"Is he as good as you?"

"How do you know I box?"

"I heard you tell Blanchard you were a judge and cautioned him before he attacked me."

"No, Dick is not quite up to my mark. I taught him all he knows last year when he was a Freshman. He is a splendid fellow. You must get acquainted with him. I would like to see a boxing bout between you."

"Not until he gets in a better humor than he was this afternoon and the memory of this gets a little older," I said, pointing to my coat.

"Right," he said, laughing, "There must not be bad blood between you; but you can come down to the 'ranch' and take a turn with me. I will be glad to have you any evening. Perhaps I can show you something that will interest you," and blowing pleasantly he walked off leaving me at the door of my room.

CHAPTER III

I VISIT THE RANCH

Hardeman's rooms were on the outskirts of the little village in a large two-story frame building. He with a number of other members of his class had rented the building, hired a cook and a janitor, and each man contributed each month to defray the general expenses of the establishment, but furnishing his own rooms to suit his individual taste and means. The building had been dubbed "The Ranch" by Hardeman, who occupied three rooms on the first floor. My first visit to the ranch, a few days after the incidents mentioned in the last chapter, gave me some inside knowledge as to how some of the occupants spent a portion of their presumably valuable time. Not knowing on which side of the hall Hardeman's rooms were located, I was hesitating in front of the closed door, when I heard some one within say:

"I'll see it and raise you ten."

There was a pause and I took occasion to knock, thinking if this was not Hardeman's room I could inquire where to find it. There was no response to my knock, but I heard a general hustling a quick moving about in the room, then a silence. I was just preparing to repeat my knock when I heard a deep voice in a serious and argumentative tone say,

"I tell you, gentleman, it is useless to discuss the matter further. This history of Greece alone proves my position correct on this question."

While the speaker was thus appealing to ancient history to support them I fancied I heard a key turn softly in the lock, and Hardeman opened the door. He grasped my hand with a look of surprise as he exclaimed,

"Why, is it you? Come right in freshy, you are at the right place; but bless my soul boy, how you frightened us!?

"Burglar?"

"Oh, no, worse than that," he replied laughingly. "Burglars don't usually announce their arrival by knocking. You see 'Old Bull' went by here half an hour ago taking his evening constitutional and" -

"I see - You thought the beast had changed his mind and charged with his horns down into the hall."

"Not exactly," said Hardeman laughing. "When I tell you that 'Old Bull' is member of the faculty you will think that we have a regular menagerie of professors, but 'Old Bull', and 'Old Tige' whom you met the other day, are the only two that can claim this distinction in nomenclature. 'Old Bull', properly speaking, is Professor Phillips, an Englishman by birth, hence his title, 'Johnnie Bull', and as genial an old gentleman as you ever met. He lectures only to our class, the Seniors, and frequently drops in on me to have a quiet smoke, a game of cribbage, and occasionally a turn with the gloves, for he is passionately fond of his national sport, boxing, and has taught me several cunning tricks, after batting my nose a time or two."

Relocking the door, he turned to three other young men who were sitting around the table, suspiciously bare of everything except a heavy cloth cover that reached nearly to the floor, and said,

- 27 -

"Gentleman, let me present my freshman Hord from Tennessee. This is the youngster that gave Doss that neat undercut on the jaw when they were hazing him. I believe I mentioned it to you."

After introducing me to each of his companions, he said,

"freshy, we are having a little game of 'Draw,' the winner to get up a supper for the crowd; if you like we will deal you a hand; if not, just make yourself at home. There are cigars, or pipe and tobacco if you prefer, and perhaps there is something in the 'lumber room' that would interest you," motioning to an open door of an adjoining room.

While he was speaking one of the party removed the heavy cover that had been hurriedly thrown over the table when I knocked, revealing a pack of cards and a quantity of poker chips.

"Nick" he said, as that, gentleman resumed his seat at the table and began to stack up the chips in front of him, "I think I am entitled to that pot."

"By no means, my dear boy, - you remember just before the freshy knocked I raised you ten and" -

"And I intended to 'call' you when the knock stopped me."

"Very probably, very probable indeed," said Nick laughing, "but you didn't call; on the contrary, while Maverick was covering up the cards you began a discourse on the history of Greece - Yes I know," he continued as the other tried to explain, "you thought it was 'Old Bull' and so did I, but my dear boy, there is a vast difference between 'calling' a hand at poker and calling on ancient history. No, no, it's my money."

After watching the game a few moments I turned to the door indicated by Hardeman as the entrance to the "lumber room." Nick was right in saying I would find something to interest me. For a moment I stood looking around in astonishment, undecided whether it was a gymnasium, an arsenal, or a taxidermist's establishment, It was a large room, twenty by forty feet. On the left as I entered was everything a professional athlete could want, from Indian clubs and dumb bells, boxing gloves of all sizes and weights, to the heaviest casting hammers and vaulting poles. The opposite side of the room furnished the arsenal. Arranged on the walls were two or three pairs of foils, a pair of elegantly finished dress swords, and just over them a pair of heavy cavalry sabers. Several vicious looking knives and pistols, from the Italian stiletto to the heavy Bowie, and from the ordinary Derringer to the latest and most improved revolver; two fowling pieces and a heavy full stocked Kentucky rifle completed the assortment. The whole was surmounted by a pair of magnificent horns from the old time Texas steer, long, tapering, highly polished and tipped with silver knobs. Suspended from one of these were a pair of fringed buckskin trousers and from the other a braided coat of the same material. Evidently no special place had been set aside for old boots and shoes, for scattered about over the floor was foot-gear of every description, from the Indian moccasin and light dancing pumps to heavy hunting and fishing boot. It was the lower end of the room that might have been taken for the shop of a taxidermist. Poised on his hind legs at the end of the room was the stuffed skin of a half grown grizzly bear, with every tooth showing and one paw extended as if to ward off the attack of two little gray prairie wolves that were stationed just in front of him. In one corner was a coyote stretched out at full speed, apparently fleeing from a full grown panther crouching, while two big jack rabbits were sitting near by watching the performance - fastened to the wall above it was the magnificent head of a bull buffalo.

The first thought, after my astonishment on entering the room was what use on earth has Hardeman for these things. My next was, what would my stern father say if he could see this display in the room of a student and know that his hopeful son was fast forming an attachment for this same student that would be as lasting as life itself. I was satisfied that even the liberal ideas of my little grandmother as to the privileges of a young gentleman at college would hardly sanction a private menagerie, with arsenal attached, simply for the entertainment of his friends.

I was so interest in examining the buffalo head that I did not hear the step behind me and was a little startled when Hardeman placed his hand on my shoulder.

"Thought the grizzly had you?" he laughingly exclaimed, as I quickly turned.

"Well I would not be surprised if any of them made a dash at me, they are so lifelike - but I hope I've not interrupted your game," I replied.

"Oh, not at all, that was over some time ago, but I saw you were interested in here and thought I would give you time to take in the whole show before coming in. What do you think of my 'lumber room' and its contents?"

"Splendid, perfectly splendid - but,"

"But splendid nonsense and folly," he added, seeing I hesitated.

"I did not say that, but was going to say I could not see of what use you could make of these," motioning to the stuffed skins and to the display of weapons on the wall.

None, none whatever, freshy, and yet I honestly believe if it had not been for the sight of them I would have left college before I had been here two months. Sit down there and I will tell you why," he said, pointing to a camp stool as he seated himself on the mate to it and refilled his pipe.

"I came here three years ago, a Freshman like yourself, without a friend or acquaintance in the University. Now I dare say you think you have been homesick since you have been here, especially the night following the loss of your 'spike,' but youngster, you don't even know the meaning of the word. "Four days after my arrival, I would have given all I ever expect to the be worth in earthly goods for just a sight of my father and sisters and the old home place in Texas. I wrote twice a day a letter to my father and to my oldest sister, and heard with equal promptness from one or the other and sometimes from both every day. My sister wrote encouraging and gossipy letters all about the boys and girls and the frolics, etc., and my father all about rounding up and branding the cattle and horses, and about the dogs, his hunting and all outdoor life and sports that I had been accustomed to share with him ever since I was old enough to sit on a hose. Well, sister's letters only made me a bit more homesick, but the old gentleman's simply made me frantic. It was like opening a fresh sore every day. I stood it about three weeks and then wired him I was coming home. In three hours after my letter reached him I had an answer by wire saying, 'Wait, am going to Washington in a few days and will call by to see you." About ten days later I had another wire telling me to meet him at Hillsboro, the nearest railroad station. I did so and when we started back here, where he said he would spend a few days with me, it required two spring wagons to bring his boxes, the contents of which he would not tell me, and did not until he had rented this building which was vacant at that time, fitted up this room just as you see it and had me invite a dozen of my classmates to a supper. He received us at the door of what I call my study. You would call it my card room. After all the boys had arrived he took my arm and said, 'Young gentlemen, come this way, we will have time to look at Nick's Lumber Room before supper,' and opening the door walked in with me."

I imagined there was a huskiness in Hardeman's voice and moisture in his dark eyes as he spoke the last sentence, which I attributed to tobacco smoke as he gave two or three vigorous puffs and coughed a time or two before he continued.

"I dare say you were not more astonished when you came in here an hour ago than I was that evening when I walked in with my father, for these skins and those weapons were arranged just as I had seen them last in what we called our 'gun room' at home. In an instant the affectionate kindness that had prompted him to do this flashed on me. He had dropped my arm on entering the room and was standing aside, evidently watching to see what effect the sight would have on me. As I turned to him there were tears in my eyes and I believe in his also, as he said with a smile on his dear old face, "Does it make you feel more at home, my boy?" I was afraid to trust myself to speak out. I squeezed his hand and gave him a look that both of us understood, but from that day to this no one has ever heard of my being homesick."

"How long did he stay with you before going on to Washington?

"To Washington? why bless your soul, he had no more idea of going to Washington than he had of flying. He spend a week with me here, and after beating me at shooting with my own pistols and making a monkey of me with the foils on both occasions, while a goodly number of my classmates were present, he left for home.

"Did he kill all of them?" I asked, motioning to the skins.

"Oh no, but they were all killed by the family, you might say, and there are incidents connected with each one that makes them more valuable to me than mere specimens. For instance, I killed that buffalo when I was 16 years old, cut him out of a herd of probably a thousand. He was one of the finest bulls I ever saw. Father killed the panther just in time to save the life of one of his herdsmen. Father and the Kitten roped that grizzly and choked him to death - rather a ticklish job if the brute had been grown, although I have seen old ones caught that way on the open prairie. The Kitten killed that coyote the day she was 12 years old. The wolf was a hundred and twenty-seven yards from her, running at full speed, which in a coyote, is equivalent to flying, when she dropped him with a little light rifle that runs ninety to the pound; these two little gray fellows she rode down and killed with her pistol."

"You said *she*, you mean *he* killed them with this pistol."

"Did I?" he replied, after hesitating a moment - then turning abruptly to the guns, he continued,

"And most of these weapons, like the skins, are associated with incidents that make them specially valuable to my father. That handsome dress sword on the right was presented to him by General Sam Houston for gallantry and special service at the Battle of San Jacinto; the other was my grandfather's who was murdered at Galiad with Fanning and his men by the Mexicans; one of those heavy cavalry sabers was worn by my father through the Texas War with Mexico, and the mate of it by my uncle, Walker DeJean, my mother's brother. He was a member of my father's company of Rangers at that time. Both of these old blades were crimson with Mexican blood for the independence of Texas; both have a history that I may tell you some time. This 'Bowie' knife was given Father by Colonel Bowie himself and this one by Davy Crockett - both his personal friends and both killed at the Alamo shortly afterward. And this little toy, not much larger than a lady's bodkin is a Spanish stiletto, most dangerous of them all was wrenched from the hands of Mexican a woman. This pair of Derringers were given to him by his dearest friend, Major Ben McCulloch."

"Were they?" I exclaimed, picking up and examining the richly mounted weapons. "Major McCulloch is a near relative of mine."

"Is that so?" said Hardeman, grasping my hand - "Why did you not mention this before? I am delighted to know it. 'Uncle Ben' as I've always called him is one of my father's oldest and best friends. But I've nearly talked my jaw-bone out of place. Come back to my den. I think the boys left about two glasses of cold punch in the pitcher. If they did, we will drink one to 'Uncle Ben's' health, and the other to our better acquaintance."

Since my spike episode I had not ventured to thrust either my person, or my opinions upon any members of the higher classes and was equally slow in accepting any advances from them, but the unusually kind interest Hardeman had manifested for me, and his frank cordial manner, made me feel I had a sincere friend in this handsome and popular member of the Senior Class. There comes a time, sooner or later, in the life of every boy, when his youthful imagination pictures himself the counterpart of some man whose life and deeds have been ineffaceably impressed on his mind. The object of his admiration may not be in the eyes of the world, an example worthy of imitation, but to him it is a model - be he prizefighter or preacher, and unconsciously his character is more or less formed by these early impressions.

Reared at home as I had been, the beginning of my University career was like opening the first chapter of my life with the world, and Nick Hardeman was my ideal. I was blind to any moral or physical defect he might have. It might have been my lonely and friendless position when I entered the University that first incited his sympathy, or my fortunate relationship to a life-long friend of his father that awakened a friendly feeling for me, but in either case as time passed our friendship grew into a brotherly affection. He coached and pressed me vigorously in my studies and with almost equal energy rushed me in athletics. He taught me how to use the foils, and by his superior skill made me almost ashamed of my knowledge of boxing.

"One must keep abreast with the times, Freshy," he would say to me sometimes when, with my ears singing from a blow on the side of my head from his glove, I would drop on the lounge to recover my wind and to protest against so much exercise. "It may be that you will need this knowledge some time - if you do all right, and if you do not why you have only taken a good bit of healthy exercise.

I soon became a daily visitor to the Ranch and spend most of my time there when not engaged in my recitations. He marked out my hours for study, and as he assisted me in all of them, I found it most convenient to have this living encyclopedia at my elbow when studying. Consequently most of it was done at his rooms. Months passed and my daily association with him was of far more advantage to me than years of intercourse with the world, would have been with no guiding hand to point out the way for me.

CHAPTER IV

A FAMILY GROUP.

It was an afternoon the latter part of December, near the Christmas holidays, that I walked into Nick's study without knocking, a custom I had long since abandoned. Finding the room vacant I called out.

"Hello! No one at home?"

"Come in Freshy," he answered from the bedroom adjoining. "Procrastination is the thief of time". "You catch me at a job I ought to have done three months back, packing away my summer duds."

He was engaged in packing clothes, scattered about over a room in a trunk he had evidently emptied for that purpose. On a table near him I noticed a half dozen old fashioned daguerreotype pictures.

"Who are these?" I asked, picking up one of them.

"My family. Sit down and get acquainted with them while I finish packing."

The first I opened was a large double case showing a strong but kind face of a man thirty-five or forty years of age, with wonderfully clear blue eyes, light hair and fair complexion; the other that of a beautiful dark-eyed woman, as pronounced a brunette as the gentleman was blond.

"This is your mother, I will venture to guess, Nick, for I can see you make an ugly shadow of her beauty, but who is the gentleman? No kin to you, judging from appearance."

"You can't always judge by appearances, either in features or manners, my boy, remember that it may be of use to you some day. Make another guess at the gentleman."

"I give up."

"Why it's my father, of course."

"And you are no more like him than I."

"Not as much in coloring, for you have blue eyes, so has he, only his are a shade or two brighter and bluer than yours, but I am like him physically, except he is a size larger and stouter. I take after my mother's side of the house in features, only, as you say, I am an ugly shadow of her beauty. But look at this, it is my sister Ellen, if you would like to see how my mother looked when she was young," and picking up a case he handed it to me. I touched the spring. The top flew up and uncovered the most exquisitely beautiful face of a woman I ever looked upon. The artist had succeeded in giving that dark rich glow to the complexion that is found only in the fairest daughters of the proud Castillian strain. It was a young girl about eighteen years of age. A wealth of soft wavy black hair clustered above her broad forehead and finely penciled brows. In the depth of her beautiful dark eyes there was a look of tenderness and loyalty to awaken all the purest love in the heart of man and stir and blood to the noblest deeds in the days of knighthood. A smile of childish innocence on her delicate mouth made the picture more complete. After admiring the likeness a moment I involuntarily exclaimed.

"how beautiful! how very beautiful!"

Nick had stepped behind my chair and was looking at it over my shoulder.

"Yes, she is very beautiful, but the casket is not more beautiful than the jewel it holds - her soul is even more beautiful in her face." Then taking the case out of my hand he looked intently at the face a moment before closing it and said in a low he as if speaking to himself: "Ellen, dear Ellen, you deserve a happy life, and I pray God you may have it."

There was a pathetic tenderness in his voice I had never had before that cause me to look up, but he quickly turned away and resumed his packing.

I opened another case. The face that looked out at me was so startlingly like Nick that the heavy pointed gray mustache which entirely concealed the upper lip scarcely detracted from the likeness.

"Now one who did not know would bet dollars to cents that he was your father Nick, and I'm willing to pay the same odds he is a near kinsman.

"And you would win the money, Freshy, for that is my uncle, Colonel Walker DeJean, my mother's brother, and the only living relative I have on my mother's side."

"What a remarkable family likeness there is between you all on your mother's side."

"Yes, it is the old Castiallin blood I suppose. My uncle says his family, the DeJeans, are direct descendants from the purest strains in the world. I am not much inclined to that kind of thing myself, but as the old fellow is a great stickler for good blood I have too much respect and love for him to ever run counter to his views on this subject. 'I am the last of my race, Nick, since your mother died,' he frequently says to me, 'and when I am gone you must sustain the honor of the family for you are my heir.'"

"Has he ever married?"

"No, and I think it is the one mistake of his life. He says he could not afford to give up his freedom; but my opinion is that the old fellow thinks there are none of the 'old strain', as he calls it, good enough for him. He is immensely rich and all kinds of traps have been set for him by designing mamas - Americans and Creoles - and he walks right up apparently blind to the very edge of the deadfall, then bows, smiles, lifts his hat and walks off to hunt up another trap."

"I would like to meet the old gentleman. I rather like his ideas about good blood."

"Oh, so do I in a measure, but I do not think every well bred man is a gentleman any more than I think every thoroughbred horse is a winner. But I've never seen a good race horse that was not a thoroughbred and I've never seen a true gentleman, it matters not how humble in life he may be, that did not have that inherent instinct of a gentleman."

While Nick was discoursing on the advantages of good blood I had opened the last of the daguerreotypes. The picture was that of a child, apparently ten or twelve years old, seated in a big arm chair by a table, but whether boy or girl I was unable to decide. It was a full size likeness, but from the waist down a Mexican blanket woven in many brilliant colors was thrown across the lap. A magnificent black and white pointer was lying on the edge of the blanket at the feet of the picture and another was sitting on the right side with his muzzle thrust over the arm of the chair, looking up in the face of the child who had one arm over the dog's neck and the other resting on the table upon which was a broad-brimmed straw hat, a pair of pistols and a small rifle. The light brown hair was parted in the middle, thrown back behind the ears and came down to the collar of what appeared to be a loose fitting jacket or blouse belted in at the waist and laced up in front instead of buttoned. The little oval face was as brown as a berry, evidently from exposure to the wind and sun, for the upper part of the forehead where the hat protected was white and fair. The delicate features, the head, the hair, the little brown hands, were those of a child, a girl perhaps, or more probably a delicate boy, but there was an expression in the steady, half serious look out of the large bright blue eyes that impressed you with the idea that you were not only looking at a much older person, but one of more than ordinary character. Judging from the surrounding I decided it could not be a girl, but the delicate, regular features made the face altogether too pretty for a boy. I gave it up and raised my head to ask Nick who it was, when I found him standing directly over me looking down with a quizzical smile on his face.

"Who is it?" I asked

"The Kitten," he replied.

"The Kitten seems pretty well supplied with claws," I said, pointing to the pistols and guns.

"Yes and no one can use them quicker or better."

"But who is it, Nick? No kin to you I know, for there is not the shadow of a likeness to any of your family."

"I'll give you another guess, Freshy, at the kitten."

"Kitten, Kitten. Seems to me I've heard you use that name before."

"How about the long shot at the coyote?" he inquired.

In an instant I remembered my first visit to the Ranch and that it was the Kitten he had said that made the remarkable shot at the coyote and had helped his father lasso the grizzly.

"Oh yes, I remember now, and this is the Kitten, is it? Well I can take in the long shot at the coyote, for I was a pretty fair shot with the rifle myself when not much older than this kid, but when you tell me that a delicate looking child like this boy had the nerve to help your father rope a grizzly bear, you must provide me with proof."

While I was speaking he had taken the picture out of my hands and was looking at it with tenderness and admiration.

"Nerve! nerve did you say? Why there is more nerve and resolution in that little body than there is in yours, mine, and a half dozen others like us, and she is nothing but a slip of a girl either."

Notwithstanding I had half suspected it was a girl, yet with the incident of the bear fresh in my mind, when Nick made this announcement I involuntarily rose to my feet.

"Is it possible? Are you sure? Do you know her?" I exclaimed.

"One question at a time," he answered, smiling at my astonishment. "I am sure of the shot because she said so, which in itself would have been sufficient, but father saw her make it. As to knowing her, I certainly ought to for she is my sister. But if you will look again at father's picture you will see she has his eyes exactly."

"I see the resemblance now," I said, comparing the pictures, "but the bear Nick, this child - and a little girl at that - helping to rope a grizzly bear! Think of it! I've always heard they are the most dangerous of all animals."

"So they are. All wild animals I've ever seen, unless wounded or protecting their young, will run from a man unless the man runs first except a grizzly. You have to give the right of way to him, but if you can catch one out on the open prairie a mile or two from cover, two good riders well mounted and quick with the rope can bag him nine times out of ten. It's his everlasting beligerent disposition that gets him into trouble just as it does some two-legged brutes, for just as soon as the horseman gets near him instead of lumbering off to the woods as fast as his big legs will carry him - as any other bear would - he rears himself up on his hind legs and shows fight. This is just what the horsemen want. They dash by one on each side of him, as close as they can, which is not very close for a horse is more afraid of a grizzly than a man, but close enough for their purpose. Two ropes fly out at the same time, two nooses light over his heard, and quick as a flash, before he has time to make at the ropes with his paw, he is on his back, his wind shut off and two horses dragging him over the prairie at a gallop. So you see after all it only requires skill and a medium amount of nerve."

"But this child, why she hasn't the strength."

"No, but the child is the best rider I ever saw; you know we have some of the best in the world in Texas. As for strength, very little is required: throw the rope and a well-trained cow pony does the rest. For the instant he hears it whiz out over his head, he braces himself and drops back on his haunches and the noose is drawn as tight as his weight and strength can make it."

"What a queer -" I started to say sport for a young girl. Yes, it does appear so, but not after you know all the circumstances connected with her life. Fill your pipe and sit down there and I'll tell you how and why the Kitten, as I call her, learned to ride and shoot."

Filling his own pipe he sat for a moment looking at the picture he still held in his hand, through the wreaths of smoke that circled around his face, then placing his slippered feet on the table began:

"Freshy, you know or ought to know by this time that I'm not inclined to make myself or my family subjects of conversation, but I love to think of this child and talk of her to any one who takes an interest in me and mine as I feel that you do, for she is inexpressibly dear to me and I know she loves me better than anything on earth except perhaps father, who has been her mother, father, playmate, companion, and teacher almost from the day of her birth, for our mother died a few days after she was born. Her name is Catherine, after our mother. Our old nurse, who had been mother's maid before she was married, could not speak English distinctly, having been born and reared on my Grandfather DeJean's sugar plantation down in Louisiana, where a patois half French, half Spanish, is spoken. She was devoted to my mother and when she died all the love and affection of her honest old heart concentrated with ten-fold intensity on the little blue-eyed motherless babe. Her whole life was devoted to the child; she would take it in her arms and rocking to and fro for hours, some soft, plaintive, negro song, scarcely a word of which any of us could understand, except now and then we could catch something that sounded like 'leetee Keetee,' which we supposed was intended for Little Katie, our mother was called Kate. When the child was nearly two years old; she was christened Catherine and father requested that we call her by his name, but this was even more difficult for the old nurse to pronounce than Katie. I compromised by calling her Kitten, but to all others she is Catherine. I was a lad, about ten years old, when our mother died and sister Ellen two years younger. Of course, we could not fully appreciate the extent of our misfortune, but I distinctly remember, child as I was, my great sorrow for my father's anguish. For weeks he would not notice the child, and I've seen old Jeanette, our nurse, gather the little thing close in her arms and look at him as he would pass by with an expression of supplication and fear in her eyes, such as I have seen in helpless animals when fearful, for their young. But, as months passed by, his grief seemed to soften into tender love for the child. It was pitiable and I often slipped away and cried from sympathy when he would take this frail little bit of humanity in his powerful arms and hold her against his broad chest as if to soothe the aching of the heart within, while great silent tears would course down his cheeks and fall upon the smiling face of the babe looking up at him with eyes so like his own. From the time she could toddle around his chair and lisp 'Daddy' they were inseparable day and night. When she was but little more than two years old, he would place a pillow on the broad flat horn of his Texas saddle and be gone for hours, often returning with her sleeping on a pillow as if in a cradle. At six she had a pony of her own, and accompanied him on his daily rides over the ranch. By the time she was ten he had taught her to shoot with either pistol, shotgun or rifle; and at twelve, with his training and daily life in the saddle, the wildest mustang ever foaled could not unseat her, and there was not a better rifle or pistol shot on the frontier. She was quicker with either than father, and I've often heard Uncle Ben McCulloch say father was the best pistol shot he ever saw, and he has seen all the best ones in this country.

"Up to this time, the Kitten, Father and I had been having things our own way. Ellen was at school in New Orleans. I was attending the local academy at home in San Antonio. Father had been instructing the little girl himself, and the child was as well up on her books as she was on outdoor sports. But when Ellen came home, having graduated from the Convent, and afterwards at a finishing school the house was turned over to her as its mistress, and we had to turn over a new leaf ourselves. It was a day or two after she arrived that I happened to overhear a conversation between the two girls. They were sitting in the library, and Ellen evidently had been questioning her sister as to her books.

"Why my dear, I am delighted to find you so thoroughly advanced in your studies and to think you have done it all without a teacher."

"Oh no, Sister, Father taught me as regular as the study hours came around, and was as careful and painstaking with my studies as he was in teaching me to ride and shoot."

"Of course he was, for dear Father never does nay thing half-way even if it be for nothing but his own amusement. I know you and brother have been delightful companions for him in my absence and it was so sweet and dutiful in you to learn all of these things simply to amuse him; but now that I am here you will have a companion and we will leave father and brother to do the shooting and riding.'"

" ' Don't give me credit, Sister, for performing as a duty things that were my greatest pleasure. But what on earth would I do without my gun and horses?' "

" ' Do? Why anything and everything that a young girl of your age should learn to do, in all of which excepting your books I fear you are sadly deficient.' "

"There was a pause and then I heard the Kitten say in a low tone that had a suspicion of a quiver in it, 'I am so sorry you are disappointed in me, Sister.'

" 'Oh no, not disappointed my dear child, most agreeably surprised in some things; but, my dear little sister, you certainly do not mean to say that you are rally fond of handling guns and pistols and riding like, like...' "

"A cowboy", humbly suggested the Kitten.

" 'Yes, a cowboy or some wild Indian' " said Ellen.

" 'If it is wrong then I must confess with shame, Sister Ellen, that I am very, very fond of these things and it will distress me greatly if you require me to give them up.' "

"There was another pause in the conversation and then Ellen spoke, 'My child, I had no idea that your taste for these things was real, but thought you did it simply to please father. I will not ask you to give them up, not entirely, but let's see if we cannot modify and compromise the matter. We will let the shooting continue for the present, also the riding, but what do you say to giving up your boy's saddle and riding like a lady?'

I wish that I could have seen the look of astonishment which I knew was on the little girl's face when Ellen made this proposition, for such a thing had never entered her head. 'Give up my saddle!' I heard her exclaim, 'and ride on a side-saddle! Why sister, do you want me to break my neck? I never in my life was on a side-saddle, and there is not an old plug on the ranch but that could toss me as high as a kite out of one' - 'But my dear child, you will be compelled to give up this way if riding sometime and learn to sit on a horse like a lady, so why not begin at once? Now that I am at home to stay I want to take up my riding again and want you to accompany me, but just think how very ridiculous we would look with you riding astride by my side. No, no, Catherine, you must for my sake change your way of riding.'

"She paused for a reply, but none came, and she continued, 'Then you must also have a governess. I had one from the time of mother's death until I went to the Convent in New Orleans. You must start in there next year and must have a teacher to prepare you. I thought you should have had a governess three years ago, but father would not consent to it.'

"Again there was a pause and after waiting a moment and no reply, Ellen asked, 'Well what do you think of my suggestion?'

" ' I am anxious to please you in every way Sister, but I do not see that you have left me any grounds to stand on for the compromise you spoke of. Now suppose you let me make a proposition to you. I will accept the governess, and will let you teach me to ride a lady's saddle like a lady whenever you wish, provided you will consent and not be angry with me if I ride my own saddle in my own way whenever I accompany father or brother or choose to ride by myself. Now what do you say to that? Of course you will not expect me to give up my shooting.'

" 'I suppose I will have to accept, provided father approves of the contract, for I see from the way you speak it is your ultimatum,' " said Ellen laughing.

"The next day when she mentioned the matter to father he said he thought her ideas concerning the child were correct, but asked what Catherine had to say about it, that unless she consented he, would not agree to it. Learning it was her own suggestion, he requested Ellen to write to the Mother Superior at the Convent where she attending school to secure a governess for the little one and send her out. And so it was that little Kitten was first broken to social harness and to a side-saddle. But scarcely two days in succession would pass that she and I, or she and father, often all three of us, would slip away from Ellen and the governess and have a dash across the prairie, A few months later I left home and came here to college. When the Kitten was 13 years old she was sent to the Convent in New Orleans, the same school Ellen had graduated from. Bless me, how time flies. Think of it, this little brown faced child is now a young lady of sixteen and Ellen writes me, very accomplished and beloved by every one in school from teachers down to the cats and dogs, but she absolutely refuses to entertain the idea of attending a finishing school when she leaves the Convent. There is evidently a secret understanding between the Kitten and father for he writes me when she comes home to spend her vacations that they still take their stolen rides together. He says that her seat in the saddle is as firm as ever, but she is a little out of practice in her shooting. And now, Freshy, you know all about her, and some day when you pay me that promised visit, you will meet her."

"But there goes the 9 o'clock bell. It is too late for us to have a round with the gloves, so get to your mathematics boy, if you want me to help you."

CHAPTER V

THE SKELETON IN THE CLOSET.

It was a typical Christmas morning, a cloudless sky with bright sunshine; but the frost chilled the white carpet of snow that covered the ground by several inches.

"A merry Christmas to you, Nick," I exclaimed as I entered his room.

"The same to you my boy, and I sincerely hope there will be more power in my good wishes for you than there is likely to be in yours for me."

He rose as he spoke to greet me, and as I offered one out-stretched hand, I noticed he held an open letter in the other, which he evidently was reading when I came in. I imagined as I looked in his handsome face that there was a shadow of sadness in his dark eyes.

"That depends upon how much it takes to make you merry. It seems that some one had already made a start in that direction," I replied, pointing to a box on the table with the lid lying by showing it had just been opened.

"A box from home?" I suggested as I caught the odor of cakes, jellies, etc.

"Yes, a box from Ellen, help yourself. She rather prides herself I think on her fruit cake, and unless I've forgotten how they smell, I think you will find one in there."

"This looks like a box of cigars," I said, picking up an unopened package lying by the side of the box, "who is this from?"

"They are cigars. The Kitten sent them from New Orleans. I suspect they are pretty good for she writes they are some that Uncle Walker DeJean brought from Havana a week or so ago. The old gentleman is interested in a factory or tobacco plantation or something of the kind over there, and while he prefers a sugar cane shuck cigarette filled with Perique tobacco - strong enough to lift the hat off your head. He always has some choice cigars made up especially for his friends."

"Miss Catherine is well I hope." "Well as can be. She writes she has developed quite a talent for painting and has sent me by express a specimen of her work as a Christmas present, but as yet it has not arrived. By the way since you have been so courteous as to ask concerning her, it reminds me she inquires after you in her letter." I looked up most agreeably surprised and I confess secretly flattered.

"It is very kind of her indeed. I did not know she had ever heard of me," I replied. But at the same time I felt quite sure from our warm friendship that Nick had mentioned me in some of his letters. So, that while I was apparently busy diving into the box after the good things, I was waiting impatiently for him to speak, which he did not do for a moment or so and then he asked, "Would you like to hear what she has to say?" "Certainly and with pleasure if you will be kind enough to tell me."

Placing the letter he was reading when I entered on the table, and drawing another from his pocket he glanced over a page or two. The old twinkle of merriment had come back to his eyes and I could see from the expression of his face that it was all he could do to suppress his laughter.

"Ah, here it is," he said turning the pages, "she says, 'How is your pet Freshman getting along? Has he ever ventured again in a spike? I will give you anything within reason if you will get me a picture of *it*. When I say *it* I mean the whole thing, coat and boy together, as they appeared after the hazing. If I could only put it on canvas as I see it in my imagination, my fame as an artist would be made. Get me the picture and you are at liberty to draw on me for all the expense necessary in furnishing your pet with anything in wearing apparel he may need from a nice apron and bib to a new spike.'"

There is nothing a boy is so susceptible and at the same time more fearful of than ridicule, and especially when the shaft is shot by a girl. The fruit cake stuck like a ball in my throat and refused to go down. I could feel that my face was crimson and I was too angry to trust myself to speak but I kept my jaws moving as if I was eating with unconcerned indifference, and while I was afraid to look up I could feel that Nick was quietly laughing at me. He soon saw that my pleasant anticipation had received a more severe jolt than he had intended and placing one arm over my shoulder, in a half jocular, half affectionate manner, said,

"Why Freshy, you certainly are not really angry? You cannot for a moment think that a sister of mine would say any thing seriously to hurt the feelings of one she has learned to know as her brother's best and truest friend. She has written in a pure spirit of fun. I wrote her a day or two after we first met telling her about the "Spike affair," I put in. "To be sure, certainly, no one would doubt that after hearing what you have just read and..."

"But stop a moment, Freshy, and listen to me," he interrupted. "In reply to that letter she wrote quite complimentary about your conduct in the affair, enough so to even soothe your anger now if you could only hear it. If I were not afraid it would make you vain I would get the letter and read it to you."

"Excuse me, Nick, one letter a day from Miss Catherine concerning myself is about as much as I can stand. I don't care to take a chance on another."

"As the lawyers say, you are 'willing to rest the case', are you? But come, enough of this foolishness, for I am feeling anything but jolly this bright Christmas morning."

"What's the matter? I noticed when I came in that you looked rather grumpy, inexcusably so I thought, for a man who had a Christmas box and two letters from home, for I guess that other letter is also from some of the homefolk."

"You are right. It is from my sister Ellen and I had just finished reading it when you came in. Get a cigar if you are through with that fruitcake, and sit down - I want to talk with you."

"Fire away," I said as I drew my chair nearer the fire. He sat for a moment without speaking, looking thoughtfully at the blazing logs, then turning to me said,

"Freshy, Ellen is going to marry."

"Why of course she is," I replied, "I am surprised she has not married before this. You certainly did not think a young lady as beautiful and accomplished as she is would not marry. It is only a question of time.

"You have covered the case entirely, "she replied. "Ellen, as you say, is beautiful, accomplished, and also wealthy. She has had many suitors, but she made her choice years ago when she was only a school girl and has clung to him with unswerving devotion. They would have been married when she quit school if father had not objected. She is madly in love with him. For a woman of her loyal heart, this means that nothing but death can change her."

"You speak as softly and sorrowfully about it, Nick, as if you were talking of a funeral instead of a wedding. I've had two sisters married myself, old fellow, and I dare say I loved them as much as you do Miss Ellen. I know I blubbered like a baby during the ceremony, but I have survived it bravely as you see."

"Yes and I could weep tears of blood and yet smile through them if I could see Ellen's happiness beyond, but I cannot. Instead, I can see her united for life to a man grossly unworthy of her. I can see her as this truth gradually dawns upon her day by day and his moral depravity appears at last, in all its hideous forms, before her blinded vision. I can see her noble heart slowly break, like a poor helpless captive, tied to a stake slowly dying from torture, with a heart too proud and brave to cry out, yet ceaselessly praying to a merciful God to send death to her relief."

I had never seen him so affected. There was an unspeakable sadness in his voice and an earnestness as if the glowing coals were reflecting the pictures in his mind. He raised his hand as if to shield his face from the fire and I saw him press back the tears in his eyes. It was some moments before I ventured to speak, then I asked,

"Who is this man?"

"Captain Carrier of the U.S. Cavalry, but rather he *was* a captain, but has resigned from the Army."

"Why did he resign?"

"To marry Ellen," he replied. "When father finally consented to the marriage it was upon the condition that he would resign and not take Ellen away from him. You see she is the only one at home; the Kitten is in New Orleans at school and won't be through for two years. I will be there after I graduate here in June, but of course I cannot take Ellen's place."

"Perhaps after all you may be deceived in the man, Nick. As a rule there is not class of men who have a higher sense of honor than our army officers. A man who goes through West Point is bound to have some polish and principle instilled into him."

"I grant you that and Carrier is one of the most polished men in his manners I've ever met, as well as one of the handsomest."

"What then, isn't he a gentleman?"

"By breeding, yes, for he belongs to one of the oldest and most prominent New England families; by instinct and practice, no, for morally he is the most deformed monstrosity I've ever heard of - every instinct in him is brutal - gambling and drinking are the least of his vices, but when drinking of course the brute in him shows in more hideous form."

"But I have heard that such conduct would not be tolerated in the Army, Nick."

"It is not, but Army life on the western frontier is as different from Army life in the East as the life of a western settler is from that of a man living in an eastern city. There is a license allowed on the frontier that would not be permitted in the East. But, notwithstanding Carrier's brutal conduct has been so notorious it would have subjected him to court martial and most probably dismissal from the service, were it not for his otherwise magnificent record as a soldier and Indian fighter. In this particular kind of warfare it is conceded by his superior officers and recognized by the War Department at Washington that he has no equal in the Army. He has only one redeemable trait in his damnable character and that is his courage. Both officers and men who have served with him on the frontier say he is absolutely without fear when scouting or fighting Indians. There is not a man in his troop but that hates him heartily and yet they cannot help admiring him for the skillful manner in which he handles them and his reckless courage in a fight. He graduated at West Point well up in his class and would have won his grade as Major long ago but for his dissipated habits. On dangerous service or at the head of his troop in action he is a superb soldier; at other times he gives full away to all of his low instincts and ungovernable temper."

"How did your sister happen to come in contact with such a character, I asked?"

"She first met him at a Mardi-Gras Ball, afterwards at my Uncle Walker DeJean's. The old gentleman has an elegant home in New

Orleans that he throws open during the gay social season in the city for the entertainment of his friends. Ellen had just finished school and Uncle gave her a magnificent entertainment, in fact several during the winter, and Carrier who was on leave-of-absence, which he was spending in New Orleans, was a welcome guest to them all. He captivated my uncle as well as Ellen, for as I said has a splendid physique, is handsome as a Greek god, polished manners, and converses well on almost any subject. As his visits to Ellen became more frequent and she began to show a partiality for him over her other admirers, uncle began to investigate him.

Of course the first inquiry the old gentleman made was about his family, for as I've mentioned to you before, he is a great stickler for good blood. He found it was satisfactory, and for a time further investigation was dropped.

Carrier soon left to join his command, which had been ordered to take the field against the Comanche Indians on the extreme western border. It was eighteen months before he saw her again, but he wrote regularly to her, not love letters, but bright, interesting descriptions of the country, their marches, scouting, and now and then a slight reference to skirmishes with the Indians, but never a word of any part that either he or his troop took in them.

Yet, on this campaign he did some of the best fighting of his life. For eight hours with his troop alone he successfully stood off six hundred Comanche warriors, the fiercest fighters of all the Indian tribes. He had five of his men killed outright and fourteen wounded, he amongst them. An arrow was shot in his thigh up to the feather, yet two days after he wrote Ellen one of his usually interesting letters and disposed of the whole affair in a P.S. by saying, 'We had another little skirmish with the heathen a day or two back; lost five men and several wounded.' It was nearly a month later when we learned through the official report in the paper that it was his troop that fought the indians and that he had been painfully wounded and again commended by his superior officer for gallantry.

Ellen had kept father fully informed of all that had passed between her and Carrier, except the love she has secreted in her heart, which I doubt if she had confessed even to herself. She had shown him all the letters she had received, which were of special interest to father as they recalled his own experience when as a young man, and Captain of a company of Rangers he fought the Indians and Mexicans for the freedom of Texas, so that when Carrier arrived a month later on a short leave, he was met with a most cordial reception from all three of us, Ellen, Father, and myself.

It is twelve miles from San Antonio where he was stopping out to the Ranch, and after he had made two or three calls father invited him to come out and spend part of his time with us and he accepted the invitation. I was prepared to worship him as a hero, but in spite of his soldierly reputation, his magnificent physique, handsome face and superb horsemanship he had not been in the house three days before I began to experience a peculiar aversion for him.

I could not at first define this sensation -- it was not fear nor yet strong enough to be called dislike, but it grew and strengthened imperceptibly but surely as ice forming on water, until I confessed to myself that I heartily disliked him. I fought against this feeling for it was evident to one, even as inexperienced in such matters as I, that Ellen loved him, and besides I had no cause whatever to dislike him. True he paid but little attention to me, but he was an experienced soldier of thirty-five and I a boy barely nineteen. There was, however, an indescribable something about him that repelled me and before he had been in the house a week I had such an aversion for him that I tried to avoid meeting him when I could do so without being observed, but the sensitive heart and keen eyes of Ellen noticed it. " ' Why do you avoid Captain Carrier, brother?' she inquired of me one evening as she was passing my door. 'Because I do not like him, my dear sister.' I replied frankly. The blood left her cheeks for an instant and then surged back in a crimson tide. 'Not like him? Why, for what reason? I should have thought that of all men he would have been mostly admired by you.' So I did until I met him,' I answered, " ' Until you met him!' she exclaimed, and her beautiful black eyes opened wide with astonishment. 'Why I am sure his manners are perfect and his person - he is - I mean,' and in her confusion she dropped her head on my shoulder to hide her blushes.

" 'I know what you would say, Ellen. He is I grant you very handsome, and I have never seen more polished manners, but, 'but what?' she asked as I hesitated. 'but he has no soul, no heart, no more feeling in him than a marble statue."

"Ah, my brother, you don't know him. You only see the automatic man, the outer shell, the cold, trained, and experienced soldier who from habit conceals all sentiment and feeling except that pertaining to his profession. If you could only hear - if you only knew him as I know him.' Her voice sank to a sigh and again she paused and hid her face on my shoulder.

"But what do you know? What reason have you for forming such an opinion?' raising her head and lookng me steadily in the face.

" 'I know nothing, absolutely nothing,' I replied, 'but I feel toward him as I imagine a child feels when its instinct tells it to fear.'

" 'How absurd, brother. You certainly do not fear Captain Carrier,' she said smiling brightly.

" 'No, no, it is not fear as the word is generally understood, but a repulsive feeling so akin to it that I can scarcely discern the difference. My only real fear is that my sweet sister loves him and I would rather see you..."

"I was interrupted by Carrier's voice calling out from the hall below; 'Miss Ellen, where are you? I am waiting.'

"It was a clear and distinct tone, but there was something like an impatient command in it that grated on my ears and I remarked, 'Listen to that command, Ellen.'

" 'Oh, no, she replied, 'we are going for a walk and I have kept him waiting.' Hastily disengaging herself from my arm she hurried down the stairs.

"A few days after this, father and I were returning from a long ride over the prairie when he suddenly turned to me after a long silence and said:

"Son, how do you like our guest, Captain Carrier?" I answered him as I had Ellen and gave the same inexplicable cause for disliking him.

"It is singular,' he said after riding some distance in silence, but I have the same feeling towards him. It is unaccountable. Perhaps it is prompted by our anxiety for your sister's welfare. He is evidently very much in love with her.'

"Not more so than she is with him," I replied, and I told him of my conversation with Ellen.

"I suspected as much myself," and last night Captain Carrier confirmed my suspicions."

"How, in what way?' I exclaimed."

"He asked for your sister's hand in marriage, Nick, and when I asked if it was with her knowledge and approval he said it was. Of course I did not consent, neither could I positively decline, for I really know nothing objectionable to him except that inexplicable dislike, which seems to have impressed you as well as me. On the other hand, he is unquestionably a fine soldier, has the bearing of a thorough gentleman, and as you say, Ellen loves him, and her happiness after all is the first consideration.

He gave me references as to his family, to his record as a soldier, and asked that I make a prompt investigation and urged a speedy marriage with as much assurance as if he already had my consent. His persistency, his arrogance and the tone of his voice in which he pressed the matter so annoyed me I told him if he insisted I could give him a definite answer then and there; otherwise I would take my time and make such investigations as I saw proper. I said I was in no hurry to have Ellen marry but at the expiration of six months I would give him an answer.

In the meantime he was to leave her free and unfettered by any pledge binding her to him in any way. He said Ellen had consented to become his wife provided I approved, and insisted that the engagement should hold pending my investigation. I declined to grant this and upon my absolute refusal to do so he turned as white as a ghost from suppressed passion, whether it was his love for Ellen, or hatred of me that caused it, I am unable to say, but am inclined to think it was the latter, for his eyes gleamed like a crippled panther as he stood with clinched hands and glared at me for a moment, then bowing, said as he turned and walked away. 'As you wish, sir.'

He leaves this evening and I must confess I am glad of it, yet he is a most charming companion at times. Unfortunately he doesn't wear well.

I think I will send for your Uncle Walker to come up and put him on the trail again, for he is a veritable old sleuth in such matters. In the meantime, I shall inquire as to his private character myself through some of my old army friends, one or two of who are officers in Carrier's regiment.'

"To make a long story short, Fresh, before the six months expired, enough evidence of Carrier's past life had been gathered to brand him a villain and to ostracise him from all decent society, but not enough to condemn him in the eyes of the woman who loved him. On the contrary it seemed to strengthen the tendrils of her heart that were twined in a burgeoning love about him. Although he required her to break her engagement to Carrier, father permitted her to correspond with him, and he, knowing his past life was being investigated, was wise enough to disclose it in his own way to Ellen in his letters to her. So when father would lay before her evidences of some damnable transaction little short of infamy, she was always ready to combat it with statements from his side of the question, which she did with such tender earnestness as brought tears to father's eyes as well as her own.

"He learned from Uncle Walker that Carrier had married a lovely young girl shortly after he graduated at West Point, but within two years she was forced to leave him on account of brutal treatment and return to her parents, where she shortly died, a brokenhearted wreck. He received a letter from an old army friend, an officer in Carrier's regiment stating that while Carrier was a superb soldier on active duty, he had ungovernable temper, who feared neither God nor the devil, was as ruthless and cruel as an Indian on the warpath, and that He would rather trust a child of his to the warmth of a grave than to the tenderness of Carrier.

Ellen was informed of all this, but it had no influence on her whatever. "Captain Carrier has informed me of all these things, and I could have saved you the trouble of prying into this private life if you had consulted me," she would say when the matter was brought to her attention.

"All brightness and sunshine seemed to have gone out of her life. The roses had left her cheeks, and there was a frightened and appealing look in her beautiful eyes like that of a stricken fawn as the hunter draws the cruel knife across its throat. It lacked only a week or ten days of the time in which father was to give his answer. He and Ellen were sitting in the library when she turned to him and said: 'Father, I have a letter from Captain Carrier this morning and he informs me that his troop has been ordered to San Antonio for post duty, and that he will be here shortly after they arrive to get your answer for my hand and my heart,' her white lips almost refusing to form the words. Rising and placing her hand on his shoulder to steady her swaying form, she continued:

" 'I know what your answer will be, my aching heart tells me you will not consent; but, oh, my dear father, do not refuse him absolutely. Give him time, give me time, just a little more time, dear father. Give yourself time to know him better."

" 'It was the wailing agony of a breaking heart - the tortured cry of a condemned soul standing on the verge of eternity pleading for just one more sight of God's blessed sunshine, one more sweet breath of life. She had fallen on her knees by the side of his chair as she spoke and throwing her arms about his neck, buried her face in his bosom to smother the sobs she could not suppress, and tears from his eyes fell upon her bowed head. For a moment neither spoke, then lifting her white face, with a look of filial love in her eyes, she said:

"Give yourself no concern about what I will do father, my first earthly duty is to you and I will perform it truly as your loving child. I will never, never marry Captain Carrier without your consent. My heart may break, my dear father, but my sense of duty to you will never swerve."

"My child, my blessed child,' said my father, God in Heaven knows it is your happiness, yours alone, I am thinking of and I would gladly give my life if necessary to secure it for you; but this man, the proofs I have of his past life, his immorality, his heartlessness, his brutal instincts and ungovernable temper are indisputable."

"Not indisputable father, for I dispute them in his absence. Yes, but from his standpoint and his version. Certainly, just as you believe them from the version of your friends and his enemies."

"Not his enemies, my daughter, for they admit he is a superb soldier, but has a most ungovernable temper and cruel disposition.'

Have you ever seen him display either, father?

No, I have not, but then....

Then wait father, and see for yourself. Time will show that you do him a great injustice,' Give him time, give yourself time. You are too noble and good to do anyone an injustice," she pleaded.

"They say love is a blind little god, Ellen, but I believe I can open his eyes,' he said as he affectionately drew her up into his lap. You asked me just now to give you, Carrier and myself more time; you shall have it. In little more than eighteen months from now you will be twenty-one years old. If you will wait until then and your love for Carrier is unchanged and he asks my consent to marry you, I will give it."

"God forever bless you, my precious father, her heart overflowing with happiness and her eyes with tears.

"I will be frank with you my child," he said as soon as she could suppress her sobs sufficiently to listen to him. "I have given you this time because I know your idol will crumble into dust long before the time expires and you will see him in his true light, as I and others now see him."

"Never, never! You will see that I am right father.'

- 66 -

When Carrier called a few days later for his answer, Ellen saw him first and told him what it would be. Later he saw father and protested, but to no purpose.

"I left home to come here to school shortly after Carrier's first visit to us and have not been back since, but father wrote me all that I've been telling you. At the expiration of the eighteen months, which was about two months ago, matters stood as they were in the beginning, except that father's dislike for the man, and Ellen's love for him, had increased. Carrier, knowing that he was being watched, was on his good behavior. Father consented to the marriage provided he would resign from the army and that Ellen should continue to live with him. To this he readily consented, for he had no friends among his brother officers and the men heartily despised him. This letter I was reading as you came in is from Ellen, glowing with happiness and telling me the wedding - a very quiet one - will take place at home on the 8th of next month. Now, my dear boy, he continued, rising and knocking the ashes out of his meerschaum, you have a full history of the 'skeleton in the closet' of our household, put there by this handsome devil, for I cannot think of him in any other sense and this is a good picture of him," taking a full size daguerreotype off the mantel and handing it to me.

It was the likeness of one of the handsomest men I ever saw dressed in full uniform of a Captain of Cavalry. His hair was very light and worn long almost to his shoulders. A heavy blond moustached and whiskers that came to a point on his chest covered the lower part of his face. His forehead was broad and high, his brows two shades darker than his hair were rather heavy but finely shaped; his nose was prominent, arched.

But the eyes were his most remarkable feature, and yet for the life of me I could not have said in what respect they differed from other people's. There were not too large nor too small - they were a dark bluish gray, fringed with heavy lashes dark as his brows, but no pen can give the faintest idea of the expression that came out of these two 'windows of the soul.' For some moments I had been trying to decide what it was that I saw or did not see in these mystifying orbs when Nick asked me what I thought of him.

"One of the handsomest men I ever saw," I replied.

"Nothing like as handsome as he was three years ago when I first saw him. He had no beard then except his moustache, but in one of the many fights with the Indians since then he was shot through the cheek with an arrow making a dreadful scar and he wears a beard now to conceal it."

"It is a face once seen never forgotten," I said still trying to discover what there was about it that caused this feeling. "Perhaps after all, Nick, you may be mistaken in the man, or that after marriage Miss Ellen's devotion may completely change him for the better."

"Never, never," he replied slowly, shaking his head.

There was a confusion of voices in the hall, a stamping of feet to rid them of snow, and the next moment a half dozen of his classmates rushed in exclaiming. "Christmas gift, old man! Christmas gift!"

"We've brought the necessary articles along with which you can pay," said one as he began to take a number of eggs out of the pockets of his overcoat and deposit them on the table. Another produced a paper of sugar, a bucket of cream followed, and last came a quart bottle of "Old Williams 'Best" North Carolina whiskey.

"You make the best eggnog of any man in college, Nick."

"And we have agreed to let you have the honor of compounding the mixture for us this morning," exclaimed another.

"Oh, I can do fairly well," said Nick, as he laughingly shook hands with the party, "provided the ingredients are all right, but I've seen fresher looking eggs than those."

"The eggs are all right. Tome mashed three in his pocket as he came through the front gate and there was not a sign of a chicken in either," said the fellow with the sugar, as he began untying the package.

In a short time, all were busy under Nick's orders assisting in making the eggnog, and he apparently the jolliest in the lot. How little they dreamed of the sorrow in his heart.

CHAPTER VI

I AM INTRODUCED TO
CAPTAIN CARRIER AND HIS WIFE

Months have passed since the eighth of January, the marriage day of the beautiful Ellen Hardeman to Captain Carrier. The Hardeman couple had left immediately after the ceremony for Europe where they expected to spend five or six months. It was now the latter part of June. The students and the citizens of the village were in the midst of the turmoil and the excitement incident to the Commencement exercised that marked the close of the session. This was the event of the year for the students and the harvest season for the citizens. The little village had a few stores and a hotel, but was made up principally of boarding houses to accommodate students who could not get rooms in the regular University buildings. During commencement week those were filled to overflowing with visitors from all parts of the South. Parents would come to see their sons graduate, or take part in the exercises of their respective classes, accompanied by their daughters, who also came to see the other girls' brothers play their parts, and especially to enjoy the flirting and dancing in the old ballroom. Although not printed in the program, this was carried on with as much geal as any other part of the week's exercises.

Nick had been chosen valedictorian of his class. "Quite an honor, Freshy, and one I do not think I should have, for I am sure there are at least a half dozen men in the class more deserving." he said to me the evening before he was to deliver his address.

"You should appreciate it all the more, I said, since you were their unanimous choice."

"Oh, I do, but there is not a member of my family here to share the honor with me. I believe I am the only member of the class without a relative present. I had a letter from Ellen last week saying that she and Carrier had just handed in New York, and that she would try and persuade Carrier to come by here on their way South, see me graduate, and all go home together, but as I've heard nothing from her since, I assume she could not persuade her 'lord and master.' "

"Lover you mean instead of master," I suggested.

"No I mean master and should have used that word alone. She doubtless looked upon him as her 'lord and lover' when she left, but unless I am greatly mistaken she has returned from her bridal trip recognizing him only as her master."

"Now that is not like you, Nick, for whatever your faults may be no one can accuse you of unfairness, and that is manifestly unjust to Captain Carrier. You haven't seen either of them since their marriage, and unless your sister has written you complaining..."

"Stop" he exclaimed sharply. "She has written me, written me often, but not to complain. She will never complain. She is one of the kind who will bleed inwardly and never utter a sound."

"Then why do you say she returns from a six months' bridal trip recognizing her husband only as her..." I hesitated at the word.

"Master," he added bitterly. "I will tell you why I use the word. I have

- 71 -

kept every letter she has written me since she has been married, have noted every expression and scanned every line and word as carefully as a miser testing his coin for a counterfeit and I have found...

"counterfeits, my dear boy, nothing but counterfeits. When she first landed on the other side, her letters were not so frequent, but they were genuine with the ring of true happiness about them. Every page reflected a joyous satisfied heart. Then they began to come oftener, evidently she found more time to write; they were newsy and interesting as ever, but there was something lacking in them. I imagined I could detect a false note, now and then, in the music of her heart that filled her first letters with love and happiness. Every succeeding letter confirmed my suspicious, and when I compared her first letters with the last there was not longer room to doubt. The music in her heart is hushed. Maybe she does not realize it herself. Only one who has watched her with loving, anxious eyes as I have can detect the discord, but it is there."

We were on our way to the "Ranch" and walked along in silence for a little way when I ventured to ask, "Were her last letters so very sad?" "No, you could not call them sad, but they were filled with thoughts of home and father once more, as she expressed it. It was not a homesick cry, but the wail of an unhappy child. I read all of this, you understand Freshy, between the lines as she has not intentionally written a word that would cause me to form this opinion."

"Nick, I hope your anxiety for her and your prejudice against Carrier has misled you in the matter."

Just as he started to reply, a woman's voice exclaimed from a passing carriage: "Oh, there he is! Stop driver, stop!"

I looked up and saw a lady leaning over the carriage door waving one hand at Nick and vainly trying to unfasten the door with the other. At the sound of the voice he turned quickly. In a bound he was by the side of the carriage and wrenching the door open caught her in his arms as she sprang out, exclaiming: "Ellen, my dear, dear sister, where did you come from? When did you get here?"

"Give me breath to answer brother," she replied between kisses, laughter, and tears. "It was only at the last moment that Captain Carrier - oh, I've forgot you've not had a chance to speak to him yet," and releasing herself from his arms, she slipped to one side giving me sight of a gentleman still seated in the carriage, but leaning forward with one foot resting on the step. I instantly recognized Carrier from the picture I had seen. There was no mistaking that handsome face, heavy blond moustache and pointed beard. Nick stepped forward and extended his hand.

"How are you Walker? Glad to see you, said Carrier. Get in and come with us to the hotel as though he had seen him the day before.

"Unless you telegraphed for rooms, you will not find a vacant one in the village, this is our Commencement week and there is an unusually large crowd here." Nick replied

"Just what I was afraid of when I consented to come by this little place. Now, what are you going to do about it, Ellen?" Her face flushed slightly as she replied:

"Oh, I daresay brother can find us accommodation for a day or two."

"Easy enough," Nick replied. "You can occupy *my* rooms. They are cool and quite comfortable, and I will bunk with my friend." and turning to me said, "Come here, Hord, and let me present you to my sister and Captain Carrier."

"Ah, and this is Mr. Hord, I am so glad to meet you. I feel as if you were an old acquaintance, brother has so often mentioned you in his letters," she said, smiling sweetly as I came up, and giving my hand a warm pressure, "Let me present you to my husband, Captain Carrier, Mr. Hord." He recognized this introduction with such a careless nod that I restrained the impulse to extend my hand, and simply lifted my hat.

"Where are your rooms brother? Let's get to them quick, I am suffocating with dust, not all to be charged to your village however, but to two days travel on the cars," she said laughingly.

"Only a short distance; we can walk if you prefer."

"Walk by all means. I've been cooped up in the cars so long it will be a relief to walk."

"All right, but what about your luggage?" inquired Nick.

"Oh, we checked our trunks through to New Orleans from New York and only have a small valise with us. Please hand it out, Captain."

"It is decidedly heavier than I care to pack around," said Carrier as he passed it out to Nick.

"I can carry it easily," said Nick, as he swung it lightly to his shoulder. "Freshy, you show Captain Carrier the way. Ellen and I will walk on."

Neither the artist who made his picture, nor Nick in his description of him, had flattered Carrier, for after having paid his fare and discharged the carriage, as he came walking up to where I stood I thought I had never seen a finer specimen of physical manhood or a handsomer face.

"Well er - I beg pardon, but I did not catch your name," he said as came up.

"Hord," I answered.

"Well Hord, which way do we go?"

"Turn this corner and down the next street."

"Street? I suppose you call it that out or courtesy," Carrier said.

"To our visitors, yes, but we allow them the privilege to call it a road if they choose."

"A road is decidedly more proper."

It was not the words, but the tone and manner in which he spoke that prompted me to say:

"Oh, we never force our courtesy or our opinions on anyone. If it's more pleasant for you to consider it a quagmire I'll not object."

"I simply prefer to call things by their proper names," he answered, looking at me sharply.

"So I observed when you spoke to your brother-in-law a moment ago."

"And that was?"

"That you called him Walker."

If you were to try to find Walker Hardeman, very few would know who you were looking for, while every student and villager knows him as "Nick" Hardeman.

"Well, I'm not asking anyone, especially schoolboys, to tell me," and without giving me time to reply asked: "How far is it to Walker's rooms?"

"Only a hundred yards or so. They are on the first floor of that large two-story frame building on the left-hand side of this street, road, or quagmire," I said pleasantly.

"Thank you, said Carrier. I'll not trouble you to accompany me further," and without looking towards me, waved his hand slightly and quickened his pace.

I knew that Nick was expecting me to join them at his rooms. So lifting my hat, I said, "Good evening, Mr. Carrier," and walked back to my room.

It was after 11 o'clock, and thinking Nick had found other quarters for the night, I was preparing to retire when he came in. "I am a little late," he explained. "Ordered our suppers sent to my rooms and it was after eight before they came. But why did you not come around? I expected you, ordered your supper with ours, and Ellen asked after you several times."

"I venture to say your 'distinguished' brother-in-law made no inquiries of that kind."

"No I cannot say he did," said Nick laughing. "By the way, what do you think of him?"

"Arrogant as a prince, which may in a measure be because of his military training but aside from this, he impresses me as a man devoid of any sentiment and doesn't have a very angelic disposition."

"I must say certainly a not very flattering report of my 'distinguished' brother-in-law. On what grounds do you base your opinions? You and the Captain surely did not have time to get sufficiently well acquainted with each other to quarrel, did you?" I detected a quizzical smile on his face as he asked the question, through the wreaths of smoke that curled up from his pipe. I asked him if he said we quarreled. Nick said, "Oh no, on the contrary, when I asked him where you were, he said rather than be annoyed by a talkative freshman, he preferred walking alone, and had dismissed you," and he threw his head back with a hearty laugh. I could feel the blood tingling in my face. As I made no reply, he asked. "Is it so?" "True as gospel" "Tell me about it, Freshy. I would have given my quarterly allowance to have seen it."

Although Nick seemed to enjoy it, immensely, I confess I could not see the humor in it; but I repeated the conversation between Carrier and myself as nearly as I could.

"Well Freshy, you can safely bet any odds you like from this time on that your friend 'Mr. Carrier' is not one of your admirers."

"After all, Nick, I may have judged him too harshly. We were not together fifteen minutes. What you had told me about him unquestionably biased me in my opinion to start with, and I may be really more at fault in speaking to him in the manner I did than he was in his replies."

"I only wish I could think you were at fault, my boy, but I cannot. You have judged him correctly.

"I asked, "what do you think of your sister's happiness, now that you have seen her?" I cannot say positively. I've not seen her long enough yet; not that I expect her to tell me anything, but her heart will speak through her eyes. She has changed some. She is more reserved, and I imagine there is less mirth in her laugh."

"I hope all of it is only in your imagination, Nick."

"I hope so," he answered. For some moments we sat in silence watching the smoke from our pipes float lazily out of the window, when he continued; "But I've seen enough to know that her marriage has changed somewhat the current of my life."

"In what way? You graduate tomorrow and are just starting in life. You have not as yet drifted into a current."

"No, but I have had one marked out ever since I was old enough to think of such things. When I was twenty-one, father gave me the old ranch, that my grandfather first settled up on the Brazos. While I expected to look after it, I had no idea of making it my permanent home, but expected to live with me as long as he lived. Of course I supposed Ellen would marry, bit I hoped it would be some one for whom I could have some respect and affection. Now all that is changed, so I shall live on my own ranch. Perhaps after all it is best."

"Is it not probable that Carrier will want to establish a house of his own," I inquired.

"God forbid, said Nick, if her life is to be an unhappy one, let her be surrounded by those who love her. But father gave his consent to the marriage on the condition that Ellen should not leave him."

"But with our sister's fortune in his hands, I replied, he would have but little consideration for this agreement, if he felt disposed to go."

"But he hasn't got her fortune in his hands, Nick said. Father, knowing that Uncle Walker intends leaving me his property, divided mother's fortune equally between the two girls and entailed it upon them. Carrier under no circumstances can do more than spend the income, some six or eight thousand a year from Ellen's portion. But as little as I fancy him, I must say that I do not think he is a man who would be influenced by money in a matter of this kind. If he wanted to go, go he would if it were a hut and a crust and leaving a palace behind him. Like all gamblers he cares nothing for money, except as it will supply his immediate wants."

"Do you suppose he continues to gamble now since his marriage?"

"I can't say much as to that. He left immediately after his marriage and has just returned, but it was one of his many 'accomplishments' before he was married," said Nick.

"I suppose he has given it up, let's hope so anyway. In the meantime, if you expect to distinguish yourself tomorrow and divide honors with post orator, John G. Sax, you had better turn in and get a wink of sleep."

CHAPTER VII

THE LAST COMMENCEMENT BALL.

The Commencement exercises closed as usual with a grand ball, the last given under the old regime, the last of its kind that ever will be given.

Destiny in a generous mood made this grand ball at the University the largest assemblage of youth and beauty and wealth ever gathered at the historic University. At the same time, she mercifully withheld from us the dark blood-stained picture, smeared by the ruthless hand of war, which many of the joyous students were to witness in so short a time.

Who could look without a shudder upon the young lovers loitering over the moonlit campus in the soft June air, see him bow his head near her blushing cheeks to catch the whispered answer to his wooing, his bright eyes sparkling with triumph, his young heart beating fast with happiness and know that the same moon should shortly shed its silvery beams on a bloody battlefield, where the night dew of Heaven beading the mask of death would moisten his pallid face, the young heart forever still.

Who would wish to know that many of the brave, boyish faces of the young gallants, now beaming with happiness, would soon be trampled into shapeless masses of flesh and blood beneath the hoofs of charging squadrons?

Fifty years have passed, but memory's mirror reflects brightly the scenes and incidents of that lovely June night in 1860. I see the ballroom beautifully decorated with palms and flowers, its massive chandeliers and candelabras filled with hundreds of wax candles shedding a bright golden light on the sumptuous scene. The joyous dancers glided over the polished waxed floor to the soft waltz music of the United States Marine Band. A few hours after the last strains of Schubert's Serenade had died away in a sweet lingering cadence under the grand old oaks, I can see the empty room dimly lighted by the last flickering flames of the candles. Here and there a scrap of ribbon on the floor, a bit of lace, a withered flower, a torn and discarded glove, and a pile of rose leaves lay scattered.

The janitors had extinguished the last sputtering light, and the ballroom had been closed an hour or more, before Nick could get away from the classmates who had assembled just outside to bid him goodbye.

"Just time to change my clothes before the wagon will call for my trunks" he said, pointing to a rosy tinge in the east that indicated the approach of another day. He had scarcely made the change before there was a rap on the door, and the gray woolly head of old Bob, the baggage man, was thrust in.

"All right Uncle Bob, I am ready for you, but you are a little early, are you not?"

"Yas suh, de road ain't none too good 'n it's twelve mighty long miles to Hillsboro, Mars Nick.

"Did you go by my rooms and get Captain Carrier's valise?"

"Yas suh, I went by; he wusn't quite ready; said tell you he would fetch it in the kerrige wid 'm, but tole me to tell you to be ready kass he's be 'round fer you terrectly 'n didn't want to wait."

"All right Uncle Bob, I'll be ready. Put this trunk on your wagon, it is light, you can handle it yourself, and I will help you with the heavy one."

The old man bent over the trunk, but instead of tossing it on his shoulder and walking out, seemed to be engaged in fixing the straps, then without looking up, asked:

"Is dat man 'round at your room eny kin to you, Mars Nick?

No blood kin, Uncle Bob but--

"dar now! I done said it," interrupted the old fellow straightening up with a pleased expression on his face, "I knowed it."

"know what?" said Nick.

"I knowed he was no blood kin to you, Mars Nick."

"what made you think so, Uncle Bob?"

"kase, when I called for the baggage he cum to de door. He had 'r bottle 'n 'r tumbler in his han'. It smelt lack sum uv your stuff, Mars Nick, 'n s'posin' he wuz some uv your kinfolks I axed him to give me a drop to sorter wake him up."

"Well, and did he give you a drink, Uncle Bob?"

The old man threw the trunk on his shoulder before answering, and as he turned to walk out said:

"no sir, he cussed me 'n tole me to git out before he kicked me out."

"D--d hog," muttered Nick, as the old man passed out. No name was mentioned, but I was satisfied the epithet was not intended for

Uncle Bob, for I heard him when he went out to help the old man place the heavy trunk on the wagon say to him, "Take this dollar, Uncle Bob, it will buy you two drinks when you get to Hillsboro."

"I wish you were going with me now, freshy, instead of waiting until your next vacation to pay me a visit," he said as he came in and seated himself in the open window. "I could give you any kind of hunting you like from Buffalo to Jack rabbits and furnish you with as good a mount as you can find on any of the blue grass farms of Tennessee or Kentucky."

"That's a pretty strong assertion, I said, for we raise the best horses in the world on our blue grass farms.

True enough and we buy the best you raise, and then improve upon what we buy."

"Do you mean to say that you have better horses in Texas than we have in Tennessee?

"Yes, for our purpose. In Texas, we ride for business, not for pleasure, and we want a horse that will go the greatest distance in the shortest time with the least distress to horse and rider. Your swift thoroughbred runners crossed with the wild hardy blood of our western mustangs gives us the best horse in the world. His own courage, and he has plenty of it, supplemented by the courage and speed of your thoroughbred, enables him to carry a hundred and fifty or sixty-pound rider ninety miles a day. At night, all he asks is to stake him out where he can get a good supper on our rough prairie grass and next morning he is ready to cover the same distance without damage to man or horse."

Nick, "you don't mean to say that the average Texas mustang can do this?"

"Of course not, only those that were properly bred. Father has four or five hundred head of mustangs as wild, hardy and vicious brutes as ever stood on four legs, some of them never even had a branding iron on them, but I venture to say he has a hundred cow ponies that can carry your weight two hundred miles in thirty-six hours and then toss you out of the saddle unless you are a good rider." I should like to own one as good as that." "Well, said Nick, come and go home with me, and I will give you the best one on the ranch. It's a great temptation Nick, but I shall have to postpone my visit until next vacation."

"Perhaps after all that is best," he said after reflecting a moment, "for by that time I will be settled, on my ranch up on the Brazos keeping bachelor's hall."

"It's more likely you will be married by that time and have a wife to boss both of us."

"Not a bit of it. I am going to keep 'shack' as we say in Texas for two years, until the kitten gets through school, and then she will come up and keep house for me. The chances are ten to one Miss Catherine will be married before then, I said. Comparing the last photograph she sent you, in which she appears in a magnificent evening costume taken with her dogs and six shooters, one would suppose she is making rapid progress in becoming a devotee of fashionable society."

"You would not think so if you had read the letter that came with it, Nick replied. She said that while her teachers think they are civilizing her by making her masquerade in the flowers, feathers, and foibles of society, her heart is aching all the time for her dear old 'Daddy' and her life on the open prairie with her horse, gun and dogs.

Then I presume, instead of enjoying the winter society of New Orleans, she will spend it at the ranch.

Yes, indeed, she goes home every chance she gets. In winter the Convent only suspends recitations during the Christmas holidays. Yet she always manges to get special permission to take two weeks, which she spends at home."

"As you've not seen her since you were at home more than three years ago, I daresay you will find her very much changed, said I.

"A little perhaps in appearance. She is seventeen years old now, but not a bit in spirit or disposition. A few days in the saddle, a little practice with her pistols, and I would match her against the best rider or pistol shot in the State."

"Well I hope -- Hello, there they are, "and as I spoke, I heard a carriage stop in front of the door and Carrier's voice calling to Nick not to keep them waiting."

"Goodbye and God bless you, old fellow," I said, returning the embrace of his arm thrown over my shoulder. "I shall step out and bid your sister goodbye."

"You up this early! she exclaimed with a look of surprise as I came out.

"After honoring me as you did last night with the only waltz you danced, you surely did not think I would let you go without wishing you a bon voyage. Why, my dear Madam, I have sat up all night for fear of missing you."

"Oh my, how very complimentary - What a dreadful tax it must have been and are you sure now that you are not talking in your sleep? Never was more wide awake in my life, Madam."

"Then I think I must reward your gallantry by permitting you to kiss my hand," she laughed as she extended it over the carriage door, "and if you do it as gracefully as you waltz, I will tell Catherine she must be on her guard when you visit us, for 'Nick's Freshman' as she calls you is simply irresistible."

"Especially when he has on a spike coat," said Nick.

"Don't mention the spike if you please. I know her opinion of a freshman with a spike and it is not altogether as flattering as one could wish.

He is still sore, Ellen, over his hazing experience and how the Kitten enjoyed my description of it. Oh well, he will be a sophomore next season, and I daresay, retaliate upon some unfortunate freshman. If I could happen to catch one of Miss Catherine's special friends, I confess it would afford me the greatest satisfaction I could wish."

"We will miss the train if we spend the day here talking. Get in Walker, and let's go," said Carrier impatiently as he pushed the door open from the inside. Only one who knew him as well as I did could have detected the flash of anger in Nick's black eyes at this peremptory order, for it came and went like an electric light.

You are perfectly right, Captain," he said smiling. "It is a self-evident fact, as old Bull would say, if we spend the day here talking, why we will be here tonight, consequently cannot catch a train of cars twelve miles away. But as we do not propose to spend the day here, and as there is ample time, there is no occasion to be in a rush."

The two men were looking into each other's eyes as he spoke. There was a mirthless smile on Nick's lips and, although I had seen him as I thought in all different moods, there was a look in his eyes I had never seen before. It was not indifference, contempt, or anger, but something stronger and deeper than all of these combined. Knowing Carrier so very slightly I could tell nothing from his expression, but his head was thrust forward like a snake about to strike. I imagined his eyes were less open than I remembered them and I could distinctly see his thin nostrils ope and close rapidly. It was only an instant their eyes met, but in that instant, each had felt the sensation an expert swordsman feels when his blade first clicks against his adversary's and he feels the iron muscle in his arm, the pliant wrist, the unwavering look, and realizes that the fight to the death is on.

Nick had taken out his watch, looked at the time, and was dangling it by the chain while talking to Carrier; replacing it now in his pocket he drew out his pipe case and taking out his briar root filled it leisurely, then turning to me said;

"freshy, I don't believe I have tobacco sufficient to last me to Hillsboro."

"Let me get you some, Nick, I suggested, and started towards the door of my room.

By no means, stay here. I know where you keep it and will help myself."

As he turned away Carrier closed the carriage door with a slam and dropped back on the seat.

"Brother won't be hurried," said Mrs. Carrier. I thought the voice was less cheery than when she spoke last, and I imagined there was a shade less color in her face.

"You have ample time, Madam," I replied. "You could almost walk the distance if you were to start now."

"freshy, I've robbed you," said Nick coming out of the door, "but as it is the last chance I'll have to get any of old man Durham's tobacco I thought I had better take all in sight."

"Get in brother," said Mrs. Carrier pushing open the door again.

"Thanks Ellen, but I am smoking and will sit out with the driver where I can enjoy my pipe and get a breath of this fresh morning air. Remember that visit, my boy." He gave my hand a parting squeeze and swung himself up to the seat. The next moment the carriage was rolling down the main street of the little village, and the first beams of the rising sun rested on his handsome face as he turned and waved me a last farewell.

A few days afterwards, I also left for my home in Tennessee to spend my vacation, but returned in time to resume my studies the first of September and occupied Nick's old rooms at the Ranch, partly from sentiment because I had become attached to them, but more on account of the fact that he had left me all of his athletic equipment; "Which I will and bequeath to my freshman to have and to hold, etc., etc.," as he expressed it in his college will which he read at a supper given to his class a few nights before he left, where the fun was a bit fast and the punch a shade strong.

Six weeks or more had passed since the opening of the session and I had fully asserted my dignity as a sophomore by assisting to haze quite a number of homesick freshmen in a manner most comprehensive to them and satisfactory to me, before I began to cultivate something more than a casual acquaintance with my studies. It was then that I realized fully the assistance Hardeman had rendered in coaching me through my freshman year. "Never neglect your duties, boy, one of which is to write to me regularly," had been his parting injunction and however much I might have neglected other things I was punctual in this, and the answers came equally as promptly. He had repeatedly and at different times mentioned each member of his family except his brother-in-law, Captain Carrier, which I attributed largely to his knowledge of the fact that I was not a special admirer of the Captain. In order to relieve him of any hesitancy on that point I inquired in one of my letters, "How is my friend, Mr. Carrier, panning out?" In his next letter he replied: "Your friend, Mr. Carrier, is fully sustaining his army reputation as a drunkard and a gambler, and I've no doubt he will present his other and more damnable traits of character as a brute with equal accuracy and promptness whenever an opportunity presents itself or his inclinations lead him that way."

x x x x

It was the memorable year of 1860. The fateful day for electing a President of the United States had come and gone. Destiny had taken part in the political contest and had chosen an obscure man from a new party to fill the highest office that was within the gift of thirty million people. The nation was stirred by this startling result as it had not been since the firing of the first gun at Lexington resounded around the world proclaiming our intentions to give our lives if necessary to maintain our rights. But all was peace and quiet at the old University. The bell in the chapel rang out its mellow notes as usual, calling the students to prayers and recitations, and they responded with light hearts and heedless care, unmindful of the ominous roar of the political sea that was boiling and seething outside. Where anxious vision could see the foam created waves tingled with red from the last sunset on a peaceful nation; a crimson sign of what was soon to follow.

When it was assured beyond a doubt that an "Abolitionist" had been elected President, we only paused a moment in surprise and said to each other; "What of it? Did not the Government hang old John Brown last year for trying to interfere with our constitutional rights? Uncle Sam is all right. Hurrah for Uncle Sam!"

Nick's letters continued to come regularly. He considered Lincoln's election a matter for serious consideration, but his grief and anxiety for his sister drove every other thought out of his mind. Carrier had gone from bad to worse, if such could be possible. When he gave up his commission in the army to marry Ellen Hardeman, he gave up his only means of support, and like most army officers, had saved nothing out of his pay. He had frankly told Colonel Hardeman this when the latter had informed him that he would never allow Ellen to leave him, and that Carrier must resign before he would give his consent to the marriage. Carrier demurred, for with all of his vices he cared nothing for money except to gratify his individual wants, however he finally consented.

Colonel Hardeman appreciating his condition, and to relieve him of any pecuniary embarrassment, settle an annuity on him of five thousand dollars subject to his own will and pleasure, independent of his wife's fortune, of which he knew nothing until he was advised by his bankers in New Orleans the morning after he was married. In addition to this Colonel Hardeman had given him five thousand dollars the morning he left as a bridal present to defray their six months trip abroad. It was now only about the first of December, yet both of these amounts had disappeared with nearly five thousand dollars more in the shape of drafts drawn on and accepted by Colonel Hardeman.

But it was not the money, for Colonel Hardeman was an exceedingly wealthy man, neither was it the manner in which the money was spent, although nearly all of it went to satiate his beastly orgies and gambling in the lowest dens of vice in New Orleans where he spent most of his time. It was the cruel, heartless indifference with which he treated his faithful and affectionate young wife; a surer, if not as quick way as brute force to break the tender, loving, loyal heart of a sensitive woman. This caused her father and brother to feel the keenest pangs of grief and anxiety. Had he welted her fair, tender cheek with his clenched hand.

One gesture of love from him would have purchased his forgiveness, and the bloom on her cheek would have returned.

Recitations were suspended for the Christmas Holidays at the University; these were passed and we had once more settled down to our studies, trusting "Uncle Sam" to take care of our political affairs. My last letter from Nick was dated from New Orleans a few days before Christmas and its contents were such as to cause me much anxiety.

He wrote: "The expected has happened, an open, and I hope an irreparable, rupture between father and Carrier. It happened in my absence. We had heard nothing of Carrier for three weeks, when father was notified by his bankers in New Orleans that Carrier had drawn another draft on him for twenty-five hundred dollars. He wired them not to pay it. A few days later Carrier arrived from New Orleans beastly drunk. Hot words ensued. Next morning he informed father that he intended taking Ellen to New Orleans with him where he intended to live in the future. When reminded of his obligation not to take her away he only laughed in father's face and ordered Ellen to get ready. She begged piteously and tearfully to remain, she is *enciente* and scarcely able to leave her room. His answer was an oath, which was not out of his mouth before father had knocked him down and disarmed him. When he arose it was to look into the muzzle of his own pistol and hear the order to march out of the house and never return under penalty of being arrested for obtaining money under false pretenses. Carrier marched, but after getting outside of the door he turned and said:

"Old man I go, but I am coming again for my wife, and by God I will have her, if I have to drag her by the hair of her head, tied to the tail of my horse, and carry you feet foremost with her."

"It was a week later when I returned home and I learned what had happened. I suggested to father that I come down to the city and see what I could learn of Carrier's movements. It is no trouble to trace him, for he is known to every detective and policeman in the city. He is on one of his wild and reckless sprees, gambling like a prince, but where he gets his money now, since father has refused to accept any more of his drafts, I am unable to say. I shall remain here a day or two longer and take the Kitten back with me to spend her Christmas at home."

It was this condition of affairs that made me more anxious than usual to hear from Nick. It was now the 7th of January and another letter was due. I had waited at the post office until after dark, but learning that the mail would probably be an hour late owing to the bitter cold and deep snow, had replenished my wood fire and was wrestling with my Greek lesson for early recitation next morning, when a knock on my door aroused me and my old boxing friend, Dick Blanchard, whose rooms were just across the hall, came in.

"Just dropped in to give you your mail. Happened to be passing the office as old Watson drove up. He was an hour late and nearly frozen," and threw a letter and paper on my table.

"Thank you Dick, I waited half an hour on the old man myself but the cold drove me in. Won't you sit down and warm?

No, thanks, he replied. I will get in my room and thaw out there. Goodnight."

I was disappointed when I saw the address on the letter was not Nick's well known writing, but the New Orleans postmark caught my eye and I opened it with some curiosity. I glanced at the signature which showed it was from Colonel Hardeman's old commission merchants, Walker & DeJean. It was dated January 3rd, and with some premonition of unpleasant news I read:

"Dear Sir: Having heard Mr. Nick Hardeman speak of the warm friendship he had for you, we send you a copy of the Picayune of yesterday morning which will fully inform you of the most horrible and brutal murder ever perpetrated in this or any other country. Mr. Nick Hardeman had just reached this city a few hours before the dreadful news came by wire from San Antonio, the nearest telegraph station to the scene of the crime. He accompanied by his uncle, Colonel Walker DeJean, left at once for home."

Nick's last letter had informed me that both he and Carrier were in New Orleans. This had caused me much anxiety, for I knew that if they should chance to meet it would most probably result in serious consequences for one or both. But, as the letter stated, he had left New Orleans, so it was with something like a feeling of relief that I tore the wrapper off the paper, prepared to read of some bloody cowboy feud up on his ranch. But icy fingers seemed to clutch my heart as I read the following startling headlines:

"A horrible double murder. The most dreadful crime ever perpetrated by a human fiend. Captain Carrier kills his beautiful young wife and her father, Colonel Lewis Hardeman. The murderer escapes but a hundred men are in pursuit."

- 94 -

I was dazed, stupefied by the awful words and it was not until I read them over the second time that I realized the horrible truth they conveyed. I rushed across the hall into Blanchard's room. He jumped up as I dashed open the door.

"What's the matter? What has happened?" he asked.

"My God, Blanchard, read that!" I exclaimed as I pointed to the headlines, every letter of which seemed blurred with blood. His face paled as he read them and for a moment we stood speechless with horror, then he said,

"What are the particulars?"

"See the paper, I've not read them." He handed it to me but I waved it aside, "Read them, Dick, I cannot," and dropping into a chair I listened to the following dispatch to the Picayune:

"San Antonio, January 2, 1861.

"A courier had just come in from Colonel Lewis Hardeman's Ranch and reports that Colonel Hardeman and his daughter, Mrs. Carrier, were both shot and killed instantly this morning by Mrs. Carrier's husband, Captain Carrier. No one witnessed the crime except Mrs. Carrier's old negro nurse, who was in the room at the time, but the faithful old creature, a French-Creole negress, is so wrought up with grief and a desire for vengeance that it is difficult to get a lucid statement from her.

"It seems that three weeks ago Carrier left the Ranch after having some misunderstanding with his father-in-law, Colonel Hardeman. Nothing had been seen of him since until this morning, when unexpectedly he rode up to the front door, dismounted and knocked for admittance. Mrs. Carrier was seated in the library on the sofa with her father reading to her, the old nurse sitting near by with some light needle work. None were aware of Carrier's arrival until they heard his step in the hall and his voice, asking the house boy, who admitted him where his wife was. Colonel Hardeman and his daughter both arose from the sofa at the sound of the voice and the next instant the door was thrown open by Carrier. For a moment he stood in the door glaring at them both, with eyes that looked like balls of fire as the nurse expresses it, then motioning to his wife, said:

" 'I am here to take you with me this time "By god you go, and go at once."

"Leave this house instantly, sir, you are drunk," said Colonel Hardeman as he made a step towards the door.

"Carrier raised the arm that had been hanging by his side just as Mrs. Carrier threw herself in front of her father with her arms around his neck. There was a flash and the bullet intended for her father went crashing through her own beautiful head. It was only the fractional part of a second, yet long enough for the bloody fiend to realize what he had done, when there was a second report, this time true to its mark the bullet sped, striking Colonel Hardeman in the forehead, and passing entirely through his head. He had thrown an arm around his daughter when she clasped him, and thus locked in a last embrace father and daughter sank to the floor dead.

"From the best information that can be gathered from the old nurse, all of this happened within a minute after Carrier had opened the library door. Closing and locking it he went out, mounted his horse and rode rapidly away toward the West. As there was no one about the house but the servants, it was some time before the old nurse's screams released her and revealed the fearful crime.

"*Mr. Nick Hardeman had left home two days before to accompany his younger sister, Miss Catherine, back to her school in New Orleans, and the foreman of the ranch was some ten miles away branding cattle. By the time he reached the house, learned the particulars, and organized a pursuing party, five hours had slipped away. As Carrier was a superb rider and splendidly mounted, he had placed fifty or sixty miles between him and his crime. With his thorough knowledge of all the country west, and his acquaintance with the different Indian tribes, these give him a big advantage in his efforts to escape the hundred or more determined men who were on his trail.*

No man in Texas was better known or more generally loved and admired than Colonel Lewis Hardeman. He was perhaps the wealthiest man in Texas. Two children survive him, Mr. Nick Hardeman and his sister Miss Catherine."

"Awful beyond expression," said Blanchard as he finished and dropped the paper on the floor. "What are you thinking of?" he said looking straight in my eyes. I had been thinking so intently that I had not even heard him read the latter part of the dispatch. I had been thinking of my dear friend, of his unutterable grief and suffering, of the inhuman fiend that caused it. It was not until the question was asked me the second time that I replied, and then expressed more the result of my thoughts than a reply to his question by saying:

"Blanchard, I am going to him."

"Going to whom?" he asked in surprise.

"To Nick Hardeman. Make my excuses to old Fet tomorrow morning at recitation; show him the paper; I am going to Hillsboro tonight to send a telegram to Nick. Will be back tomorrow and will leave tomorrow night if he wires me where to meet him.

"But my dear fellow, you will freeze to death tonight. Wait until morning."

"But before he was through speaking, I was drawing on my heavy riding boots, mounted a good stout horse, and inside half an hour was breasting the blizzard on the road to Hillsboro twelve miles away. It was some time after midnight that I reached the little station and aroused the sleepy operator.

"How long before I can get an answer to a wire from San Antonio, Texas?" I asked.

"Night message, not before ten o'clock tomorrow."

I wrote the following and told him to send a special delivery from San Antonio out to Hardeman's ranch:

"We will hunt him together. Can leave at once. Wire where I can meet you. Am waiting at Hillsboro."

It was ten o'clock the next day before I received a reply to my message saying Mr. Hardeman had left home some days before for the West, his whereabouts unknown. The message was signed by "Coleman." Manager of the ranch.

Thinking that Colonel DeJean had returned to New Orleans and that he could give me the desired information concerning Nick, I wired him. In a short time the answer came from the old commission Merchants, Walker & DeJean, saying: "Col. DeJean left the city with

Nick, as he wrote you. Have heard nothing from them since. Do not know where to reach either." Weary and disappointed I started back to Chapel Hill through the blinding snow storm.

Lights were twinkling in the little village when I dismounted at my rooms. Blanchard, anticipating my return, had a glowing wood fire blazing in the chimney, and on the hearth a saucepan steaming with hot punch. To his anxious inquiries I could only shake my head and hand him the telegrams I had received. Pulling off my top coat and heavy boots, and swallowing a glass of punch, I threw myself across the bed and for eight hours was wrapped in that dreamless sleep of utter exhaustion.

CHAPTER VIII

PLAYING SOLDIER.

There could have been no better illustration of the, patriotic sentiment of the best and most intelligent people of the South at this time than was shown by the five hundred students at the University of North Carolina. There were many representatives from every southern state. They were young, honest, intelligent and unprejudiced by party politics or sectional strife. They were Whigs and Democrats by birth and training, according to the political faith of their fathers, yet all alike had been taught in the same school of patriotism to love and respect the country and the flag for which their forefathers were so largely instrumental in establishing and for which many of them had given up their lives, from King's Mountain, S.C. to the City of Mexico. They were the descendants of a home loving people. This inherent instinct was part of their religion. They were the lineal descendants of those who, in dictating the Declaration of Independence and the framing of the agreement afterwards known as the Constitution of the United States, were careful to preserve the sovereignty of their respective states in forming a Union of the Colonies to fight the common foe. The sanctity of their home," the sovereignty and their state, the honor of their country, and the love of her flag were the cardinal virtues in the youth of the Old South. They were instilled into them from the cradle, and their character was built upon them.

South Carolina had passed an ordinance of secession on the 20th of December, and with one or two exceptions all of the students from that state had returned to their homes with a view of enlisting in her defense, should any attempt be made to coerce her back into the Union. But our faith in Uncle Sam was yet unshaken.

There will be no war, we had said to our South Carolina schoolmates in bidding them goodbye. A little sect of Abolition fanatics, we agreed had by an unfortunate combination of circumstances gained control of the government for the present, but they dare not violate the Constitution or abridge the rights it guarantees to the people - either South or North.

Our faith was sublime, but our judgment poor.

My father was an intense "old line Whig" in politics, consequently opposed to secession. "Make our fight if we must make it, in the halls of Congress under our Constitution and our flag," he had written me shortly after the election of Mr. Lincoln. But when South Carolina actually seceded, I wrote him again and mentioned what I considered the patriotism of the South Carolina boys in leaving school to defend their State if necessary from the "vile invader." I sprinkled the letter quite liberally with these oratorical expressions with a view of mentioning in a mild and unobtrusive postscript that my quarterly allowance would be due in a short time, and if he could let me have it a few days in advance it would be gratefully appreciated by his most dutiful, etc. His reply was as crisp as the exchange he enclosed. "Attend to your books and let South Carolina attend to her own affairs; she has been a 'thorn in the flesh' since the days of John Calhoun. After your own state secedes will be time enough for you to come home", was his reply.

But I found it very much easier to use the enclosure in my respected parent's letter than to follow the advice it contained, for stirring events and startling rumors were crowding upon us day and night, and studies were correspondingly neglected. It was late in the afternoon of February 2nd. I had just laid down *Abbott's Life of Napoleon* and reluctantly picked up one of my studies, when there was a confusion of footsteps in the hall, followed by a rush of five or six Texas boys into my room.

"Just dropped in to shake your paw and tell you good-bye, old fellow", they shouted.

"What's the matter? You look as wild-eyed as a lot of lunatics. Sit down."

"Haven't time. Not a moment to spare", said one.

"We leave for home tonight", put in another. "Old Texas has done it."

"Hurrah for old Texas!" and they gave a general yell.

"Have any of you sense enough left to tell me what you are talking about?" I said, grasping one of them by the collar. "What has old Texas done?"

"Seceded, man! Passed the ordinance of secession yesterday", he answered.

"Rats! 'Go tell it to the marines', I don't believe a word of it", I replied

"Then, how does that strike you?" said one of them producing a telegram. "It came this morning to Hillsboro and was sent up to me by the mail coach this evening. "We are all off for home tonight", and another general shout went up.

The despatch was dated at Austin, Texas, February 1st, '61, and read "Legislature passed the ordinance of secession today. Come home at once."

Bright, joyous, buoyant with life and hope, my warm friends and classmates, yet, only a hurried handshake, a light laughing jest, and they were gone out of my life forever.

Not a day passed since the news of the horrible murder of Colonel Hardeman and his daughter had reached me, that I had not thought of Nick, but not a word more had I heard of him. I knew so long as there was any chance whatever of catching Carrier he would not give up the chase, and that their meeting would be the death of one, perhaps both. In the meantime, weeks and months were slipping away rapidly, each pregnant with big events destined to make an epoch in the world's history. Records and deeds of the past were forgotten or overshadowed by startling issues of the present.

South Carolina had seceded from the United States on the 20th day of December, 1860, and Texas followed in February, '61. General Ben McCulloch had been placed in command of all the state troops and to him had been surrendered the arsenal with all of its ordnance supplies and all other United States property in the state. I knew if Hardeman was in Texas, he would have been with General McCulloch and have written me. Yet nearly three months passed and I had heard nothing of him. North Carolina had not yet seceded; the old state, upon whose soil the sentiments, afterwards embodied in the Constitution of the United

States, were first expressed and so generously sealed with the blood of her sons, was loath to sever the contract she had made, notwithstanding it had been so flagrantly violated by her northern sisters, but no choice was left her, and on the 20th day of May she formally withdrew from the Union and cast her lot with the Confederacy.

The "war spirit", however, prevailed over the state well before this formal action was taken by the Legislature. It had penetrated the little village of Chapel Hill to such an extent that Captain Ashe, an old soldier of the Mexican War and a resident of the village, had organized a company with the view of offering their services to the Confederacy in the event the state did not secede. My roommate and myself, with a number of other students from distant states, joined this company and were sent to Raleigh, where we united with other companies, organized into a regiment, the First North Carolina Volunteers, afterwards known as the "Bethel Regiment". We elected D.H. Hill to be our colonel, and formally offered our services to the Confederate Government.

What a glorious old regiment it was! From its ranks in after years more distinguished soldiers came than from any other single regiment in the Confederate Army; it was made up mostly from students and ex-students of the University, the best blood of the Old North State, supplemented with a liberal supply of the same kind from other states. How blissfully ignorant we all were of the real life and hardships of a soldier.

My roommate, Ernest Wittick and I were only privates, yet we spent hours in discussing the momentous question as to whether each of us should take a trunk or make one answer for our joint wardrobes. We finally decided to take only Wittick's, a big double decked affair that two years later would have held all the clothes of a regiment. Wittick was notably one of the best dressed men in college on all occasions. He was as fastidious in his taste as a woman, and no society belle knew better what to wear and how to wear it. Having ample means, he gratified his taste for good clothes. Our young lady friends had contributed lavishly such things as they thought necessary for a soldier's comfort from fine toilet soaps and extracts, beaded slippers and tobacco pouches, to smoking jackets and embroidered shirts, the latter worked by their own fair hands. One more thoughtful than the others sent in a manicure set.

Wittick would not trust me to do the packing, so calling his attention to such things as I wanted, I left him surrounded by this elaborate assortment and turned in for the night. I was just on the verge of sleep when he roused me. "What is it?" I asked.

"Do you want me to pack you one or two nightshirts? I find only one here."

"Oh, go to thunder, Wittick! I don't care whether you pack any."

"All right, old man, you needn't get huffy about it. If you prefer to use those you draw from the government instead of your own, I have no objection, but I am taking no chances myself."

"You blooming idiot: what are you talking about? Do you suppose the government is going to issue nightshirts to soldiers?"

"That's just what I don't know and I don't propose to speculate on it. Hence your humble servant has taken the precaution to pack in three of his own; but if the government issues us tents to sleep under, I don't see why they wouldn't issue nightshirts to sleep in. "You just wait, my fastidious youth, your eyes will be opened and you will see, said I." Wittick did see and that very soon.

We left the village for Raleigh the next morning for our camp of instruction, and in a few weeks were mustered into the Confederate service and our officers commissioned. The regiment was made up largely of wealthy young men who had brought servants with them. We had two in our mess, a cook and a general utility man to brush clothes, look after our laundry, run errands and the like. Since we were paying all expenses for our servants, Colonel Hill looked leniently, but rather with a grim smile, upon all this display of the privates, for the old fellow was a West Point man who had seen hard service in the Mexican War, and later became one of General Lee's most trusted army commanders.

A few days after we had been mustered into service, and he received his commission as Colonel, the regiment was called out on dress parade, and "General Order No. 1" was read out by the Adjutant announcing that the regiment would start for Richmond, Virginia, at ten the next day. Only forty pounds of personal baggage would be allowed to each private. Only commissioned officers would be allowed a servant, and only one to each company; the men were to supply themselves with cooked rations for two days. Tents must be struck and loaded at half past nine and the regiment move at ten. A look of consternation was on every face. After we had marched back to our quarters, the boys began to hurl curses loud and deep at the Colonel.

"What does the old creature mean anyway?" asked one.

"Mad, crazy as a loon. How in the devil's name does he expect us to live?"

"We are good for two days whichever way the cat jumps," said Dick Blanchard. "You heard what the order said about cooking up two days rations." Dick was quite as fond of good eating as Wittick was of good clothes.

"But who's going to do the cooking? That's the important question."

"You, of course," said Wittick who up to this time had been sitting quietly apart. "A man who is as fond of eating as you are certainly ought to know how to prepare it."

"Just listen to the 'walking fashion plate for young gentlemen's correct clothes', will you? It's dollars to cents he is thinking more of his back than his belly," replied Blanchard.

There was a general laugh, for all knew Wittick's weakness for good clothes.

"Laugh away, gentlemen, I confess I'm no glutton. I would rather be found dead in a clean shirt and an empty stomach, than stuffed like a prize pig, slovenly clad in dirty linen, as most of you seem to prefer. Forty pounds of baggage!" he exclaimed contemptuously, "and that to include gun and accoutrements. Why, old Hill certainly must expect us to fight the Yankees naked."

He little thought how true he was speaking at the time, for eighteen months later, as Captain of a four-gun battery of field artillery at the Second Battle of Manassas, this fastidious youth of immaculate linen, this dude of the regiment, fought his guns with such savage fierceness and heroism as to win the highest praise from the unemotional and silent Stonewall Jackson himself. Jackson had just finished his famous march around Pope destroying his supplies and defeating his army in detachments, and was now resting his weary troops on the Manassas battlefield waiting for Longstreet to come to his support and for Pope's attack with his concentrated force. So continuous had been the fighting, day and night for forty-eight hours that Wittick's guns were scarcely cool when he received orders from old Stonewall in person:

"Place your battery on yonder knoll, Captain, as quickly as possible, and hold it until you are relieved."

Then turning to one of his staff near him, he said:

"Tell A.P. Hill to support that battery."

Seated on his long-bodied sorrel, he watched through his glasses the cloud of dust that marked the progress of the battery to the hill, saw the guns wheel into position, and immediately go into action. A grim smile of satisfaction lit up the stern face of the old warrior for an instant; for the quick action of the battery told him that the enemy were making for the same vantage point from the other side, but Wittick's guns had reached it first. More anxious still, he watched a brigade unwind itself from A.P. Hill's light division and start in a double quick to support the battery now enveloped in smoke and drawing the concentrated fire of three Federal batteries; for he knew that nothing could live long and take such punishment. It was not half a mile away, but how slow the gray line seemed to go. Yet every man in it, sinewy and thin-flanked as grey hounds, were straining their hard trained muscles to their limit in the race to reach the hill in time, and they did.

But when they formed in line of battle just under the crest and the Colonel sent word for the battery to withdraw, he found that two of the four guns had been shot to splinters, a wheel shot off of another, leaving only one in action with not enough men left to man it. And Captain Wittick ,what of him? They found his fastidious youth of immaculate linen, this dude of my old regiment, bareheaded, stripped to the waist, his white skin streaked with powder and blood, the fragment of a shell having cut an ugly gash in his shoulder, cheering his few surviving comrades as he rammed home the charges himself or sighted the piece as required. It was that night, after the utter defeat of Pope, that old Stonewall learned the fate of Wittick's battery.

"Magnificent, good, very good!" he exclaimed. "Let him be supplied at once with guns we have taken from the enemy."

It was such gentle blood that flowed in the veins of Ernest Wittick and that fought in the ranks under such leaders as Lee, Jackson, Stuart, Forrest, and others that established the undying fame of the private Confederate soldier as well as that of his leaders.

x x x x

The very morning that General Order No. 1 was read in our camp of instruction, we left for Richmond, Virginia, where we were mustered into the service of the Confederacy for six months, as long a time as they would accept troops at that time. We thought this sufficient for us to "eat up" all the yankees. On the other hand, the yankees were only accepting volunteers for ninety days as they thought this ample time to either "hang all the rebel traitors in the South or run them into the Gulf of Mexico".

Our regiment was sent to the Peninsula and landed at the historic village of Yorktown. We were the first armed body of rebels that had marched through the streets of the old village since Cornwallis surrendered to Washington seventy-five years before. We were also the first and, at that time the only Confederate troops on the Peninsula. We soon learned that up to this time we had only been playing soldier, but now we were to experience the real article. It was drill, drill, drill from morning until night, varied only by throwing up fortifications, company drill, battalion drill, regimental drill and dress parade every evening. Wittick expressed the general feeling of the regiment when he said:

"Old Hill is pious enough himself, but he does not give his men time enough to say their prayers."

As we became more proficient in drill and better disciplined, General Magruder, who was in command of that department, began to test General Ben Cutler, commander of the Federal forces at Fortress Monroe. We would be marched down to within sight of the fortress, show ourselves and march back. This was repeated several times. "Old Ben" evidently had his good eye on our movements and was only waiting to accumulate "a sufficient force to catch and hang" all of us, as he expressed it. On the tenth of June, '61, he sent out five thousand troops to accomplish this task. Colonel Hill decided to make the fight at Big Bethel Church some ten or twelve miles below Yorktown. Our regiment had been strengthened by the addition of a four-gun battery from Richmond, consisting of three twelve-pound smooth bore guns and one six-pound rifled piece. Our fighting strength rose to about one thousand men.

Bethel Church was a few paces to the right of the road over which the enemy were advancing, and our line extended from the rear of the church across the road, with our extreme left drawn sharply back to protect our flank and give us the advantage of a little open field across which the enemy would have to move in order to reach us.

The result of this battle, the first of the War between the States, is a matter of history and of no special interest to the reader. However, an incident occurred during this little engagement which shows the irony of fate. My company was on the extreme left with the little open field in our front. There was no concert of action by the Federal forces; they made their attack by regiments or battalions separately, or independently of each other, and we whipped them in detail.

It was like a lot of boys fighting a bumblebees' nest -- one would rush up, get stung, run back, the another would come up and be repulsed likewise. In one of their spasmodic attempts to carry our line, a regiment started over the low rail fence on the opposite side of the little field not more than one hundred and fifty yards from us and directly to our front. We fired a volley and they promptly fell back into the bushes, but a young officer immediately jumped on the fence, threw one leg over it, and with drawn sword called on his men to follow. He was a target for a half dozen guns on our right, instantly followed by the report of a single shot. He threw up both hands and fell back dead amongst his men. This last shot was fired by a negro boy, our Captain's cook, who had asked permission to carry a gun and join in the fight. We afterwards learned that the officer he killed was Major Winthrop of Massachusetts, and it was a Massachusetts regiment he was trying to rally. So it was that in the first battle of a war, in which the abolishment of slavery was the leading cause, the principal officer killed in the engagment would be from the State of Massachusetts, the cradle of abolition, and should be killed by one of the race he was fighting to liberate.

By the time our six month enlistment expired the war was on in earnest. A number of big battles had been fought. McDowell's grand army had been utterly routed at Manassas. McClelland had replaced him in command, and it was evident that the next advance of the Federal army would be by way of the Peninsula.

Confederate troops were being concentrated there. When our regiment was mustered out many of the men immediately reenlisted in other commands from their states. Wittick and I decided to return to our homes and enlist with troops from our respective states, he in artillery and I in cavalry. Both of us had seen enough "foot service" to convince us that we preferred riding to walking. We stopped overnight in Richmond on our way home, and were seated in the rotunda of the old Spotswood Hotel when our attention was attracted to a group of officers gathered around a gentleman dressed in citizen's clothes. Where every one was in uniform, this of itself was sufficient to excite our curiosity.

"Who do you suppose he is, Wittick? Some fellow trying to get a government contract. He's applying in the wrong quarter for that. Those are all field officers, and if I am not mistaken in their appearance, they have been on the fighting line. He must be of some importance, however, from the interest they take in what he is saying. Perhaps he is a member of the Cabinet."

"You can bet your last penny he is not that, or a member of Congress either." said Wittick, "If so, he is not in uniform. Uniform! Why a Cabinet member or congressmen do not wear uniforms.

Don't they though? Did you ever see one that did not have on a plug hat and double-breasted coat? Have you observed our civilian's style of dress?" he said, nodding his head toward the group. No, I have not. Well, I have, and it is a bit peculiar. His clothes are alright and fit him perfectly, but that hat of his is decidedly out of line. Who would expect a well dressed, you might say an elegant looking gentleman, wearing a Texas sombrero with one side pinned up with a little brass star? Maybe its a gold star, Wittick; if so, how would that suit your fastidious taste? God or brass, I am curious to find out who the old guy is. Wait here a moment."

I watched him walk over to the register, call the clerk's attention to the group, and, instead of returning to me, quickly joined the party of officers. In a few moments, however, he returned.

"Well, why don't you ask who it is?" he said as I quietly continued to smoke my pipe. Because I do not have enough curiosity or impudence as you seem to have to ask a stranger why he prefers to wear a certain style of hat. But he is no stranger, at least not to you. Guess who it is."

Just at that moment the group around him broke apart; smiling and lifting his hat as he bade them good night I had a full view of a strong sun-tanned face that I knew, but for a moment could not recall. Just then one of the officers said to him:

"General, you will be sure to join us tomorrow?"

"With great pleasure," he replied, turning his face to the light. As he did so, I recognized him.

"General Ben McCulloch, by all that's lucky! I exclaimed, and rushed out after him. "This is General Ben McCulloch", I said placing my hand on his arm just as he was stepping into a carriage.

"Yes, sir, it is. What can I do for you?"

He shook my hand warmly when I told him who I was.

"Yes, yes, he answered to my rapid fire of questions. Nick Hardeman is alive in with my army. He is a Major in his Uncle DeJean's regiment. Yes, saw your father last week - spent a day at your house as I came over here. Now you must excuse me. I have an engagement with Mr. Davis and some of his Cabinet and my time is rather limited. I suppose your have been soldiering long enough to know how to do without sleep, and as I have some matters to talk over with you, and you doubtless want to hear more of your home folk and Nick, if you will wait until I return, we will have our chat." Thank you, General, I will wait for you."

At eleven o'clock I bade my old roommate, Wittick, farewell as his train left carrying him to his home in Alabama, where shortly after, he joined a battery of field artillery as a private and surrendered at Appamatox with an empty sleeve and the rank of Major.

It was well past one o'clock before General McCulloch returned.

"You are a McCulloch in looks but not in size", he said, after turning up the light in his room, and looking me over critically from head to foot.

I am not certain, General. I have three or four more years of growth left, but if I can measure up to the McCullochs in everything but size, I'll be perfectly satisfied.*

I suppose I ought to thank you in the name of the family for the implied compliment", he said, with one of those rare smiles that made his usually serious and thoughtful face look as soft and gentle as a woman's. I think they are a fairly good sort myself, but rather inclined to be rash and hot-headed at times, owing to the Scotch-Irish blood.

---

*General Ben McCulloch, born in Tennessee, had fought in the battle of San Jacinto under General Sam Houston in Texas' war for independence. Then he was commisioned a Captain of Rangers in Texas fighting indians and mexicians.

In the Mexican War that followed, he fought under General Taylor at the battle of Buena Vista, and was promoted to major by Taylor, who called him; "a bold, daring...scout and desperate fighter."

When the Civil War broke out, Jefferson Davis, President of the Confederacy, who had served with McCulloch at Buena Vista, commissioned him brigadier general in the CSA, the same date as General Robert E. Lee.

McCulloch had greater experience and competence than the militia general Price, so Davis decided to maintain a split command. McCulloch was killed by a sniper at the battle of Pea Ridge, March 7th, 1862.

I have heard that the most distinguished member of the family", I said bowing to him, "is a trifle inclined that way himself."

"Doubtless you have, yet if you had been with me half an hour ago, and heard some comments on my operations out West, as reported to him by General Price, you would have thought that some of the gentlemen considered me over cautious, even to the point of timidity."

The sarcasm in his tone did not escape me. He stood before the fire a moment looking intently at the blazing logs, then began walking up and down the length of the room with his hands clasped behind. Evidently his interview with Mr. Davis, or some of his Cabinet, had not been a very cheerful one, and, as many of us at that time thought Mr. Davis a demi-god who could do no wrong. I remained discreetly silent.

Mr. Davis, a West Pointer himself, is very much inclined that way" he continued.

"Yet you hold his commission, one of the first issued, as a Brigadier General in the Confederate army, and you are not a West Pointer, I offered.

"No, my military lessons were learned from actual experience in battle. It is from experience of this kind that the tactics taught at West Point are formed. Mr. Davis and I served together under his father-in-law, General Taylor, we were good friends and comrades. Knowing his predeliction for West Point men, I feel it a distinctive honor that he should have selected me, a civilian, one of the first to commission as a Brigadier General in the Confederate army. General Robert Lee's commission and mine are of the same date, and up to this time I am the only civilian that holds that rank.

"It was a strong proof of Mr. Davis' friendship for you", I said quietly.

"You are not very complimentary, young gentleman", said the General with a smile. "I would not accept such a position if I did not feel capable of discharging its duties."

He walked up and down the room a time or two, and then as if giving expression to his thoughts more than continuing his conversation with me he continued.

"And yet strong pressure is being brought to bear upon the President to persuade him that I am not the proper commander for the Department assigned to me."

His recent victory over Lyon and Seigle at Wilson Creek on the tenth of August was yet fresh in the minds of every one, and McCulloch was the idol of the western army at that time. He evidently saw the look of surprise on my face, and stopping in front of the fire, said,

"You look surprised, but you do not understand the situation."

After a turn or two up and down the room he continued.

"General Price is a brave, courteous and cultivated gentleman, but a better politician than a soldier. Yet he allowed Frank Blair, Tremont, and Harvey to beat him in politics by playing upon his Union sentiments and keeping him undecided as to what action he would have Missouri take, until Lyon had accumulated a sufficient force in St. Louis. Then Lyon drove him and his militia out of the state and did not stop pursuit until Price and his disorganized militia had fallen back upon my army for support.

Price had five or six thousand followers, and he at once proposed that we jointly advance and give Lyon and Seigle battle. I objected from the fact that his troops were absolutely disorganized, not over half of them armed, and these with shotguns and squirrel rifles, horse pistols and scythe blades converted into spears with not a dozen rounds of ammunition each.

My own force, not over three thousand, were fairly well armed and disciplined. While I was perfectly willing to give Lyon a fight, I wanted something like an even chance with him. I knew he had some six or seven thousand troops well armed, drilled, and provisioned. He had enough artillery and cavalry to make it hazardous to attack with many undisciplined and poorly armed troops in my force. I called General Price's attention to these conditions and urged him to organize his command at once. His ardor for battle was stronger than his discretion and he chafed under the delay required. This was the first discordant note between General Price and myself, but he went diligently to work organizing his men into regiments and brigades. In the meantime I sent word to General Hardee, who was commanding some two or three thousand troops at Pitman's Ferry, seeking his opinion of General Price's suggested advance into Missouri; and if he would support us. He replied that he would not make the move with less than four thousand disciplined and well armed men with at least six good batteries of artillery. I showed this message to Price, but it had no weight with him. He was as urgent as ever for an advance.

In the meantime three or four weeks had passed, and he was getting his troops into a more orderly condition. I knew there was no better fighting material in the world than these Missouri men, but it would be murderous to rush them up in disorganized, half-armed mass against Lyon's veterans. General Price was at my quarters one night urging me as usual to name a day for our advance, when one of my scouts came in and reported that Lyon and Sigel were advancing on us with about seven thousand men."

"Now it is fight or run', said Price jumping to his feet. Which is it? Fight, I think, but sit down, General,' I replied, let's discuss the matter".

Price said, "I think it best to call a council of the Brigade commanders at my headquarters at once when all of them can be heard, and I will at once issue the order for them to assemble.

But there is a matter we must have understood between ourselves, General, before the council assembles."

"And that is?", he said, turning to me with a look of surprise.

"Who is going to command our united forces to fight Lyon, I said.

Why as two-thirds of our force is mine, and I hold the rank of Major General, Price replied, I think I am the proper one to command.

Doubtless from your standpoint, General, but you certainly know that as an officer of the Confederate Government commanding regular Confederate troops, I cannot turn them over to any one unless ordered to do so by our government. Now as to rank, I think a Brigadier General in the Confederate army outranks a Major General of militia, especially when the state he represents is not a member of the Confederacy!"

This was the second discordant note between General Price and myself. After a little discussion as to the question of rank he finally consented to let me take command. Two days later the battle of Wilson Creek was fought and won. Lyon was killed and Seigle retreated rapidly up into Missouri. Price made immediate preparations to follow and urged me to join him. It was against my judgment, and even if I had been inclined to do so, it would have been in direct violation of my orders from the Secretary of War at Richmond.

Declining to join Price in his advance into Missouri was the third discordant note between us. I moved my troops back into Arkansas and thought nothing more of the matter.

About three weeks ago I received a request for Mr. Davis to come to Richmond, and tonight when I met him and some of his Cabinet I heard very distinct echoes from the discordant notes I have spoken of confirming my opinion that General Price is a better politician than a soldier. He has sent representatives to Richmond who have reported me as unwilling to cooperate with him, ascribing motives foreign to anything I have thought of. It is gratifying to know, however, that Mr. Davis and his Secretary of War approve entirely of my action but 'What are we going to do with Price?' is the question bothering the War Department now. The result will be, that a ranking officer will be sent out to take command of our forces, since Missouri has at last decided to join the Confederacy."

"Who will it be?" I inquired.

"That I am not at liberty to tell," said the General with a smile. "But enough of this. It is half past two and I must get a few hours sleep. I want to talk to you about your personal affairs. When I spent the night with your father on my way out here he told me where you were, that your term of service would soon expire and you would probably return home to join the Army of Tennessee. Now I have this proposition to make you, I want another staff officer who has had some military training, who will obey orders implicitly and promptly, and who is always in condition to do so unless sick or wounded."

His steel gray eyes seemed to bore into me as he spoke the last few words.

"I don't drink anything but water myself", he continued, and will not have a drinking man on my staff. But I am willing to take you on faith. As a staff officer, I offer you the rank of Captain, and if you prefer it to the Army of Tennessee, it is yours."

My heart felt as if it would thump through my ribs as I thought of being with dear old Nick once more, of campaigning with him, of fighting by his side, or talking over our college days as we sat and smoked around our bivouac fire.

Grasping the General's hand, I tried to thank him, but tears came instead of words.

"There, there, my boy, don't try to say it. Your face expresses all and more than you could say if you tried a month. I will have your commission made out tomorrow and have you assigned to me as an aide on my staff. As you leave early in the morning, I will get the papers made out and give them to you when you join me out West, which I hope will be soon. For the moment go home, see your father, whom I told of my intention, attend to such matters as he may require of you, then come to me. Now to bed."

I followed his advice so far as going to bed, but not to sleep. What bright anticipations! What glorious, vivid scenes crowded my brain. I could hear the soft mellow notes of the cavalry bugle sounding "boots and saddle". I could see the best riders and the best shots in the world forming into dense columns and hear the thrilling notes of the bugle sounding the "charge". I could see the sweep of the columns "by fours" upon the enemy, with Nick's brave bright face in front leading his matchless squadrons. Ah! Youth, Youth, glorious Youth, the garden of life, but where the flowers never bloom but once.

It seemed but a few moments since I had left General McCulloch when a knock on the door startled me from my revery, and a voice called out:

"Six er clock, boss. Your train leaves at seben. Jes time to git your breakfus 'n ketch it."

An hour later I was on my way home, which I had not seen for two years.

CHAPTER IX.

HOME COMING AND PLANTATION LIFE IN ANTE-BELLUM DAYS.

"Wake up, young man, wake up! We are at your stopping place." It was the voice of the conductor accompanied by a vigorous shake that aroused me from sleep.

On my way home from Richmond I had stopped a day or two at Chapel Hill to get my trunk and other belongings I had left when I joined the army, and the only all rail route at that time to my home in Tennessee ran through South Carolina and Georgia. It required nearly two days and a night to make the trip with the little wood-burning locomotives. It was before the advent of sleeping cars, and I thanked the conductor for his information as I yawned and stretched myself with a sense of relief. Looking out as we pulled into the station I could scarcely realize it was the quiet little town I had left two years previous. The depot platform was swarming with soldiers; the bright yellow-braided uniforms of the cavalrymen mingled with the blue-trimmed jackets of the infantry and the red-corded caps of the artillery. Not a familiar face did I see. I stood for a moment on the car step before getting down, when I heard someone exclaim:

"That's him! I seed him! That's my young marster! Let me by, gentlemens, ef you please."

I looked in the direction of the voice, and saw an arm and a black hand holding an old silk hat and a carriage whip above the crowd while the other, judging from the commotion, was evidently working the body of its owner through it.

"Let the old man pass; boys, he seems to be on a hot trail for somebody", said a voice in the crowd, and the next moment old Andy stood before me clasping the hand I had eagerly extended still holding his hat and whip, lightly and half carelessly on my shoulder, his honest black face beaming with pride and pleasure.

"Marse Ben! Marse Ben! I shorely is glad to see you"

And I'm just as glad to see you, Uncle Andy. How are all at home?

"How you is growed, to-b-shore, to-be-shore! exclaimed the old fellow in honest admiration still holding my hand as he eyed me from head to foot. "To be sure" was a favorite expression of the old man's to emphasize his opinions, and he always pronounced the three words with a deliberate pause between each other.

"Uncle Andy", as I had called him from infancy, was about forty-five years old. He was the gardener and assistant about the stables, and had held me on the back of my first horse when my legs were not much longer than the prongs of a carving fork. He had taught me to trap birds, snare rabbits, fish and swim. His care and affection for me in my infancy and his admiration of me as a child and young man were heartily returned, for Uncle Andy was a wonderful man in my childish imagination, and my affection for him strengthened with age. It was natural that my heart beat faster and with feelings stronger than simple pleasure when I felt the warm pressure of his honest black hand and saw his face beaming with happiness.

"N won't ole marster be proud to see you?" he continued. Uncle Andy, you haven't yet told me how he is. Well he might be better, Marse Ben, 'n he might be wus; dese times don't seem to suit him."

"Well, let's get out of this crowd and we can talk as we drive home."

He swung my heavy trunk on his shoulder, walked to the rear of the depot, and, as he deposited it in an express wagon drawn by a mule, he said in a half apologetic tone: "Ole Marster wouldn't let me bring de kerridge, said some uv de soldiers might take er fancy to de hosses 'n take 'm fum me, so he made me hitch old Beck to the carry-all. It's good enough for me, Uncle Andy, besides he couldn't have sent anything that would have made me feel more at home than you, old Beck, and the carry-all, for I've known you three all my life."

"You shorely has, 'cause old Beck was foaled jes two years after you wus born; she's nigh on to seventeen and you's nigh on to twenty."

"And the Devil, Uncle Andy, how is the old fellow looking? Is he still fighting a blind bridle?"

The old man smiled with a chuckle and shook his head as if it was a question beyond debate.

"I aint seed him since las spring, when ole Marster sole him to Captain Will Sikes."

"Sold him! I exclaimed. "Why, what on earth did Will Sikes want with him?"

"That's zactly what old Marster axed him when de Capen cum up to buy him. 'Why, Billy', old Marster say, no one on de place kin ride him but Andy 'n de ole brute 'll kick at de sight uv er collar'. Capen, well he laugh 'n say 'all right, Square, I'll risk it 'n ef he is sound I'll give you two hundred dollars fur him'. Old Marster made me go 'n bring up de Devil; Capen Will looks him over 'n says "I takes him, Square, 'n here's four bran new fifty dollar Confederate bills'. Ole Marster he sorter smile and turn up his nose when he took de money 'n say 'All right, Billy, he's your hoss, it's bout er even trade. De ole hoss is wuth nothin 'n your Confederate money is wuth less'. Mind you, old Marster don't set much stress by that kind uv money, but howsomever, he sold de Devil fur it."

In order that the reader may not think that Uncle Andy and I were on intimate terms with his satanic majesty, it is proper to say Devil was a magnificent chestnut gelding that had been my saddle horse for the past ten years. His dam had died when he was only a few weeks old, and my father had given me the little long-legged, delicate looking colt. I was only six years old, but Uncle Andy and I mothered him through his coltish days and he grew up to be a strong handsome three year old, but he would fight all attempts to work him. It was natural that the farm negroes should call him "The Devil". I was thinking how I could replace him when the old man noting my silence asked,

"Is you sorry he sold him?

"Well, I am disappointed, I expected to take him with me out west. He was so well suited for my service."

"Is you goin' in agin, Marse Ben? he asked quickly with an anxious note in his voice.

"Yes, just as soon as I can see my father and attend to anything he may wish. Then I will join General McCulloch's army in Arkansas. I want to take two good horses with me."

"You'll hafter have somebody to look after 'm fer you, wont you?" he asked after a pause.

"Yes, I thought I would take one of the young boys with me."

There was another pause and then turning to me he said in a low earnest tone:

"Marse Ben, tek me."

"Why, Uncle Andy, you are too old."

"Me too ole? Who me! Now Marse Ben you shorely is jokin', to-be-shore, to-be-shore; why. d'aint a man on d'plantation kin do more hard work 'n I kin, 'n as fer hosses - I done forgot more 'bout hosses 'n dese young boys'l ever learn."

"That is so, Uncle Andy, but you must be close to fifty."

"But I don't feel it, 'n supposin' I is 'n you gits hurt? Some uv de Yankees is liable to shoot you, now what would de young boys know what to do fer you?"

"Oh, they have surgeons, regular doctors to look after cases of that kind; besides, what would you know about it?"

"Who me! me! Why shorely you aint fergot, Marse Ben who waster pick d' thorns and rusty nails outen your feet, open de biles 'n stone bruises, and bind 'm up with slipperty-elm poultices, 'n tote you on his shoulders wid your legs 'cross his neck from one good fishing hole to 'nother up 'n down da creek when your feet was too o sore fer you to walk? You shorely aint fergot it, is you, Marse Ben?"

The appeal was irresistible; memories of my childhood days and the affectionate care of the old man filled my heart, and grasping his hand I said:

"You shall go with me, Uncle Andy. We've been partners all my life and we'll chance it together to the end."

Negroes are an emotional race, but they rarely ever express their joy in tears. They will laugh, sing, shout and dance for pleasure, but rarely tears, yet the old man's eyes were dim with tears as he squeezed my hand.

One must have been born in the old South, owned slaves and reared with them from infancy on a plantation to realize the strong ties of friendship and affection that existed between master and servant, or to understand the unwavering loyalty of the slaves to their former masters during our Civil War, or even after their emancipation.

The butler, the cook, the mistress' housemaid, and the coachman were strictly the "upper crust" of plantation society; then came the gardener, the young ladies' maid, and the houseboy and so on down in the social scale to the field hands.

My home was five miles out on the turnpike leading from Murfreesboro to Nashville, and the quiet of the country was in direct contrast to the turmoil and fuss of the little town we had left a mile or two behind. The road on either side for miles was lined with primitive forests of magnificent trees that towered above the dense undergrowth, and occasionally a field of fall-sown wheat that already was covering the dark rich soil with a carpet of green. Every foot of the road was familiar to me. I had gone over it almost daily from my childhood and I was equally as familiar with the surrounding country, for there was not a farm within ten miles of my home that I had not hunted over with my gun and pointer or following my fox hounds.

We passed through the forests and were now in the rich cultivated lands, half gathered crops of corn and cotton lined the road on either side. It was a scene of peaceful quiet and prosperity. No one would have thought that we were driving over historic ground, that in less than eighteen months one of the great battles of the Civil War would be fought here, the Battle of Stone's River. A mile or more to our left a line of timber, mostly cedar, marked the boundary of the cultivated lands; through these woods the wild Rebel yell would resound over the fertile fields as the victorious Confederates of Hardee's corps drove Rosencranz' right wing back upon his center. The heavy hedges on either side of the road and the railroad cut on our right would mark the spot where the terrific onslaught of the Confederates was checked by Hazen's gallant brigade of Federal troops and saved the day for Rozencranz. To our right, just beyond the railroad cut, the clear waters of Stone's River glided over its pebbly bottom. We were almost in sight of McFadden's Ford where on the following day General Bragg, made another of his blunders, demonstrating his inadequacy as commander of an army, by sending Breckenridge's brigade of Kentuckians to capture an inaccessible position on the high bluff across the river. It was certain death for them. This operation was equaled only by the deadly destruction Hood later brought down on his army at the Battle of Franklin. The gallant Kentuckians never faltered, but charged through the icy December waters of the river, waist deep, under withering Union fire that made the water run with their blood. They gained the position, but the unsupported small force that survived was unable to hold it."

No vision of these great events overshadowed our thoughts as we jogged along that bright December afternoon. A mile or two further we turned into the lawn gate of my home. Everything was just as I had left it. The magnificent old forest trees that I had played under as a barefoot boy stood thick as ever over the two story brick house with it solid walnut pillars supporting the porches in front looked as solid and hospitable as ever. However, I saw a marked change in my father as he met me in the hall. There was a careworn look in his eyes; his iron gray hair was almost white, his strong, square shoulders were stooping, and his step was not as firm. My father was not an emotional man, but his affection for his children was deep and strong. However I was unprepared for his warm greeting, especially since he was, or had been, an intense Union man, had voted against secession, and strenuously objected to my entering the Confederate Army. But my ovation, my joyous welcome home, came later. It was after supper I was passing through the hall when the house girl said:

"Some uv de folks is out in de back yard 'n wants to see you."

As I stepped out on the back porch I was greeted with,

"Howdy, Marse Ben, Howdy, Howdy, Howdy! How's your been?" from a dozen or more throats and twice as many hands were stretched out to me as they crowded up on the steps to clasp the two I gladly extended. On the outer edge of the group I heard some one say:

"Stop, 'Riah, stop. He aint gwine have none uv your foolishness now. He's er grown up man."

And a voice that I knew even before I knew my name answered:

"Turn me loose, Bob, turn me loose, I'm gwine to hug my white chile."

"You certainly shall, Aunt Maria, and I intend to hug my black mammy", I said as I jumped down from the steps to meet her.

The next moment her big, black arms were around my neck and mine around hers. There were but a few days difference between my birth and that of her youngest child. My mother was then quite feeble and could not supply the necessary amount of nourishment for a lusty baby like myself. Aunt Maria had been called in as a wet nurse.

It was several days after my return home before I mentioned my future intentions to my father concerning the army.

"So you accepted General McCulloch's offer of a position on his staff?"

"Yes sir, it was very kind of him, as well as yourself, for I expect you were instrumental in having him make it."

"Not at all, sir, none whatever. I presume my opinion would have little weight, as you were already in the army contrary to my advice."

"I am very sorry if I offended you, sir, in doing so, but I had enlisted before I received your letter advising me to wait until our own state seceded. I considered it a question of constitutional rights that affected every Southern state and the only way left to assert them was by force of arms."

He smoked a few moments in silence, then knocking the ashes from his pipe said:

"I suppose when you say constitutional rights you refer to secession and slavery. Granting that they are, is either of them, or both combined, comparable to the preservation of the Union? It was a fatal mistake made by the framers of our Constitution that they did not limit the sovereignty of the states to the sovereignty of the United States. This amendment to our Constitution could have been made, almost without a dissenting vote in Congress, any time previous to the past five or six years, this would have settled the question of secession forever and there would have been no war."

"But it would not have settled the slavery question, sir", I suggested.

"The slavery question would have settled itself. There may be differences of opinions as to the right of secession, but there are none concerning the question of slaves as property and the right to own them. Mr. Lincoln could not have raised an army of five thousand men, outside of two or three New England states, had he made the call for the purpose of freeing the negro instead of preserving the Union."

"But he is an 'Abolitionist', sir, and was elected by the Abolition Party."

"That does not make him a violator of the Constitution. He believes in abolishing slavery, not only from a humane view, as he see it, but more for the progress and development of the nation. I think, recognizing slavery as a Constitutional right, his sense of justice would not allow any but fair and legal means to abolish it, certainly not a resort to armed force. He is not of the John Brown type of fanatic or the more villainous set that were urging him on."

"How do you think the question would have been settle then, sir?"

"Either by an act of Congress, the government paying for the slaves, or by the owners voluntarily giving them their freedom."

The answers were so unexpected and looked so unreasonable to me that I made no reply.

While we were on the slavery question I thought it a good time for me to open my negotiations with the old gentleman about taking Uncle Andy with me out West. It was some minutes after he stopped speaking before I could make up my mind to broach the subject. Uncle Andy and I had several conferences concerning it, the old fellow was as anxious about it as I was timid, only that evening when looking over the horses trying to decide which would suit us best he remarked:

"You aint said nothin' to old Marster yit 'bout me goin', is yu Marse Ben?"

And I had promised I would ask him right away, so I opened the subject by saying I would need a couple of good horses to take with me.

"Are you going by horseback?" he asked.

"I thought it best and most economical, sir. Under present conditions I doubt if I could get prompt and reliable shipping facilities and am satisfied I could not find as good horse in the West as we have here without paying exorbitant prices."

"When do you think of going?"

"Just as soon as I can get through with the matters you have asked me to attend to for you."

"I sold your old horse to Billy Sikes, but there are a half dozen or more on the place that will possibly suit you. Take any you like."

"There is another favor I hope you will grant me, sir", I said with a lump in my throat and after a moment's pause, "I will be very grateful if you will let old Andy go with me."

"Does he want to go?"

"Yes sir, he is very anxious to go, spoke to me about it the day I returned home. I will feel better satisfied to have him with me than a younger servant."

"In that case, father said, "you may take Andy with you. I hope he realizes the great risk he faces. He should be a big help to you. May you both be careful." Suddenly his eyes misted, and he bowed his head. Then he looked up at me and gave us his blessing.

After thanking him there was a pause of several minutes. I got up to leave and convey the news to Uncle Andy, who I knew was anxiously waiting for me on the back porch, when my father said:

"Son, I will want you to go by our plantation in Arkansas and buy a year's supplies for the negroes. Owing to the uncertainty in shipping I will not attempt to send them as usual by boat from this place."

He had his farm in Tennessee supply his cotton plantation in Arkansas with all the necessaries: mules, meat, and clothing, for carrying on the work. Notwithstanding that it made from two hundred and twenty-five to two hundred and fifty bales of cotton each year, our Tennessee farm made more clear money.

CHAPTER X

I JOIN THE TRANS-MISSISSIPPI ARMY AND MEET OLD FRIENDS AND OLD ENEMIES.

It was two weeks later. I had finished all the duties my father had assigned me and was anxious to get away. General McCulloch had impressed upon me the importance of reporting to him promptly and I had already been detained three weeks longer than I expected. Andy and I had selected our horses and all other minor details were complete.

It was after supper, my father was enjoying his usual smoke looking reflectively in the big wood fire when I told him I had settled up all the matters he required of me, and if there was nothing more, I would leave early the next morning. He continued to smoke in silence a moment, then knocking the ashes from his pipe he turned to me with the most serious and solicitous look I had ever seen on his face.

"My son", he said in a low and slightly tremulous tone, "if there was ever a shadow of success in our undertaking, notwithstanding the disasters it will eventually bring upon this country, I could see you go with at least the satisfaction of knowing that success would be gratifying to you, but there is not, in my opinion, the remotest possibility of it. The South has made two irretrievable blunders to start with; first, in trying to establish a Confederacy of the Southern States, which would be the beginning of the downfall of this nation, and the other is in selecting Mr. Davis for its President."

I was so astonished at this statement that I sat speechless for we all thought at that time that President Davis was "parexcellence" the man for the job. He evidently saw my look of astonishment.

"Do not misunderstand me", he said. "I have great respect for Mr. Davis. He is in many respects a man of great moral character, and from his point of view, a true and sincere patriot. But the faults of great men are as strong as their virtues. Mr. Davis is an egotist. To some extent this is pardonable, for he has cause to be, but he is a man of such intense prejudice that he will allow it to warp his judgment of men to such an extent as to disqualify him to sponsor the birth of a nation. But this mistake aside, the South has no navy. Even if she had the men and means to build one, every Southern port will be blockaded before she could do so. Then, cut off from the outside world, the real struggle will begin and it will be the beginning of the end. Today the North can arm, equip and put in the field ready for action two men to the South's one without stopping a wheel of her various manufacturing industries. The South can't even supply the troops she has with suitable arms. The North will replenish her army with recruits from the outside world; from what source can the South replenish hers to fill the places of thousands killed in battle or die in hospitals?" He paused a moment and continued.

"I do not doubt the heroism of our people, the result is inevitable; they cannot successfully contend against the world." He again paused and lit his pipe. I could see that he was deeply moved as he tossed the taper in the fire. He smoked a moment in silence.

"I am not saying this", he continued, "to discourage or dissuade you from your purpose, for every pulsation of my heart is in sympathy with my people, but", and his voice was hard and sharp. "I condemn with equal bitterness your leaders moved by passion and personal ambition who have brought this great unnecessary calamity on our people at a time when they were so utterly unprepared for it."

I thought it prudent to say nothing, for my faith in President Davis and our other political leaders was sublime, but I lived to see in after years how prophetic were his words.

"Will you start in the morning? What time?" he asked after a pause.

"I would like to get a very early start, sir", I replied.

He walked over to his secretary, unlocked a drawer, and placed upon the table some papers and a buckskin belt that gave out a significant sound of coin as he put it down.

"Here are two drafts on the State Bank of Tennessee for Five Hundred Dollars each", he said, as he handed them to me. "I want you to use them in buying meat and such other supplies the negroes need on the plantation in Arkansas. The bank in Helena will cash them for you, and here is the trash I sold your old horse for", he said pushing over to me a big package of Confederate bills. The one on top was for One Hundred Dollars, and as I turned up the corner of the package I saw it was made up of Fifty and One Hundred-Dollar bills.

"But sir", I exclaimed, "Here is very much more than the Two Hundred Dollars.

"Keep it, I have no use for it, but here is some money", he said, pouring some gold coins out of the belt, "that will be useful to you when you need it. There ought to be two hundred and ten dollars there, and I advise you to carry it around you in this belt."

"But, father, I'm robbing you", I said as I stood up with tears in my eyes, "I will take this Confederate money. It will answer all my purposes. Keep the gold you will need it."

"I have all I will need, my father said, on deposit in Louisville and Cincinnati. Now, if you want an early start, it is time and were in bed. As I may not be up in time to see you off, I'll bid you good-bye now", he said rising and shaking my hand.

He was stern, hard man. He loved his children, but was not demonstrative. On the other hand I inherited all my mother's tender, loving, impulsive nature, and while I never remembered receiving a caress or any demonstration of affection from my father, my heart was in my mouth and tears in my eyes as I threw my arms around his neck and hid my face on his shoulder. I felt a gentle pat on my arm that I valued more than the gold he gave me.

As I withdrew my arms there was a timid tap on the door. It opened slowly, and old Andy, hat in hand stepped just inside. He gave a quick glance at my father then at me, and his eyes began to wander in an embarrassed way around the room. The old man fingered the brim of his hat, looking down at the floor. "I come to tell you good-bye, Marster", he said.

"Why certainly, Andy, certainly, replied my father. "Good-bye," and may God protect you and my son, extending his hand, which Uncle Andy took with as much reverence and more pride then if it had been a king's.

"Take good care of yourself Andy, and don't let the Yankees catch you, if you do, they'll set you free, and then you will have to work!" he said with a smile.

It was before sunrise when I mounted my horse next morning. I glanced up at the window of my father's room; the curtains were closely drawn. It might have been imagination, but I thought I saw them move slightly and I lifted my hat in silent salute. Riding through the gate at the end of the lawn I stopped to take a last look at my old home. Never had it appeared so beautiful, and never had I looked upon it with the same feeling that now moved me.

I little dreamed that when I saw it again its massive brick walls would be pierced with cannon shot and the brick on the outside chipped by bullets from small arms, or that the white ash flooring in every room and hall downstairs would be stained with human blood, ineffaceable after more than fifty years; or that the magnificent forest trees thickly scattered over the lawn would be scarred and mutilated by shot and shell. The house was used as a hospital by Rosencranz after and during the battle of Murfreesboro. It was a marker on the firing line of battles in 1864 when Hood attempted to take Murfreesboro after the battle of Franklin. A battery of Federal guns went into action on the brick walk not ten feet from the front door. Windows have been cut in the opening made by the cannon shot, carpets cover the blood stains on the white ash floors, fresh wood and bark cover the ugly scars on the old trees that shade the lawn, look through the window and you will again hear the boom of the cannon as the shot ploughs its way through the wall, lift the carpet and you see the dark blood stains cut through the fresh bark and see the fragments of death dealing shells

xxxx

Owing to excessive rains and high water in the Mississippi and its tributaries it was three weeks before I reached Helena, and much to my disappointment I found only a small quantity of the supplies I needed. This necessitated another vexatious delay. For weeks I was scouring the country trying to buy sufficient meat to furnish the negroes, and it was the latter part of February before I again turned my face to the West, nearly two months later than I should have been. At Little Rock, I saw the first evidences of war west of the Mississippi. There was a hospital of wounded soldiers, and I met a number of officers at the hotel, some wounded and all just from the front. From there I first heard that Van Dorn was in command of the Western army and was starting into Missouri with the united forces of Price and McCulloch. Learning the location of the army as near as I could, I started early next morning on my hundred and ten mile ride to join it.

It was in the afternoon of the third day out that I began to come up with the stragglers, broken down men, some occasionally wounded, shortly after passing the last of these I came, to where the roads forked. Both branches gave unmistakable evidence of troops having passed over them, but which was Price's division and which McCulloch's I was unable to decide.

"Now which way, Uncle Andy", I said stopping, undecided which road to take. "If we follow the road that carries us to Price's division we will probably have to ride four or five miles more to get to McCulloch."

"The road to your right will carry you to General McCulloch's command", said a deep clear voice almost at my elbow.

I was startled, for I had seen no one. Turning my head quickly my eyes rested upon a striking personage. He was a man fully six feet in height and at first glance one would have guessed his age at sixty-five or seventy years judging from a full but neatly trimmed and perfectly white beard and mustache that covered his face, and the long iron-gray hair that dropped from under a fur cap to his shoulders, but to look into his keen, bright black eyes, note his erect form, his quick action, would have pronounced him fifty years. He wore a close-fitting jacket of dark heavy material and a pair of buck-skin leggings laced up to his knees. On his right side from a strap passed over his left shoulder hung a bullet pouch and a powder horn from which he supplied the ammunition for the long, heavy, full stocked rifle resting in the hollow of his left arm. He had evidently just stepped out from behind a large tree on the edge of the road and heard me express my uncertainty as to which road to follow.

"You startled me", I exclaimed, "but I am obliged to you for the information."

"Are you carrying despatches to the General?"

My instinct and slight military training told me this direct question from a stranger was unnecessary and I paused before answering. He saw me hesitate and quickly said,

"I beg your pardon, sir. It is non of my business, but I know General McCulloch personally, have done considerable scouting for him since he has been in command, am about his headquarters very often, and as I've never seen you there, I very naturally supposed you had despatches for him."

"That is alright. I have not despatches for the General, but am aide-de-camp on his staff, and the reason you've not seen me is because I am just now reporting for duty. I am from Tennessee and have unfortunately been delayed nearly two months."

"This is not your first experience then. You have doubtless seen service with Tennessee troops?"

"No, it is not my first experience, but not with Tennessee troops. I have seen service in Virginia with North Carolina troops."

"I understood you to say you were from Tennessee and I naturally supposed you were a Tennessean."

"So I am, but was a student in the University of North Carolina at Chapel Hill when the war began, left the University and joined the First North Carolina Volunteer Regiment, offered our services to the Confederate government and was sent to Yorktown on the Peninsula."

He had removed the gun from his arm, resting the butt on the ground, and with his hands crossed over the muzzle was looking at me with the same steady look that had not for an instant moved from my face since our glances first met. When I mentioned being a student at

Chapel Hill and enlisting with the North Carolina troops, I thought I saw a look of pleasure or pride flash for an instant in his eyes.

"You say the road to the right leads to McCulloch's camp? How far is it?" I asked .

"Very near nine miles by that road, but," he paused a moment as if considering. "There is a much nearer way through the mountains that will cut off half the distance if--"

"I will cheerfully pay a guide to show me the near cut - in gold", I added as I saw the shadow of a smile in his eyes.

"You've not told me your name. Thompson is mine."

"And mine is Hord, Ben McCulloch Hord", I said extending my hand.

"Your name indicates relationship to the General, are you?"

"Yes sir, he is a relative."

"Then I will show you the way to his headquarters without money and without price - even in gold". This time there was no doubt about the laughter in his eyes.

Motioning me to follow, he turned abruptly into the thick underbrush, and after going through it a short distance, we came to a broad well beaten path that soon began a gradual descent that became steeper as we advanced. After going perhaps a mile or more through the dense forest with only an occasional glimpse of the sky through the overhanging branches, Thompson, who had been swinging along in front with a swift easy stride, turned sharply to the right, and I rode out on a projecting point of land that gave me the most beautiful landscape view I had ever seen.

It was a valley probably three-fourths of a mile long and at its greatest width a half mile, oblong in shape, and so even and perfect were its sides it looked as if Nature in a fantastic mood had dipped it out with a spoon. The mountains heavily timbered, sloped down almost abruptly on every side. From my elevated position the land looked as level as a billiard table, it was divided off into plots of different sizes, and, aside from the fruit orchards, every foot of it seemed to be in a high state of cultivation. From the upper end of the valley somewhere below me a stream gushed out of the mountain and emptied into a lake fringed with willows, that covered an acre or more of land in the widest part of the valley, passing out at the lower side on through the farther end of the valley and disappearing at the foot of the hills.

"Well, what do you think of it?" asked Thompson.

"Well, what do you think of it?" asked Thompson.

"Beautiful, beautiful, a scene to inspire the pen of a poet or the brush of a painter."

"It is much prettier later on when the fruit trees are in bloom and the forest has on its summer coat."

I reluctantly turned from the view to follow his as the path once more lead us into the timber. The descent became more pronounced and as we wound around great boulders I caught the sound of falling waters, another turn brought us to the source of the stream I had seen from above. It was a bold spring gushing from the mountain in volume and velocity almost sufficient to drive a mill wheel. Flowing five or six feet over a broad flat rock it fell, making a miniature cascade, into a little pool three or four feet deep and twice as wide, then, dashing over the lower side, on down the hill to the valley below.

"What a magnificent spring!" I exclaimed.

"And as good as it looks", said Thompson, who had followed a little path over the mouth of the spring. "Ride across and sample the water." Taking a gourd from a crevice in the rock and handing it to me as I dismounted. It was as clear as cut glass and deliciously cool.

"It doesn't vary two degrees in temperature or an inch in depth winter or summer", he said. "Harnessed as it comes out of the mountain and it has by actual test eight-horse water power sufficient to throw it over the top of my house."

"You live near here?"

"Yes, not more than three hundred yards by direct line, but seven hundred by the path we go."

"You own the spring?"

"Yes and the valley you admired so much. You were two hundred and eight feet seven inches above the level of the lake from your view point, and this spring from the top of the rock it falls over is ninety-two feet four inches."

I suspected from his manner and the brief conversation I had with him, when we first met, that he was no ordinary mountaineer and hunter, but was unprepared to hear him give in a quiet confident way geometrical proportion of heights and power of water. He must have noted a look of inquiry in my face, for he added after a moment's hesitation:

"I have studied civil engineering."

"Then Nature did not do all the beautifying?"

"I helped a little", he said with a smile, "except the fish pond, I did most of the excavating, but nature furnished the water."

"Fish pond! you mean the lake I saw? Is it stocked?" I asked eagerly.

"Stocked full; almost too full, with black bass and white perch. Are you fond of fishing", he added having noticed my interest in his replies.

"Nothing I like better, and next to catching, I love to eat them."

"Perhaps you can be accommodated both ways."

"I would love to 'wet a line' in the lake and feel a two or three pounder fighting at the end of it, but I must be getting along. I'm now nearly three months behind time." And I prepared to mount my horse.

"But that won't interfere with your fishing. You can catch a mess and eat them too without delay except in the cooking. Come this way."

"I followed him to the edge of the little pool, and pointing to a rope he told me to pull it. I did so and up came a fish box made of slats, the water lashed into foam as I drew it up. It was a sight to gladden the heart of any fisherman. More than two dozen black bass and big white perch, weighing from two pounds down to half pound, were flopping about in the box.

"A good catch, Captain, for one haul. Now pick out a mess for our supper and we'll go down to the house and have them cooked. Why, you haven't half enough", he said as he strung them on a twig, and picking out more than twice as many, he closed the box and pushed it back in the spring. "Now for the house."

Once more we began to descend the winding path. The house was on an elevation that sloped gradually down to the level of the valley in front, and was one story built of cypress logs dressed down so smooth one could scarcely see where they joined. The corners were fitted as closely as cabinet work. There were two front rooms and three in the all. There was no passage between the front rooms, but a porch extended full length supported by small cypress trees just as they stood in the forest. On the upper end of some of these posts the branches had been sawed off a foot from the body of the tree and from each of them hung bark baskets of mountain fern and evergreen vines. There were windows and doors that opened out on the porch from each room. Rosebushes and shrubs, just beginning to take on a tinge of green, dotted the sloping ground in front.

"Hold this horse a moment, and I'll show you where to feed him", said Mr. Thompson, passing my bridle rein to Andy as I dismounted. I knew at once from his tone and words that he was born and reared in the South. He gave a sharp rap on the door. I was standing a little to one side when it opened and a pair of round arms and pretty hands reached up to host's neck and an anxious voice said,

"Oh, Fred I'm so glad -"

"The sentence was never finished. She had come forward sufficient to catch a glimpse of me, the arms were quickly withdrawn and she stood blushing like a girl.

"It is all right, Lucy, I will have that kiss anyway", said Mr. Thompson laughingly as he suited his action to his words.

"Captain Hord, this is my wife, Mrs. Thompson. The Captain is a member of General McCullochs' staff, Lucy, and I'm showing him the nearest way to the General's headquarters. He will take supper with us and says he is fond of fish", showing her the string.

"I hope, Madam you will not judge my appetite by that string of fish. It was your husband's selection."

"We are all fond of fish", she said with a smile that dimpled her cheeks. She must have been a beautiful brunette as she was a very handsome woman yet, fifty or fifty-five years old, for her dark wavy hair smoothed down over her brows and coiled on the back of her shapely head was liberally sprinkled with gray. She had dark brown eyes quickly expressive of her feelings, and a girl of twenty might have justly envied her smooth velvety looking skin and the roses in her cheeks. Not the least of her attractions was her gracious manner and soft speech.

"I will go and show your servant where to feed your horses, Lucy, maybe the Captain would like a bath after his long ride. Would you?" he asked turning to me.

"I beg you will not put yourself to any inconveniences, Madam, I -"

"Not the slightest, none whatever", she said, interrupting me. "Sit down, make yourself comfortable and excuse me a moment until I can give the fish to the cook."

I took occasion to examine the room in her absence. I was admiring one of the paintings when, Mrs. Thompson said from behind me,

- 148 -

"You are fond of art." She had entered the room without attracting my attention.

"Very much, these are excellent," I said.

I saw a flash of pleasure in her eyes as she inquired.

"Did my husband show you that view where you arrived?" pointing to a large painting across the room.

We walked over to look at it, and as she drew the curtain back from the window to give us better light, I stood once more on the projecting point of the house looking down on the beautiful valley.

"Do you recognize it?" as I stood in mute admiration before the canvas.

"Recognize it?" I exclaimed. "Who has ever seen that valley could fail to recognize it? But this picture is even more beautiful than the valley now, for the artist caught it when the orchards were in bloom and the forest had on their summer coats, as your husband expressed it."

"Suppose I were to tell you it was not a professional, but an amateur that did it?"

"Then I would say that the amateur is throwing away his time and talent."

"But suppose it was a woman?"

"I would say the same."

"I do not think my husband would agree with you."

In an instant the truth flashed in my mind that she was the artist. I stepped back and looked at her in amazement.

"Are you?" I started to ask, but the question was unnecessary. Her pretty mouth had again dimpled her cheeks with a smile and the laughter in her eyes as she nodded her head confirmed my suspicions.

"I plead guilty, Captain. All of us love to hear our work praised, especially if we think it sincere. I hope you will not think me unusually vain for listening to your praise and leaving you to guess who did it. Really I did not come in expecting to find you looking at my works, but to tell you your bath is ready. See how an old woman's vanity has made her neglect her hospitality. Come this way."

"Had your bath?" inquired my host, as I returned to the living room

"Yes and enjoyed it immensely, but was wondering where your water comes from?

"I take it from the spring above and convey it to the house in cypress boxes underground that will carry a two-inch stream sufficient to supply all of the out buildings as well as the house."

Then I learned that he was a native of North Carolina, had graduated at the old University at Chapel Hill in the class of 1842; had chosen civil engineering as a profession, came West many years ago, and owned more than four thousand acres around his little valley farm.

When I entered the supper room, the linen was immaculate and in the center of the table a large glass bowl was filled with magnificent roses and fringed around with violets. It was a supper long to be remembered, in a soldiers' life.

I cannot find words to express my thanks for your kindness Madam", I said as I was taking my leave.

"Then don't try", she replied, extending her hand graciously.

- 150 -

Postpone it until your next visit, which we hope will not be far off."

Little did she or I think how soon her wish would be realized. Mr. Thompson and I began our ascent out of the valley at the other end. The path was rough for a short distance but soon broadened into a passable road. Here my host stopped.

"You can easily find your way from here, Captain. Follow this road for a mile and you will come to a big public road that crosses it, turn to the right, and you will soon see the camp fires of General McCulloch's troops. I will doubtless see you tomorrow. Until then", and we shook hands.

"See me tomorrow." I knew what he meant. He was joining the fight - this old man. Every incident of the last few hours flashed through my mind: his beautiful home, his "happy valley", his loving wife. What could she do alone in these wild mountains? Yet he was going to risk it all and take a chance on his life.

"Mr. Thompson", I said still holding his hand, "you are a much older man, and I hope you will not think me presumptuous. I am not superstitious nor have I any premonition of disaster to either of us, but let me beg of you not to risk your life in the fight tomorrow."

"You will risk yours", he said looking me in the face with a smile.

"Yes sir, but I am a young man and carry only my own life to fight, and the life of one man is a small piece in a battle. You will carry far more than your own life on the fighting lines. If you were killed, your death however painful would be a mercy compared to the lingering, heart-breaking death for the one left. Besides, you can serve the Confederacy more effectively as a citizen than as a soldier."

He made no reply but squeezed my hand, turned and walked swiftly back on the road we had come. We rode forward in silence. The events of the evening, and reasons why these people should be so far removed from their homes, were occupying my thoughts which were interrupted by Uncle Andy.

"They shorely is quality folks. Marse Ben; to-be shore, to-be-shore." As I had arrived at the same conclusion, I heartily agreed with the old man's opinion.

A mile further on, we came to the public road mentioned. It was filled with infantry marching to our left. As the last of the column passed, and we were about to ride out, I heard the rattle of wheels and tramp of horses that told me the artillery was close behind. As the first gun came up an officer rode up and stopped within a few feet of me to fill his pipe.

"What troops are these?" I inquired.

"Price's".

He lit a match, and cupping the little flame with his hands to protect it from the wind, threw the light on his face. I saw from the red bars on the collar of his jacket that he was a Captain of artillery, but it was his face that impressed me. It was brown as a berry and covered with dust and a week's growth of beard, but there was something familiar about it that I could not define. Just then his horse gave a vigorous shake, the match went out, and so did the tobacco fly out of the pipe, for the rider swore at it for wasting his "precious weed" as he proceeded to refill it. He struck another match, again cupping it with his hands. I scanned his face carefully and my memory at once recalled him. It was

Dave Scales, a friend of Nick Hardeman, a member of the old Ranch Club at Chapel Hill. We were classmates and had graduated at the same time. Hardeman from Texas and Scales from Missouri. All the members of the Ranch Club knew me well as "Nick's freshman, and his warm friendship caused a kindred feeling for most of them, especially Scales, who, owing his long legs the boys had dubbed "Shanks." The match went out just as his identity came to me.

"Old Shanks Scales, as I am a sinner!" I exclaimed.

"What's that! Who are you? There's but one man West of the Mississippi River that calls me Shanks. Who are you?" he asked eagerly pressing his horse close to mine.

"Strike another match, Shanks, and see if you memory is as good as mine."

He did so, and by the little flickering flame looked closely at my face and clothes and shook his head as the burnt match dropped from his fingers.

"I can't make you out, sorry, but you are not one of us. You are too clean looking and your uniform too spanking new. You must be a fresh man."

"Why. Shanks", I said as he pronounced the last two words. "You have guessed it the first time out of the box."

"How? What! I never called a name."

"But you've just said I was a freshman."

"Yes, well, what of it?"

"How would Nick Hardeman's Chapel Hill freshman fit in?"

The words were scarcely spoken before he had almost pulled me out

- 153 -

of the saddle with his vigorous welcome. Nick had told him of my staff appointment, but as week after week passed and they heard nothing, had given up all hope of seeing me. I explained my unfortunate delay but hoped I was in time to get in the game soon.

"You'll have a chance tomorrow, Freshie. After two days chasing we've at least brought old Sigel to bay and we'll give him the finishing touch tomorrow. We are going around, that is Price's division, to strike his right flank at Elkhorn tavern, while your people under McCulloch will strike his center and left flank. Yes, I am Captain of artillery, these were my war dogs that just passed, six beautiful Napoleons, all captured from Lyon and Sigel. You'll hear them barking tomorrow in the thickest of the fray, for I have as good set of boys as ever cut a fuse or rammed home a charge. But I must catch up with them. Good bye, old boy, and good luck to you - same to Nick - will see you both in a day or two."

A soldier's greeting and a soldier's parting. His "war dogs" did bark and bite great chunks of human flesh the next day, fought to the very muzzles in saving Price's beaten army, but the lifeless body of their gallant captain was borne from the field on an empty caisson.

I soon reached General McCulloch's headquarters. He with two other officers were inspecting a map spread out on the log upon which two of them were sitting, the other standing by holding the lantern. I waited until they folded up the map, indicating the conference was over, before presenting myself. After a look of surprise, and a not very cordial greeting, he said:

"You are late reporting for duty, sir."

I felt keenly the rebuke in his tone, especially as the other officers were present. I at once explained my delay, reminding him of his instructions when we parted in Richmond to first go by home and attend to such matters as my father required and then report to him as soon as possible. Then I gave him as briefly as I could a report of myself since leaving Richmond. He was satisfied with my explanation, shook my hand warmly, and presented me to the other officers, General McIntosh and Colonel DeJean, as one of his aides-de-camp. My cool reception and confusion had prevented me from giving more than a casual glance at these gentlemen. So when the name DeJean was mentioned, and I looked fully in his face, I knew at once that I was shaking hands with my friend, Nick Hardemans', uncle for the likeness in the old daguerreotype shown me years ago at college had not faded from my memory. He was of magnificent physique, handsome, faultlessly dressed from his plumed cavalry helmet to his polished boots and silver spurs. His dark complexion and black eyes spoke of his aristocratic Creole blood, and his white mustache carefully trimmed and waxed might have likened him to one of Napoleon's marshals dressed for either a ballroom or a battlefield.

"And this is our long-expected friend from Tennessee", he said smiling as he shook my hand a warmly. "I feel as if you were an old acquaintance. I've heard Nick speak of you so often. He will be surprised and delighted to see you, for all of us, like the general, had long since given up the hope."

I thanked him and express my eagerness to see Nick.

"Why, I think we might manage that tonight", he said, turning to General McCulloch. "What do you say, General, our young friend here is very anxious to see Nick. Can you loan him to me for an hour or two, I will guarantee his safe return in that time?"

Both of them laughed, but I did not catch the point until General McCulloch said seriously

"Well Colonel, with your guarantee."

I felt the blood rush to my face.

"I beg your pardon, General", I said interrupting, "if I must have a guarantee for my prompt return I would prefer to stay."

"That is alright, Captain, he said, dropping his serious look and tone for one of amusement. "It is alright, the colonel and I were having a laugh at your expense. You can spend the night with Nick if you wish, just so you report to me at five o'clock in the morning. Better leave your traps here. What have you?"

"Two saddle-bags of clothes, my servant and his horse."

I saw him give a quick glance at Colonel DeJean and remark,

"You will need the horse more than the servant. However, we will provide for you tonight and make definite arrangements later. Here Williams." This is Captain Hord of my staff, quarter his servant and horse close by and see that rations are issued for them."

After putting Andy and the luggage under care of the courier. I mounted my horse, joined Colonel DeJean and started to his camp located on the extreme right of our forces. Nick had charge of the picket line and we found him stretched out on a blanket reading a letter by the light of a little fire.

"Here's a stray', Nick, and I think he belongs to your herd", said the Colonel as we stopped just beyond the firelight.

"Too far from the range, Colonel. He don't belong to me unless he carries my brand."

"Better look him over before we disown him", replied the Colonel.

I had dismounted, and the moment I stepped in the circle of light he recognized me.

"Sit right down here and give an account of yourself, Freshie", he said after our embracing and hand shaking was over, "and, Colonel, will you please send Captain Thornton out here to take charge of my pickets while I am listening to this young man's excuses. Now tell me all about yourself."

As the reader, if he has been sufficiently interested to follow, is already familiar with these incidents, it is only necessary to say that Nick only interrupted the recital occasionally to ask of some old mutual friend.

"And now", I said, filling my pipe after I had finished, "tell me about yourself. Begin where you started in pursuit of Carrier. I learned from the papers all about the tragedy."

"Well, Uncle and I followed him to the border of New Mexico, where we lost him. Knowing he had interest in some silver mines in Mexico, we decided to separate, uncle going south and I north. At a little mining camp in New Mexico, I struck his trail again and followed him to San Diego in California. There I lost him for a time, picked up his trail again in Los Angeles. Just a week after my arrival, he killed a prominent rancher in one of his drunken rows and the fellow's friends would have hung him if they could have caught him, but he fled, they guessed to San Francisco. I followed and I lost him entirely. It was the middle of January when glancing over a San Francisco paper I learned that my state had seceded from the Union and General Mcculloch was in command of all the forces in the state. I abandoned the pursuit, returned home, found my uncle organizing his regiment, which he armed and equipped at his own expense. I organized a troop myself for his regiment, was elected major, and here we are.

"Where is Carrier do you think?" he asked.

"In the Federal army without a doubt. They know nothing of his private life after he resigned. His reputation as a fighter against the Indians is good, and when he asked to be reinstated, they were not only glad to get him, but I dare say they would give him the rank of Colonel based on his military record. They likely assigned hm to their Western army, since he had made his reputation as a soldier in the West."

"Where is Miss Katherine"? I inquired. With friends in New Orleans, I suppose." Nick said.

"The 'Kitten', bless her brave loyal little heart." There were tears in his eyes as he spoke. "It hurts me when I think of her, yet there is not a waking hour I don't think of her. We are the only two left, my friend. No, she is not in New Orleans. Uncle begged her to take the old house servants and go down there and open up his house, but she said she could not live so far from me and the old home, so she is up on the Ranch with her horses and dogs, and I expect she is better satisfied, as they afford her recreation.

Old Mr. Gibson and his wife and daughter are living at the house with her. The old man and my father were life-long friends. He has been general manager of his different ranches since father first owned one. Her old nurse and all the other house servants are there. I expect that it is the best that can be done.

How the poor child begged to come with me! Wanted to bring two servants, the old nurse and her husband. They would keep close in rear of the regiment, and be near if I should be sick or wounded. They didn't want any wagon or tent, and only such baggage as they could carry on their horses. She had been with us on our hunting trips and slept out in the open with us for weeks.

Her arguments were simply unanswerable for I knew all she said was true, and when she concluded by saying: "And you know brother, I can beat you either riding or shooting", I have never seen her equal in the saddle or with the pistol. I simply surrendered and told her to see the Colonel. Of course, he objected, and no persuasion could move him.

"We write each other two or three times a week. Wish you had arrived a few hours sooner, I sent my last letter to her this evening, it would have pleased her very much to learn that my 'long expected freshman', as she calls you, had at last made his appearance. When I wrote her that General McCulloch had appointed you to his staff, it gave her almost as much pleasure as it did me. And, every letter I got from her, she would ask if you had arrived.

When more than a month passed, and we heard nothing from you we had given up all hope of you joining us and the General made another appointment. We must get some sleep, for unless I am very much mistaken we are going to have the stiffest fight with Sigel tomorrow we have yet had, and none of us are happy with the situation."

"I saw Price's troops moving to our left as we cam in. Where were they going, and what is the situation, Nick?" I asked, as he began to spread our blankets down before the little fire.

Price is attempting a flank movement to strike their right at Elkhorn Tavern. It is nine miles over a rough mountain road, placing the two wings of our army out of supporting distances of each other, while Sigel's line will not be two miles from extreme right to left on ground he can move his forces easily from one point to another as needed. Price said he could reach his position by seven o'clock in the morning. General McCulloch says he can't reach it before ten. We are ordered by Van Dorn to wait until we hear Price's guns before we attack, but the question is, will Sigel wait until Price gets on his flank before he attacks us. General McCulloch, who knows him well, thinks not. He has been reinforced this evening by General Curtis with three thousand fresh troops, and the probabilities are we will have his whole force to fight for hours before Price can fire a gun."

"Why didn't General McCulloch object?" I asked.

"How could he? Price suggested the movement and was backed by Van Dorn, who is the commander-in-chief. The plan was against his judgment, and he couldn't object if his superior ordered him to fight ten times as many.

But let's get under these blankets, boy, we've only a few hours to sleep and a hard day ahead of us. A minute more and both of us were sound asleep.

CHAPTER XI

THE BATTLE OF PEA RIDGE.

"Wake up, Captain, it is five o'clock." The voice accompanied by a vigorous shake from Nick's orderly roused me from a dreamless sleep.

"Where is the Major?" I asked, looking at the vacant place by me.

"Gone an hour ago, told me not to disturb you until five o'clock. Your breakfast is ready, sir," pointing to the little fire a few feet away where a pot of coffee was simmering and some slices of bacon boiling on the coals. "This is not our kind of bread, sir", he said, drawing a half dozen big army crackers from a haversack, "but we captured some Yankee commissary wagons yesterday and the boys are trying them for a change from our 'corn dodgers' ".

Then minutes later I had finished my breakfast and dismounted at General McCulloch's headquarters. He was just sitting down to breakfast with two of his staff.

"Won't you join us?" he said, after introducing me as the "long missing member" of his military family.

I thanked him, told him I had breakfast, but would like to find my old servant and give him some instructions, if he would not need me for ten minutes.

"Hadn't you better make it twenty, Captain?" he said with a smile and a mischievous twinkle in his eyes.

"Make it twenty them, sir", I replied, "and I'll promise you shall never have another opportunity to prod me about being tardy."

"It's a bargain", he said with a laugh, and called an orderly to help me find Uncle Andy.

We found the old man in a heated controversy with the quartermaster's sergeant over the amount of corn issued him for his horse.

"What's the matter?" I asked, walking up unobserved by Uncle Andy and placing my hand upon his shoulder.

"Does that old man belong to you?" asked the sergeant.

I told him he did.

"Why, the old fool wanted me to give him shelled oats for his horse. I told him neither the men nor the horses were living on 'pie crust', and now he wants enough corn for his horse to fee a team of army mules."

I explained the matter to the sergeant, and telling Andy to take the feed we went a short distance in the thicket where he had tethered his horse.

"Now listen carefully to what I say, Uncle Andy, and do exactly as I tell you." I took off the belt containing the gold and from my pocket a package of Confederate bills. "Belt that gold around your waist next to your skin and don't take it off day or night, hide this package of money about you where it is not likely to be found. Do not touch the gold and never show more than ten dollars of the money at one time, for I've not doubt there are men around us here, white or black, that would cut your throat for a five-dollar bill." The old man's eyes were opening wider and his black skin taking on an ashy hue as I continued.

"Now listen carefully, Uncle Andy, if I am captured or killed, you go directly to Mr. Thompson in the valley, give him the money and then make your way to Helena. From there take a boat to Nashville. I guess the Yankees will have the river open by then. Here are three hundred dollars of Confederate money and ten dollars in gold. Mr. Thompson will change it into greenbacks for you to pay your way home. Leave your horse with Thompson and get you a worthless old mule or horse to ride, for the first man that you met would take your good horse from you. Now here's a note to Mr. Thompson and a pass through our lines for you, showing that you are my servant." By this time the old man's eyes were glassy and his face had an ashy green look.

" 'Fore Gawd, Marse Ben, don't give me all dis money. Don't do it, Marse Ben, somebody is shore to find it out and kill me before I gits home."

"But, Uncle Andy, the chances are you are not going home. I'm only telling you what to do in case I get killed or captured, and I'm not counting on either. You stay with the headquarters wagon and I will always know where to find you, and you will know where to find me. We are going to have a pretty stiff fight today, and I may want a fresh horse before night, so you have this one ready."

I left the old fellow sitting on the ground, his knees drawn up to his chin, his hands clasped around them, the picture of despair.

"Take the Captain down the line and acquaint him with the location of the different commands so there will be no confusion or delay in delivering orders should I have occasion to use him for this purpose", said General McCulloch to one of his staff when I returned.

- 163 -

"That is General McIntosh", said my guide, pointing to a large man in a general's uniform "and this is his brigade. Come and I'll introduce you."

"A new member of the General's staff? I met him last night", said the General as I was presented.

"Rather an old member, General, but a late arrival", replied my brother officer.

"Well, sir, you are in time to help us give Sigel another thrashing today."

The troops were forming by regiments as we rode back, and by seven' o'clock, when General McCulloch rode down inspecting them, the division was formed for action with a strong line of skirmishers in front.

"Well, General, we are all ready to move as soon as we hear from Price", he said to General McIntosh as the latter rode up and joined us.

"I am afraid it will be some time yet before we hear from him," replied McIntosh, looking at his watch. "It is more than nine miles around the way Price went, ordinarily the roughest road on the mountain and my scouts report that the Yankees have made it more so by felling trees across it. Price said he could make it by eight o'clock this morning and it is now half-past seven. I wonder how near up he is."

"Sigel can tell you", said General McCulloch. "He has the best scouts and the best cavalry in the Federal army, and I'll venture to say, knows within a half mile of where the head of Price's column is now, and he will give us the information within the next half hour."

"You mean', said General McIntosh, "if Price is not up close enough to strike Sigel's right flank within the next two hours, Sigel will at once concentrate his whole force on us."

"Exactly, and it will be decided with in the next thirty minutes. If Sigel opens the fight, you may know Price is not near enough to strike him; if he waits for us to attack, Price is threatening his flank. In either case, gentlemen, we are ready", he said waving a salute to McIntosh and staff as he turned and galloped back to the right of the line.

We stopped a moment, the General was saying something to a surgeon when a shot rang out far down to the left in front of McIntosh's brigade, quickly followed by another and another until a crackling noise like a burning prairie swept along our entire front.

"Ah, I thought so. Price is not in this fight", I heard the General mutter to himself as he looked at his watch.

Our skirmish line was heavy. They were ordered to hold their ground stubbornly and fall back slowly, for we were fighting for time to let Price get up. The underbrush was so dense we could not see our skirmishers but the fighting came closer every moment. The men were obeying orders, fighting for every inch of ground, but falling back slowly to our battle line closely pressed by the enemy. Covered by the thick underbrush they were within fifty yards of our line before we delivered our fire and followed it up with a vigorous assault that pushed them back on their second line, then the firing ceased for a few minutes, and we re-aligned our force on the ground gained to meet another attack that we knew would come soon.

"We could not see through the dense thicket, but were close enough to hear the enemy give orders to advance and prepared to meet the shock. It came like the roar of a tornado sweeping over the thicket. Up to this time our second line had not fired a shot. The fight was raging furiously. McCulloch, who could only judge of how it was going by the proximity of the firing, had sent in one courier that never came back, and another had just dismounted for the same purpose when a captain, supported by a soldier, both wounded, came out of the brush and reported that our line would give way unless supported General Parsons, in command of our second line, was near by.

"General, you can go forward at once", said McCulloch.

In a few moments we heard above the roar of musketry the wild Rebel yell that told us Parsons was in the game and had struck hard, for the firing moved farther from us. Again there was a lull in the storm of battle. Up to this time the fight was made on both sides with small arms. Not a cannon had been fired. Owing to the dense undergrowth and the short space between the contending lines, it was not safe for either side to use artillery, but now a gun boomed out in front beyond our extreme right, then another and another until a shower of shells went hurtling over us. I looked in the direction of the firing, and a smoke crowned hill told me a battery of the enemy was in action, and as the shells began to burst above us, were rapidly getting our range. McCulloch scanned it closely through his field glasses for a moment and then turning to me, said:

"Captain, you know where Colonel DeJean's command is. Ride over and tell him there is a six gun battery on a hill almost directly in his front, and to take it or move it from its present position."

As I turned to obey the order he dismounted and, throwing the reins to an orderly, started through the brush toward the front, but called to me to tell Colonel DeJean, if the ground was such that he could not use cavalry, to dismount and fight them as infantry. I found the command a little in advance of where I left it early that morning. They were drawn up ready for action, the men standing by their horses.

"I will ride forward and take a look at the ground", said the Colonel, after I delivered the order. "Remain here until I return, I may want to send a message to the General."

"How is the fight going?" asked Nick as the Colonel left us.

I told him the situation, and that we had to put in all of our strength to check the last attack, and that nothing had been heard from Price.

"And this lull in the fighting now means that Sigel is doubling his strength in front of you before making another assault", he said.

"I fear it is. If so -"

"If so, the situation looks bad, but not hopeless, my boy. Here comes the Colonel. Let's hear what he has to say."

"Tell the General I will attack immediately with cavalry." Then turning to Nick he said, "A hundred yards in front the ground is open right up to the guns."

I watched the command move forward before turning to ride back and had gone but a short distance before I heard the wild shout of the Texans as they swept forward towards the battery. There was an ominous quiet on the fighting lines below me, a calm before the storm,

I thought, as I rode rapidly forward. Coming in sight of the place where I had left General McCulloch, I saw a group of officers, including General McIntosh, some members of his and General McCulloch's staff and a number of couriers, and within the circle a surgeon was bending over the body of an officer on a stretcher.

"Who is it?" I asked one of McIntosh's staff as I rode up.

"General McCulloch", he replied.

"Wounded?"

"Dead. Shot by a Yankee sharpshooter in a tree the doctor says, judging from where the ball entered and where it came out, but -"

The sentence was not finished. There was a terrific noise, a shock and blinding smoke from a shell that exploded directly over us killing one of the couriers and wounding a number of others present. The battery that for a short time had directed its fire in another direction was again concentrated upon us. It evidently was the first shot fired in that direction since General McIntosh's arrival, but they were coming thick and fast now. I saw him wave his hand for the group to disperse, then speak to one of his staff who, looking around, saw me and motioned me to him.

"You know where Colonel DeJean's forces are. Ride back as quick as you can, tell him General McIntosh is in command, and to attack that battery at once." And without giving me time to explain mounted his hose and rode rapidly down the line, and I rode as rapidly in the opposite direction anxious to get from under the terrific shell fire.

"I could scarcely realize that the broken shattered troops that I rode up to on returning were the same gallant squadrons I had seen swing out in battle formation not a half hour previous. Some were dying and many wounded men and horses lying around. I needed no one to tell me the attack had failed.

"Where is the Colonel?" I asked a boy captain who was reforming his troop.

"Dead. Killed at the muzzle of those d--d Yankee guns. But we'll get 'm yet." As he looked up at me I saw tears in his eyes. I knew if the Colonel was killed Nick was in command, and a little further on I found him re-forming the regiment for another attack.

"The fight seems to be going against us", he said when I reported the death of General McCulloch. "But General McIntosh's order was not necessary. I am re-forming now to attack the battery."

The lines were advanced under cover to the edge of the opening and halted for final alignment.

"Let me go in with you, Nick?" I asked as he rode out in front with this little bugler by his side. "General McCulloch is dead. I'm unattached, have no command, and can offer my services where I please. Let me in?"

For an instant the fighting fire faded from his eyes. It was the old smile, the look of warm friendship of our college days, that lit his face as, pressing my hand, he said.

"By my side, boy, eight by my side. Sound the charge, Tommie," he said to his little bugler.

We broke from cover in three lines, squadron front, and started for the battery at full speed. The guns were still training on our infantry below with shell, and before they could change the direction of their fire and load with grape and cannister, we had covered more than half the ground between us. Excepting those worn by the officers, there was not a saber in the regiment. The men were armed with six-shooters and double-barrel shotguns loaded with buck shot, the most effective and deadly weapon for cavalry service then known, and up to this time we had not fired a shot, but the battery had our range now, and we were facing a withering fire. I could almost hear the deadly thud of the iron as it mashed through the flesh and bones of horses and men, but on we rode. We were winning the fight, the gunners were deserting their pieces and running to the rear. I had been riding knee to knee with Nick, but as we almost reached the muzzle of the guns he drove his horse a half length in front. I saw him rise in his stirrups, swing his saber to make a deadly 'right cut' at a gunner who stood with a rammer poised over his head ready to strike, then the earth seemed to open beneath us and the fires of hell burst forth. A regiment of infantry supporting the battery, concealed in the brush not ten feet behind it, rose in two lines and delivered their fire in our faces. I saw Nick's horse plunge forward on his knees, doubtless pierced by twenty bullets. Nick reeled backwards in the saddle, his arms above his head, then fall limp in his saddle as he swayed over and fell against my horse, his blood spouting over my knee and arm as I leaned over to catch him. At that instant came the sharp commend.

"Right wheel! Wheel to the right, quick. Guard against cavalry.

A dozen or more men on my left swung to the right carrying me and my horse in the rush. Not a hundred yards from us a column of Federal cavalry were coming down at full speed on our flank. They poured a stream of fire on us from their carbines as they came that crumpled up our little squad like dry leaves in a furnace. I felt a sharp pain in my left side as if a hot iron rod had passed through me, I grew deathly sick, the roar of battle died away, a black pall seemed to fall over the earth. I felt as if I was being hurled through space and then - oblivion.

When I regained consciousness, I was lying on my right side in a log pen that had at one time been a cabin. A fire was burning where a chimney once stood, and around it were grouped a number of men evidently talking, for I could hear a roar but could not distinguish words. They looked like giants by the firelight. Finally one of them came over and must have kicked me for it felt as if he was pulling my leg off. Then another giant rushed over from the fire, then the darkness came over me again. Now I was at home up in the cedars by the big cool spring, and I was awful thirsty, but somehow I couldn't swallow the water. I would dip my face in it, but could not get it in my mouth. The darkness lifted again. There was the fire, but the giants were gone, yet there was the water trickling down my face. I was burning up with thirst, but could not get one precious drop of it. I stuck my swollen tongue out and turned my head a little to try and catch a drop as it ran down my cheek. Instantly a black object bent over me and I heard a rumbling noise that my scattered senses gradually gathered into speech.

"Is you 'wake, Marse Ben? Does you know me? It's your ole Uncle Andy, Marse Ben, don't you know me?"

"Water, water", was all I could manage with my parched tongue.

"Yes, honey, yes, honey, all you want, but don't you move, Marse Ben, don't you move a finger. Doctor say it'll kill you if you does. You shall have all the water you want."

Feeling that my face was immersed in cool water was not altogether imagination, for the old man, as I learned afterwards, had been sitting by me all day, continuously bathing my face, mingling his tears with the water. Greatly refreshed by the water mixed with a little brandy, the Federal surgeon had left with him, I was able to listen intelligently to Andy's report of our disastrous defeat.

"They ges naturally killed all uv our folks, Marse Ben, 'cept d' ones what got away", sid the old man.

When General McCulloch's body was brought in, he thought I was also killed, and to his frantic enquiries, was told I had been sent to the extreme right of our lines. Mounting his horse, he rode as fast as he could in the direction indicated, and rushed into the midst of the bleeding and battered remnants of our cavalry falling back from the last unsuccessful attack. When shot, I had fallen across the neck of the trooper's horse next to me, who throwing his arm over me, had carried me back with the retreating squad, and was preparing to ease me down as dead when Uncle Andy came up. He relieved him of his burden and carried me in his arms to the deserted cabin close by to avoid being trampled by the horses and men from our retreating forces, closely followed by a regiment of the enemy's cavalry. In the afternoon, a Federal surgeon with his ambulance squad had found us in the cabin, examined my wound, dressed it, and after enquiring who I was, told Andy I had one chance in fifty of getting well if I kept perfectly quiet for twenty-four hours, but if moved or received the slightest jar, I didn't have on chance in a thousand.

Our relation to each other, for Andy had explained that I was his "young marster", and the old man's affectionate solicitude evidently appealed to the surgeon's sympathy, for aside from the flask of brandy, he left a tin of condensed milk and two jars of extract of beef with instructions how to use them, for neither Andy nor I had ever seen or heard of either up to that time.

But there was one incident in the old man's story of what had happened that I could not understand, and it was a year later before it was fully explained.

"There wuz er big man wid red whiskers standin' by when the doctor was axin' me who you wuz", said Uncle Andy in relating the incident. "n' when d' doctor walked over to d' fireplace he made me tell it all over agin to him n' den he axed me ef you ever went to school in North Carolina n' I tole him you shorely did. Then he called d' doctor and said, "Doc, call a stretcher. I've found an ole fren here n' I want to tek him to d' hospital.' N' d' doctor he say 'Ef you move him it'l kill him'. N' d' big man say 'I'll tek d' chance' n' d' doctor he say 'I wont', n' d' big man say 'He's my prisoner n' I'm gwine to have him'. N' d' doctor he say 'Look here, sur, I ranks you when it comes to wounded men n' I say you can't move him'. N' d' big man he turned round and kicked your leg as he walked by, n' d' doctor he jumped at him n' said "you dam brute, you tech d' boy again n' I'll report you n' have you 'duced to ranks'. That doctor shorely wuz white folks, Marse Ben, 'cause when he left he give me five dollars and says "Be keerful with your young marster, old man.

Keep him still or somthin' may bust inside uv him n' ef it does it'l kill him' "

I was too weak for the incident to impress me, but it was recalled to my memory a year later under more startling conditions.

It was the morning after the battle. Andy had bathed my face, and I had just finished my cup of beef tea when a tall figure filled the doorway, and the next moment Mr. Thompson stepped in. He said he had just finished going over the battlefield thinking perhaps the burying squad had neglected some of our poor fellows, and that the last troops of the enemy had withdrawn marching North toward Missouri; he also informed me that General McIntosh had been killed a few moments after General McCulloch; that Price did not get into action until nearly ten o'clock, after McCulloch's division had been defeated, and that Sigle and Curtis with their united forces then turned upon Price and defeated him.

"But you must get out of this", he added looking up and around the open and almost roofless cabin.

I told him of the doctor's orders not to move me for twenty-four hours.

"Then we must make you more comfortable", he said.

And giving Andy a note to his wife, sent him back over the road he had shown us two nights before. By noon he retuned accompanied by Mr. Thompson' manservant with blankets and pillows and a basket of delicacies suitable for an invalid. Three days later I was carefully placed in a hammock provided by Mr. Thompson, with Andy supporting one end and his servant the other by stout ropes passed over their shoulders and under their arms, and carried me to the beautiful little home in the valley. Dressing my wound with the tenderness of a woman and almost the skill of a surgeon with the motherly care of his wife, I improved rapidly and in a few weeks was able to sit up, but the old adage that "haste makes waste" proved true in this instance, for I had a severe chill and despite the best efforts and incessant attention, I drifted into a lingering case of malarial fever that carried me once more into the shadow of death, and it was six months before I felt strong enough to attempt carrying out my intentions, after the death of both General McCulloch and Nick, of returning East and joining the Army of Tennessee.

The latter part of September, Mr. Thompson having secured me a passably good horse and Andy a mule, we gratefully packed our belongings, bade our good friends farewell, and started on our return journey to Tennessee. Our objective was, Helena Arkansas, where we expected to cross the river and join General Johnson' army in Mississippi. But, on reaching Helena, we found an old friend organizing a regiment of cavalry, and at his solicitation, I abandoned the idea of going east and organized a troop myself. Soon after, the regiment was completed and mustered into the Service. Orders came from the command to report at Little Rock to join General Price in a raid into Missouri, but to leave one troop to gather up all stragglers from the army east of the river, and to enforce the Conscript Law, which had just been passed, in that Division. My troop was selected for this unpleasant duty, the Colonel explaining to me his reason for doing so, that while my troop was "gilt edge" in both men and horses, I had not sufficiently recovered from my wound to stand the extraordinary hard service he felt sure his force would undergo.

I drew up my troop in time the next morning to let the regiment pass and listen at the jibes thrown at my fellows as it rode by: "Be good little boys and we'll bring you some pet Yankees when we come back". "Take care of the old women and the babies, boys, and keep your clothes clean." Such sallies were general, followed with a chuckle all along their line.

I applied myself diligently to my duties, and between drilling and scouring the country over collecting conscripts and stragglers, my men had no time to look after the old women and the babies, for I was determined when we joined the regiment again no troop should look better, drill better, or have better mounts. How they would behave under fire was another thing. So when orders finally came for me to join the regiment at Cotton Plant, Arkansas, and bring all the conscripts and supplies with me, I felt a bit proud as I drew them up in line after drill, read the order to them, saying that Curtis was starting towards Helena with a large Federal army and that we would strike them probably at Cotton Plant, to have them greet the message with a cheer.

There were no organized Confederate troops south of White River at that time except my company. Curtis in all probability would cross his army at Des Arc, ten or twelve miles below Cotton Plant, sweep all over the country south of White River to Helena and thus cut me and my conscripts off. Cotton Plant was seventy-five or eighty miles north, and with no encumbrance it would be nothing more than moving from one camp to another with my troop, but I knew it would be rather a close shave to carry out five hundred or more unarmed conscripts that required guarding almost like prisoners, and a dozen wagons with supplies; so I decided to move at once and issuing orders to cook up two days rations, had the wagons packed and before sunrise next morning, the "Conscript Camp" was deserted and they were miles away on the march with a strong guard in the rear to keep up the stragglers.

CHAPTER XII.

I MEET THE LITTLE SCOUT.

When I reached the village of Cotton Plant, I turned the conscripts over to the recruiting officer and joined my Colonel at supper. With a number of brother officers gathered around his camp fire, I eagerly listened to the history of their Missouri campaign under General Price, from which they had just returned. They had been attached to Shelby's brigade of Missouri cavalry, a magnificent body of troops most ably commanded by Colonel John Shelby. As the advanced guard, this brigade had opened the way for Price's army, participated with distinction in every battle fought, and, as the rear guard, was the salvation of his army during it's disastrous retreat. The camp fire lit up the bronze faces of my comrades, and as I listened to them tell of the charges and countercharges of Shelby's "Iron Brigade", as brave and reckless in defeat as in victory. I flushed with disappointment when I thought of the light duties I had been engaged in during this bloody engagement.

"And to think", I exclaimed, "while all this was going on, I was engaged in collecting a miserable gang of conscripts. One day's service with you would have been more of a soldier's life than years such as I have been doing."

"I doubt if you could have stood it, Captain. It was dreadfully hard service, in the saddle day and night, and you not fully recovered from that puncture they gave you at Pea Ridge", said Captain Jo Green, the oldest officer in the regiment except the Colonel.

"Green is right about it, Captain", said the Colonel. "When I was ordered to report to General Price for the Missouri campaign and leave one of my companies to gather up these conscripts, I was governed entirely by the physical condition of its commanding officer in making my selection: I anticipated extra hard service on this raid, and no-." He was interrupted by a staff officer handing him a paper.

"Gentlemen", he continued, addressing the party, "I have just received an order from General Parsons to move the regiment at five o'clock in the morning to the ford on the river four miles above this place. Our scouts have reported that the Federal commander will cross his right division there. General Parson intends to contest the crossing sufficiently long to enable him to get his unarmed troops and wagon trains over the river. Issue the necessary orders to your troop sergeants at once, and then to your blankets, for you must be up at four". With a wave of the hand he dismissed me.

As I was passing him he lightly placed his hand on my shoulder and giving me a kind smile, said,

"Well, Captain, it is going to be infantry's day tomorrow, not much use for cavalry in contending for a river passage like the one we have above, but I dare say opportunities will be plentiful after the Yankees are once over on our side.

"By the way, I want to congratulate you not only on the manner in which you performed the duty assigned you, but on the excellent appearance of your troop. Your men and horses look fit."

"Thanks, Colonel, I made it a rule to drill them an hour at least every day. It was good fro the men as well as the horses. Otherwise they would have grown fat in the conscript service."

Good night said the Colonel. We may have more to do tomorrow than we think, so you had better turn in and get a good night's rest."

Cotton Plant was a little village on the east bank of the Cashé, a deep, little stream spanned by a high narrow bridge. At this point it was six or seven miles east of Unite River, into which it emptied its sluggish waters twenty miles below. The land between the two streams was low and marshy, covered with dense brakes of tall cane interspersed with virgin forests.

Every year when the winter and spring freshets came, all the land between the two streams overflowed for three or four miles above Cotton Plant down to where the two streams met below. There was a road that ran through this swamp from Cotton Plant to White River, and this was only available in the dry summer months. It was over this obscure road from Cotton Plant to White River that General Parsons decided to pass with his unarmed conscripts, in order to avoid the Federal army. A division was reported to be crossing the same stream at the regular ford above. The east side of the Cashé was above overflow. The land was very fertile, and vast fields of corn and cotton extended for miles around. A broad public road ran almost parallel with the river for twenty miles above. Learning from his scouts that a division of the Federal army would cross the river at the lowest ford available, and send a body of cavalry down the road to Cotton Plant as soon as they crossed, they would discover his conscript camp and wagon train. So

General Parsons decided to contest the crossing long enough to let him to safely cross the deep little stream into the protecting swamp on the west side.

We had 2,500 of 2,800 infantry men, six pieces of field artillery, and our regiment of about 800 cavalry, -- a weak force to oppose a division of not less than 8,000 troops of all arms. However, the nature of the ground was decidedly in our favor and greatly lessened the disparity in numbers.

By five o'clock the next morning our cavalry was in line, and moved up the road a mile, when we halted.

"Captain Green", said the Colonel, turning to him. His troop had the column followed directly by mine, "I will leave you and Captain Hord here. Let the infantry and artillery pass, see there are no stragglers, and wait here for further orders."

The cloud of dust made by our cavalry, as they moved on up the road, had scarcely settled before another cloud behind notified us that the infantry and artillery were coming up. In a few moments they swung by, making us the butt of their wit and jeers, as the infantry always did when passing the cavalry.

"That's right, boys, don't git any further up or some of you might accidently get hurt", said a long lank fellow with a sergeant's stripes on his jacket.

"Look, boys, look! See that fellow with all the gold braid? Now ain't he a cute", said on pointing to me.

"Dick, hush: he's a mighty purty boy, but that aint gold braid on his arms. Them's chicken in'ards", said a villainous smooth-faced rascal by his side.

As they passed Green's troop, I could hear them handing out the same class of compliment to him and his men. Green was a tall raw-boned fellow, florid complexion, with a full yellow beard that covered almost his entire face except a pair of twinkling blue eyes and a very prominent red nose.

"Look at the old gentleman with the corn silk all over his face", said one, "and a red beet in the middle", said another.

"Gee whiz, partner! what kind of liquor do you drink, and what did it cost you to color that nose?"

"Run a lawn mower over your face, Uncle, then dump a load of fertilizer on the stubble, and it will help the next crop", was the advice given him as the last company passed.

It was a hot sultry day in August, the road ran for miles through vast fields of cotton and the sun began to pour down its merciless rays upon us. The men threw themselves on the grass in the fence corners, taking such advantage of the shade as the rails offered. Two hours or more had passed, and yet we heard no sound of firing.

"The Yankees are taking it very leisurely", said Green, after listening for some time for the firing to begin.

"Possibly they have decided not to make the crossing at this ford", I suggested, "or our scouts were mistaken."

"That is not likely if little Walker made the report for -- Ah! did you hear that?"

"They have struck our skirmish line", I said as the pop, pop, pop of the guns distinctly reached us. The firing soon became a continuous roar of small arms for a time, then gradually ceased.

"They have either won the crossing or have been driven back", said Green rather anxiously from the top of the fence, where he had climbed up to get a better view with his field glasses.

"He had scarcely ceased speaking when for the first time the artillery opened fire.

"Hurrah!" shouted Green, shaking his old slouch hat over his head, as he leaped down.

"What do you make of it now", I asked.

"Clear as daylight. The boys have driven them back, and they have brought up their artillery to try and shell them out of their position. Our guns have also opened. Get the troop ready, sergeant, we will soon get orders to move", and his blue eyes were twinkling with as much pleasure as a child's with a new toy.

The steady roar of the artillery and small arms told us that the fight was on in earnest. One hour passed and yet no orders came for us to move.

"What in the devil's name do they mean by keeping us standing here like stumps in an old field", asked Green as he paced up and down the road impatiently listening to the guns. "I'll give them twenty minutes more, and if they don't send for us, I'll move up if I am courtmartialed and shot for it."

Green was my superior, and I was eager to follow him.

"Just say the word, Captain, and I'll take chances with you", I said as he again mounted the fence to scan the distant woods about three miles away.

"Just ten minutes more", he said, glancing at his watch.

In a moment he called to me, "get up here, Captain, your eyes are younger than mine. See if you can detect anything moving beyond that cotton field on the right. The road turns in that direction above us."

He gave me his glasses as I seated myself on the fence by him, and focused them on the point indicated. The road ran straight ahead of us for about a mile, then turned abruptly to the right in the direction of the woods, where the fight was going on. Looking carefully, I could see a small cloud of dust rising above the cotton field, moving rapidly in our direction. I reported it to Green.

"A courier with orders no doubt. Let me have the glass and when he comes around the turn in the road, I will know more definitely."

In a short while I could see a dark speck as it came into the stretch of road ahead of us. A moment more and Green lowered his glasses and jumped down.

"What do you make of it, Captain?"

"Orders without doubt. Judging from the way they are coming, it means hurry. Form the troop in fours, sergeant", he said, and turning to me, "Captain, please have your troop formed the same way and be ready to move at once."

I gave the necessary orders and went forward to join Green, who was standing by his horse at the head of his troop, waiting for the rapidly approaching courier.

"I suppose there is not doubt but that the orders are for us to move forward", I suggested.

"None whatever for it is little Walker himself who is bringing them. The distance was too great for me to recognize the lad, but I would know his horse in a thousand."

"And who is little Walker?"

Green turned to me with a look of astonishment, but instantly remarked, "Oh, I forgot you were not with us on our recent campaign. Why little Walker is as well known in the army as the commanding general. He is chief scout for the department headquarters, with a roving commission to go where and when he wishes, serve where he chooses, and report where he please."

"A sort of free lance", I suggested.

"The General has implicit confidence in his ability, and well he may, for a better, more successful and braver scout never straddled a horse - but here he is."

A smooth-faced lad, apparently not over sixteen or seventeen years mounted on a black gelding, pulled up in front of us.

"Who is in command here?? he asked, touching the rim of his sombrero.

"Captain Green, at your service", replied Green.

"Captain, General Parson requests that you move up promptly. I am instructed to act as your guide."

"Prepare to mount! Mount! Forward! Trot! Gallop!" were the commands that came crisp and sharp from Green, and in less than a minute our troops were swinging in columns of fours over the dusty road in a hard gallop, towards the distant woods, where the roar of the battle was incessant. Little Walker was riding boot to boot with Green in front. His easy seat in the saddle and the supple motion of his body with every stride of his horse spoke of the superb rider that he was.

I moved up by his side in time to hear him say to Green, "I think we can stand them off for five or six hours longer."

"Then we are alright", replied Green, "for our wagons and conscripts will be safe on the other side of the Cashé by that time."

"Our little force of thirty-five hundred, all told, will be on this side, four or five miles from a crossing in an open country, with a division of about eight thousand Yankees in front of us. The situation is not as cheerful hooking to me as it might be, Captain", said the lad, shaking his head and looking at Green.

"The Colonel told me last night that he thought the work today would be all for the infantry and artillery", I replied.

"When we withdraw from the ford, and they cross over, our cavalry, supported by the artillery, will probably have to cover our retreat, and it depends upon how hard they press us as to the amount of work you will have. But the stubborn little fight we are giving them at the ford may make them a little cautious about pressing us too closely", said the lad.

We had reached a point where the swamp land on our left extended up to the edge of the road, and within half a mile of where the fighting was going on above us.

"Keep to the road straight ahead, Captain", said Walker to Green, "and you will find a courier just beyond that point of timber who will give you instructions from the General. You bring your troop with me, Captain, and I'll show you the position he wished you to occupy", he said, turning to me. "Better throw your men into single file, as it is nothing but a narrow trail after we leave the road."

I gave the necessary orders, and in a few moments, led by the little scout, we filed to the left into the dense swamp, through which we advanced not more than a hundred yards and came to a halt.

"Better dismount your men here, Captain. The ground in front of us is lower and more swampy and unsafe for a horse. He would sink to the girths further down on either side of this little cowpath.

I had the men dismount and fasten their horses securely in the bushes. The scout had ridden a few steps to one side, and I followed him. As I parted the dense brush and rode up, I found him dismounted and examining a peculiar looking little gun he evidently had just drawn from the leather case hanging over his arm that up to this time had not attracted my attention.

"Where is your horse?" I asked, looking around and seeing nothing of him.

"Lying down over there behind that big cypress tree."

"Sick?"

"Oh, no. He is only going to play the part of quarter-master during the fight."

"I don't understand."

"Why he is an a 'bomb-proof' position", he answered looking up at me with just a faint suspicion of a smile. "Push aside that clump of bushes and see if you don't think so."

- 187 -

"I rode a few steps, pressed aside the bush indicated and sure enough, close behind a huge cypress tree, the black gelding, unfastened, was lying as quiet and comfortable as if in a pasture, nibbling the tender leaves from the young cane within his reach.

"You found him alright, did you?" he asked, when I returned after securely tying my own horse.

"Alright and making his breakfast on the young cane near his head."

"I hope you did not fasten your horse near enough to disturb him."

"No. But your horse is not tied, and after he nips off the cane near him, he will get up and help himself to a fresh supply and probably go over and get acquainted with mine."

"No danger of that, Captain, I have known him to remain in the position for five hours. It is one of the several tricks I've taught him that are very useful to me in scouting. He is very intelligent, and has saved me more than once with his head as well as his heels from falling into the hands of the Yankees."

I had never seen a repeating magazine rifle with metal shells until that time.

"One of the new Whitworths?" I inquired as I watched him take six long brass shells from a small leather box on his belt, and load them into the rifle's magazine.

"It is a later invention even than the Whitworth, but not near so heavy nor so accurate at very long range" said the scout.

"How far will it carry accurately?"

"The inventors claim a thousand yards. I have never tried it over five hundred, but at that distance, I can put four out of five shots in a space the size of your hat, and at three hundred I can put them all in a space not larger than your hand."

"Wonderfully good shooting", I remarked in a rather a skeptical tone.

He had not looked up, and there was nothing boastful in the way he mentioned his skill with the rifle; but he evidently detected a tone of doubt in my voice, for his face flushed to a deeper tan, and looking up at me with a pair of big blue eyes in whose depth were unquestionable sincerity and truth, he replied, "Those who know and have served with me, think that I am quite a good shot, and not given to exaggeration."

The look and manner in which he spoke removed all doubt from my mind.

"Forgive me, Walker", I said extending my hand, "but it was so far beyond anything I could do, or that I have ever heard of being done with a rifle, I could not suppress my doubts, which I assure you I no longer have."

"Thank you," he said accepting my hand. "I hope I may have an opportunity soon to at least partially substantiate late my statement."

"A beautiful little gun. Where did you get it?" I asked, making a motion to take it.

"It came from Europe, but do you not think I had better show you your position?" he said, changing the subject, and tucking the rifle under his arm. "Judging from the hot fighting above us, we may expect a flanking column down this way at any moment. Walk with me a little way to the front. I can show you the ground, and you can place your men as you think best."

We returned to the path where the men were in line, and turning to the right, he followed it a short distance, when he called my attention to the ground on either side.

"You can see, Captain, this marshy ground is partly covered with water. While it will support the weight of a man, a horse would sink to its girths. It continues this way to a lagoon or cypress "break" as the natives call it, covered with water from one to three feet, utterly impassable for man or beast, except over a narrow bridge, made of small trees thrown crosswise, one above the other, until they afford a dry passage four or five feet wide from one side of the lagoon to the other. This little path leads to the end of the causeway on this side and extends pretty much through the same kind of ground for some distance on the other. Wait a moment. We are near the end of the path. Let me have a look to see if the Yanks have come up on the other side."

He stepped through the bushes quietly and noiselessly as a shadow, and in a moment called me to come on. The lagoon was a black sheet of water, probably two hundred yards wide, free from undergrowth, but out of which stood a forest of tall cypress trees, their conical-shaped roots or "knees" projecting in great numbers above the surface.

"An easy place to defend", I said, after looking over the situation.

"But a very important one", replied the scout. "If they find this crossing, and I dare say they have a native guide looking for it, and should pass over a regiment or two of their cavalry, they would be between our troops and Cotton Plant, our only way of retreat when the time comes, but could also strike us in the rear of our left."

"What do you think is the distance across?" I asked.

"Between two hundred and two hundred twenty-five yards."

"My guns won't be very effective at that distance."

My troop was armed with double - barrel shot guns, loaded with buck shot and ball cartridges, but useless at any distance over a hundred and fifty yards.

"If you will accept my services for the fight, Captain, I think I can supply the need at least of one long range gun."

"With pleasure, my boy, and I will be further obliged if you will go back and bring up the men, while I select the positions for them."

As they came down they were placed on the right and left of the path under shelter along the edge of the lagoon, where each gun could cover the crossing at some point. Instructing the men not to fire until ordered, I returned to the path near the end of the bridge, and found the scout waiting for me.

"Captain, I have found a place well protected", he said as I came up, "where I can cover the bridge for fifty yards or more from the other end, and if you will allow me to fire at will, I think I can give them some trouble before they can get that far out. Ah! hear that? They are coming."

"Go ahead, and use your own judgment". He turned and glided like a shadow into the thick underbrush.

I had an acute sense of hearing myself, but it was a half minute before I could hear what the trained ear of the scout had caught, that rumbling sound, familiar to every cavalryman, that told of a large body of moving horses. A moment more; and they came in sight around a bend in the path, not more than fifty yards from the end of the bridge on their side.

The footing was evidently wider than on our side, for they rode in double file, two abreast, down to the end of the bridge and stopped. An officer rode up and closely scrutinized the line of bushes on our side, then the bridge. How to cross his men over this narrow passage, whether in single or double file, seemed to give him most concern.

Cautiously two of them rode out in double file, ten or twenty feet from the end, evidently to test it. Satisfied they could cross in this way, two others started, when a keen whip-like report of a rifle came from the extreme right of my line followed almost instantly by another, and both horses of the second file fell dead across the end of the bridge. The two troops in front, out on the bridge, openly exposed to fire from the ambush, instinctively looked for cover, and whirled their horses around on the narrow bridge at the same time.

The result was what might have been expected, both went over the sides into the, stagnant mire and sank into soft mud up to their bodies, struggling ineffectually to extricate themselves. The riders, apparently unhurt and supporting themselves by holding to the ends of the logs, made their way to the bank and took refuge in the brush.

It was so unexpected, and done so quickly, that for a moment, the Federal officer was confused. Then we heard him order his men to dismount, lead their horses back, and be careful not to get off of the solid ground. He did not dismount himself. His horse was standing across the road and just at the heels of the two that had been killed. His attention was divided between watching his men and looking anxiously up and sown our side of the lagoon trying to locate the points from which the shots had come. He turned his head for an instant giving an order to his men, when with a sharp crack of a rifle his horse dropped dead in his tracks. The officer quickly freeing himself from the saddle, withdrew with the last of his men up the road to where the brush afforded more protection. I was watching the point where they had disappeared, with an occasional glance at the horses as they struggled to pull themselves out of the mire, when a soft quiet voice said:

"Well, Captain, nobody hurt yet."

Looking around, the little scout was standing near enough to have touched me, yet I had not heard even the crackling of a twig as he came up.

"I thought I would fortify our position on their side", he said, "and make Uncle Sam pay for the fortification, so I piled up their horses on the end of the bridge as well as I could without dragging them up with a rope."

"You did it splendidly and in a way little short of marvelous."

"Not marvelous; a horse is like a steer. Shoot him in the brain, and he will drop in his tracks without a struggle, and it only requires good shooting to do it. What do you think will be their next move?"

"Deploy their men as skirmishers along the border of the lagoon, they can reach us with their carbines, then bring up artillery, shell us, drag the dead horses out of the way, and under cover of the battery make another effort to cross."

"It is impossible for them to do so without first moving the horses and when they attempt that some one will get hurt. I have three cartridges yet in my gun and six more in my box. I will guarantee to put a man out of the commission with each shot before they move the horses."

"Then we can hold the place as long as necessary", and calling a soldier I sent a note to the commanding officer advising him of the situation.

We neither heard nor saw anything of the enemy for some time, when the little scout stretched on the ground near me closely watching the other side through a pair of field glasses, exclaimed: "they have deployed as skirmishers, and are coming up on both side of the path. I can see the bushes moving as they advance and now and then catch a glimpse of one."

"If you can see the end of the bridge well enough to shoot from here, you might as well get ready, for they will soon make an effort to move the horses out of the their way," I said.

"If you will permit me, I prefer my first position, which is some twenty or thirty steps beyond the extreme right of your line. They will not be able to locate me so readily, for when I fire, they will very naturally look at this end of the bridge for the shooter," replied the scout.

"You are right. Go ahead, but remember you have only nine cartridges."

"All of them shall count", he said and turning he disappeared in the bushes as silently as he came up.

Motioning my orderly to me I explained the situation, and had him pass the order for the men not to expose themselves, for in all probability when the scout fired, we would receive a fusillade fired at random.

For some moments everything was quiet and motionless on the opposite side. Then I saw a cavalry hat cautiously thrust out of the bushes, then another, until four light felt hats with yellow cords were stuck out of the bushes rather prominently near the dear horses. I smiled, and wondered if the little scout would bite at the bait thus temptingly shown and waste four of his valuable cartridges on empty hats, but not a sound broke the stillness. Soon a head and shoulder, then the body of a calvaryman came out followed directly by three others, crawling on their hands and knees. When the first one was near enough and he reached out to put his hand on the leg of the dead animal, a shot rang out from our side, simultaneously with a scream of agony from the wounded trooper as he pitched forward on a shattered shoulder. The little scout was watching the proceedings. As I expect, a volley came from the other side, but rattled harmlessly against the trees and brushwood around us. The wounded man was lying in plain view in the open road and we could hear his moans and cries of pain as he made repeated attempts to crawl to cover, which he finally did, dragging his shattered shoulder and leaving a trail of blood behind him. The firing ceased as suddenly as it began and for ten or fifteen minutes there was not a sound or sight of conflict except the dead horses at the far end of the bridge. Then came a single pistol shot, evidently a signal, for a tremendous fire poured in upon us, mingled with wild cheers, and at the same time a dozen men leaped from the brush and began to drag the dead horses out of the way, or throw them into the swampy mire on either side of the bridge.

The incessant roar of the guns, mingled with the shouting, drowned all other sounds, but, watching the men around the horses, I saw one, two, three, four fall in rapid succession, the little scout was still on the job, keeping up his score. When the fourth man fell, the others abandoned the dangerous task and made a rush for cover.

In a few moments, the firing ceased. With the exception of the cries of the wounded men on the other side, everything was as quiet as before the firing began. I passed the word down the line asking if any of the men were hurt and had received the assurance that, with the exception of a slight flesh wound, all had escaped. My courier returned bringing me notice from the commanding officer advising that he would begin drawing off his troops from the ford in half an hour. As soon as the infantry passed, I was to move back on the main road and join my regiment, which would cover our retreat to Cotton Plant. The scout was to report to him at once. I had just finished reading the order, and telling the courier to find him and deliver the message, when he came out of the bushes near me.

"Well, Captain, we have baffled them so far," he said.

I looked at him in amazement saying, "I expect this is the only time, on record where one gun stood off a regiment for an hour or more of as good soldiers as those were across the way."

"Oh, we had every advantage of them", he offered. Unless they had wings, they could never have crossed that lagoon except over the narrow bridge, and with your shotguns you could have made a slaughter pen of it before they could reach you, even if they had been regular infantry instead of cavalry."

"If they attempt it again, I will have to depend on my shotguns, for I have just received an order from General Parsons to send you to him at once."

"Then I must be off. I will probably see you again before we are safely over the Cash"; and touching the rim of his sombrero, he quickly disappeared in the brush to find his horse.

No further attempt was made to cross after he left, and soon orders came for me to join my regiment. When I reached the road, I found it drawn up ready for action, supported by two pieces of the artillery. A cloud of dust not a mile below us marked the retreating column of our infantry. The stubborn resistance we made at the ford gave the enemy a very exaggerated idea of our strength, and they advanced cautiously, even when they realized that we had withdrawn.

Their skirmishers were deployed, advancing slowly through the wide fields of cotton and corn feeling for our lines. It was half an hour or more before they realized there was nothing in front of them, and another half hour before their cavalry was sent up to the fort, making contact with us. Although they outnumbered us two to one, the conformation of the ground, and our method of fighting, minimized the disparity in numbers. The road was broad and level, wide enough for squadron front, enclosed by a high rail fence with fields of cotton and corn on either side. We were fighting for time; the clouds of dust across the open fields revealed our retreating infantry, now some miles away from the bridge that marked their safety. Our regiment was divided into four squadrons about two hundred each. The width of the road enabled us to present a front equal to their own, and our tactics were to fight them by squadrons in detail, meet their charge with a counter-charge, and when we were forced back by the weight of numbers, after a hand to hand conflict, shotguns and six-shooters against carbines and sabres, we would ride through our troops to the rear and reform, leaving a fresh squadron in front to meet their next rush, which would go through the same maneuver. Fighting in this way each squadron had been in action twice. Men and horses were showing the strain upon them. Our ranks were getting thinner every moment. I could see an anxious look upon the grim dusty face of our old Colonel as he rode in and out of the lines encouraging the men, the reins of his bridle thrown over the horn of his saddle, his bridle arm hanging loosely by his side with blood dripping from the end of his fingers, the result of a carbine shot as he led the first squadron in its charge. I was reforming my troops in rear of our column after our second effort, when he rode up.

"Captain, take your troop down the road and report to Captain Green. You will find him just beyond that bend in the road. Promptly, if you please." He turned and galloped back to the front.

I found Green some three hundred yards below the point indicated, standing in a gap where the fence had been thrown down.

"Ride in, Captain, have your men dismount some distance back in the field and report on foot. I'll show you your position. How is your ammunition?"

"We have plenty. It was not necessary to fire a single shot this morning at the lagoon."

"Didn't they attempt to cross?"

"Yes, but that little scout piled a few dead horses across the bridge and then stood off the whole Yankee force with his rifle."

"That little kid is more and more a wonder to me every day. But we have no time to lose now. We are going to trap those Yanks in an ambush. Place your men in the fence corners. Mine are concealed just above you. Have three or four men in each corner, but don't crowd them, for each shot must count and hold your fire until I give the word."

Up to this time not a shot had been fired by either of the two pieces of artillery supporting us, but they were kept close in the rear of our squadrons. As I turned into the gap where Green was standing, I noticed the two guns 100 yards down the road, one on either side of the road ready for action.

"It looks as if our artillery is going to help us. I noticed as I rode up they appeared to be in position", I said to Green, after placing my men. Then we stood listening to the fighting in the road above us.

"The 'old man' intends to give them a rather stunning surprise, Green said. He told me, before they first struck, us to keep the artillery well out of sight. He wanted to spring it on them when most effective. The squadrons will soon begin to form behind the guns there, when the last squadron breaks in retreat, the Yanks, finding they have no support, will follow close behind them. By the time they have ridden into the full span of our ambuscade, our boys will have passed behind the guns, giving them an open range for firing their grape and cannister at the head of the charging column at a distance not exceeding fifty yards. At the same time we will open fire from our ambush. There goes the first squadron to form behind the guns, right now!"

"There goes the charge", I replied, nodding my head towards the fighting up the road where a wild, fierce "Rebel yell" rose above the noise of battle. In a few moments they also galloped by to join the others behind the guns.

"By George! those boys have been roughly handled", said Green, noting some of the swaying figures supported in their saddles by their comrades, others with bloody heads and faces, and then a number of riderless horses. "There is only one more squadron and a piece between us and the Yanks, and there they go now!" he exclaimed.

As the wild familiar yell again rent the air, the Colonel came at full speed down the road from the direction of the fight.

"Captain Green", he said, pulling his horse up close to the fence, "the artillery fire will be the signal for your men to fire, and try to make every shot count. Then mount your men as quickly as possible. I will charge with the regiment after serving them two rounds from the artillery. The last squadron is engaged now and will come by in a few moments."

Glancing up the road, he exclaimed; "They are coming now!" and wheeling his horse, dashed down to where the squadrons were re-forming behind the guns.

Since the enemy had struck us early in the afternoon, they had been steadily pressing us back, sometimes fast, sometimes slow, but we always presented a fighting front to them. Their charges met with counter charges. In this way they had driven us back, for more than two miles, but without once breaking the formation of our column. Now, not an eighth of a mile above us our last squadron had charged. After a short clash of arms, I heard their bugle sound the retreat, and the heavy hoof-beats of the pursued, as well as the Yank's pursuing horses, made the ground tremble. For the Federals finding no support behind this squadron for the first time and noting the wild disorder of the flight, gave their short yep, yep, yep battle cry and followed in close pursuit, thinking they had at last broken our formation and routed us.

As our troopers passed I could hear the officer ordering the men to form fours in order to pass between the guns and they were obeying like the tired veterans they were. Not more than thirty steps behind came the front files of the enemy bending forward with drawn sabers and urging their jaded dust-covered horses with the spur. In this order they almost reached the guns. The distance between pursuer and pursued was short but sufficient, for the two pieces double shotted with cannister had been trained on the road in a way to make their fire most destructive and as our last men passed behind them, they belched forth their death dealing fire almost into the faces of the Federal column, which withered and crumpled up as if they had rushed into a white heated furnace.

Then we opened fire from our hidden positions on their flank. The men had been ordered to fire one barrel, then other, in order to give an exaggerated impression of our numbers, as well as to make both shots count. Then they were to draw their six-shooters and continue the fire. Our line of ambush extended a hundred yards along the line of fence and at this distance the Federal troops were not twenty feet from the muzzles of our double-barrel guns: a man could have hardly missed his target if he tried.

Our first volley that immediately followed the crash of artillery threw them into confusion. Our second demoralized them, and as our men drew their pistols there came in rapid succession two more shots from the doubly charged pieces of artillery, which converted the demoralization into a rout. As the clear notes of our bugles sounded the charge, the rout became a panic. A moment more and the regiment led by the old Colonel galloped by us in pursuit of the fleeing and demoralized enemy.

Green and I mounted our men and returned to the road. It was a sickening sight.

"Regular slaughter pen", said Green, as he looked up and down the road at the mangled bodies of men and horses, some dying and many dead.

"And it's still going on", I said, as the sound of firing from our pursuing column reached us.

"Yes, the old man is a regular tiger when he once draws blood, and when he gets licked for half a day as he has this afternoon, he is apt to take a heavy toll when he gets a chance."

While we are speaking the firing ceased, and soon after, as the dust cleared away, we could see our men returning.

"You did excellent service with your guns, Captain", I said to the young officer commanding the battery, a mere lad scarcely twenty years old.

"Oh, they were so close to us it was only necessary to shut your eyes and pull the lanyard. I was afraid at one time we were not going to have a hand in the game at all."

"I confess I was afraid several times that you were not", I replied with rather a forced smile.

"The only encouragement I could get from the Colonel when I ventured to ask how things were going up front was to 'keep the guns close up in the rear and be ready for action at any moment'. Here he comes now at a gallop."

A moment more and he joined us.

"Captain Green, draw your men up on the side of the road so the columns can pass."

"Captain Brown", he said turning to the young artillery officer, "you have done well. See if you can't do as well in dropping a half dozen shells in that cloud of dust you see across the field. Our friends in blue are on the back track. They have passed the bend in the road, as you can see from their dust, and I think a few shell thrown amongst them would hurry them up, but wait until our men pass you."

When the regiment rode up, the Colonel ordered them on to Cotton Plant.

"Take it leisurely, men," he admonished them as they passed down the road. "I think the game is over for the day."

"Now you may try your guns, Captain", he said, turning to Brown as the last troops passed.

"Load with shell and cut the fuse for eighteen hundred yards", were the orders of the young officer, estimating the distance with his experienced eyes.

The first shot proved the accuracy of his estimate as well as his skill as a gunner, for he sighted the piece himself, and the white puff of smoke we saw as the shell exploded in the cloud of dust told us he had their range.

"Give them a few more like that Captain, and you may then limber up your guns and follow the regiment into Cotton Plant."

"You two gentlemen", he said, turning to Green and myself, "will hold your troops here for an hour. I do not think we will be attacked again in this evening, but be on the alert. At the expiration of the time follow us to Cotton Plant. Meantime I will ride on and see if I can find someone to look after my arm, it is beginning to feel uncomfortable."

"I am sorry and hope it is not serious, Colonel", I said,

Apparently he did not hear me, for he made no reply.

"A peculiar and eccentric old man", said Green as he watched him ride away, "but a gentleman and a soldier every inch of him."

"I've never seen him in action until today. He seemed rather to enjoy it, but I rather think he might have used the artillery sooner than he did."

"Enjoy it!" exclaimed Green, "he fairly reveled in it. As for the artillery, that was his greatest pleasure in the game; he wouldn't have missed the surprise of turning the trick on them just at the time when they thought they had us beat, not for twice what it cost us. That is one of his peculiarities", continued Green. "He is as bloodthirsty and cruel as an Indian in a fight and cross as a wounded bear, but aside from this I believe he is the most tender-hearted man I ever saw, and most careful, and considerate of his men and horses."

"Something of a West Pointer, I take it?"

"Not at all, a Mexican War veteran. Got his military training under Houston, Taylor and Scott, for he served under all of then. I think he is Texan by birth, but now a resident of this state, but yonder come orders, I think."

Down the road towards Cotton Plant the little scout came galloping toward us.

"Gentlemen", he said saluting, "I was ordered by General Parsons to advise your Colonel that everything is safely over the river and that he can now withdraw his regiment. I met the Colonel some distance up the road and he asked me to ride here and repeat the order to you. But before you move Captain", he said to Green, "with your permission, I will ride forward on the road a little beyond your pickets, take a look at the situation and draw in your pickets with me as I return."

"Certainly", replied Green, and as the lad rode away he added:

"There goes another I understand even less than I do our Colonel."

"Who is he? Where is he from?" I asked.

"Those are questions that have been asked by nearly every man in the army, for nearly all of them know him by sight, but no satisfactory answer has been given to either of them yet. Some say he is from New York, others from New Orleans. Some say he is from Texas, others from Kansas, and some mysteriously whisper that he is a runaway scion of some royal family in Europe", said Green laughing.

"I suppose", he continued, "they form their conclusions from his reserve, courteous and refined manners, and the little foreign rifle he carries. He also has an inexhaustible supply of money: greenbacks, Confederate, and some say he is equally as well supplied with gold."

"What does the lad himself say?" I enquired as Green stopped to light his pipe.

"Nothing, absolutely nothing. He admits slipping through the Federal lines out of St. Louis and joining Shelby's brigade when they ran up on a raid within twelve miles of that city, and when asked where he is from he says he joined the army at St. Louis. But when some persistent enquirer asks where he was born and lived before the war, he replies, 'What difference does it make so long as I do my duty as a Confederate soldier?' and he says it in such a way that the subject is dropped."

"Rather a mysterious little personage."

"And remarkable as well", continued Green, "You know lads of his age, sixteen or seventeen years old, we have plenty of them who have run away from home to join the army, after they mingle with the rough soldiers for a while, become the toughest specimens in the army, drinking, gambling, cursing, using the vilest language, forming the most dissolute habits and giving more trouble generally than half a dozen older men, but this lad is an exception and a remarkable one as well. He has none of the usual vices, and not a man in the army has ever heard him say or do anything that would offend the senses of a refined woman. He has been well reared, whoever he is, and has the strength of character to maintain it with all the odds against him."

"A paragon of virtues", I said, smiling at Green's admiration of the lad.

"You are not far wrong in saying it", he replied. "A young boy absolutely unknown and without any 'pull' as far as any one know, who can join an army and inside of a year's time become as well known, and I dare say more admired then, the commander of the Department, has something to be proud of."

"He certainly had", I admitted, "but what has he done to win all this notoriety and admiration?"

"Well, he has beyond doubt the first quality desired in a soldier, Courage, not the hot-headed impetuous kind one would look for in a boy of his age, but the cool deliberate kind that will go up against the cold steel without flinching: the men know this and love him for it. They have seen him tested a hundred times and never falter or get rattled. Then he is courier and chief scout for the commander-in-chief, and in this way comes in contact with all the officers and many of the privates, and his unvarying courtesy to all alike wins their respectful regard. Then there is 'Little Walker's Brigade' ", said Green smilingly, "it is as well known in the army as the headquarters outfit.

"Little Walker's Brigade? I do not understand." "Well, that is the name the men have given it", said Green, "They all know of his wonderful skill as a marksman. In the first action he was in after he joined Shelby, when the enemy was five hundred yards away out of reach of the others, he began pumping lead into them with his little rifle and making every shot count, one of the privates standing by called to some of his companions, 'Great Scott, boys! look at that little fellow shoot. He is worth a whole brigade of such cattle as you', and the name has stuck ever since."

"A well deserved compliment, and true", I said as I thought of his morning's work at the lagoon; "but what about the 'outfit' you speak of?"

"Well, it consists of Walker, his servant who speaks a jargon that no one but Walker can understand; his two horses, and little burro that packs his luggage wherever he has to go. He attaches himself for a time to any command he chooses, and all of them welcome him. Of course the general at headquarters always knows where to find him and what he is doing. "Now said Green, knocking the ashes out of his pipe, "you know as much about him as I do or any one else, unless it be our Colonel; the lad seems to like the old man better than any one else, if he shows any preference at all, and I have heard the old gentleman say, 'The boy is as game as a pebble, the best mounted man in the army, the best scout, and the best shot in the world'. Now when the old gentleman unbuckles himself to say that of any one, it is a safe bet that there is something out of the ordinary."

I told Green of my morning's experience at the Lagoon and of the boy's extraordinary shooting.

"That was with his rifle," he replied, "I am told by those who have seen it that his skill with his pistols is simply marvelous; that a man mounted and going at a gallop can toss two walnuts in the air at the same time and this boy can draw his belt pistol and break both of them before they hit the ground."

"Did you see him do this, Green?"

"No I did not; but the man who did, told me."

"It sounds a bit fishy to me, but after that I saw him do with his rifle this morning, I have less reason to doubt it."

"Those who have seen him shoot say he is quick as a flash of light and shoots with almost equal accuracy from any angle."

"One of the best field shots on quail I ever saw, shot from his hip, never looked at his gun, but kept his eye on the bird."

"But he had a hundred or more shot in his gun and each shot was a chance to hit", said Green, "This boy has only one shot and one chance. How do you account for that?"

"Mechanical skill perfected in that line, but I confess I don't see how he can do it with a rifle. There was not more than a second's difference between the shots this morning. Yet if the muzzle of his gun had moved the fraction of an inch at that distance from the target, he would have had a clean miss, but he never missed a shot."

"They also say he can dress a wound as easily as he can make one. After one of our sharp little engagements up in Missouri, old Bowls, our brigade surgeon, was kept pretty busy patching up the boys. Little Walker happened to pass by one suffering from a severe flesh wound that Bowls had not reached. He got down and bandaged it up himself. Just as he finished, the old surgeon came up, looked at it and said, 'Young man, I'll have to make you my assistant. That job is as well done as if I had done it myself'. Here he comes back with the picket."

"I believe I will dismount and give my horse a little breathing spell. I have not been out of my saddle an hour since I left you at the Lagoon." he said to me as he dismounted and loosened the girth of his saddle.

Standing with one hand and forearm resting on the bowed neck of his horse and the other on his hip above his belt pistol, facing Green and myself seated on the ground a few feet distant, it gave me an opportunity to have a close view of the boy and gratify the curiosity aroused by the facts just related.

He seemed to be a lad not older than seventeen, about five and half feet tall, and at first glance I saw nothing out of the ordinary in his face. He had a smooth oval face which exposure to the hard rough life of a soldier had not yet erased its youthful lines. Cleansed of the streaks of sweat and dust that covered it, he doubtless would have passed as a handsome lad. He had a good mouth and chin that showed more firmness and strength of character than had the average boy of his age. But his most impressive features were his eyes. They were unusually large, and blue as the bluest Italian skies, fringed with heavy lashes that were two shades darker than his long, nut brown hair, which was thrown behind his ears and reached almost to his shoulders. He looked you steadily in the eye when talking, with a thoughtful expression more usual in a man of fifty than a youth of seventeen. He was not dressed in the gray jacket usually worn by our men. Instead he wore a coat made of fawn-colored material which I thought was cloth, but afterwards found to be the finest quality of tanned deer skin as soft and pliant as flannel. The body and sleeves were as loose fitting as a lady's blouse, the latter reaching to just above the wrist and fastened with strings of the same material instead of buttons. In fact, the coat was buttonless, the front also being laced up with a string. The shirt was gathered in at the waist by a narrow band covered by his pistol belt, and the rest reached half way to his knees. As he stood, I could only see enough of his pants to note they were of the same material and as loose fitting as the coat.

So far I had seen nothing in his dress to indicate the liberal supply of money Green had spoken of, but when I came to his boots, in my survey, I saw at once where at least a good sum had been hidden, for in those days a fine pair of officer's boots was the most expensive article of his wardrobe. These seemed to be of the finest French calf-skin, and evidently made to order, for they fitted the slender arched foot like a kid glove and looked as soft; the tops were made of stouter material up to the knees with "flaps" when turned up would cover the knees and legs for some distance above. They were, however, turned down and fastened with string just below the calves of his legs; on the heels was a pair of silver Mexican spurs, evidently more for ornament than service, for they were as small and light as a child's toy, and the rowels were doubtless made of silver quarters.

Yes, he is a little thoroughbred gentleman, just as the Colonel says, I thought, looking up at the serious and firm little face. I mentally added, one who under no circumstances will ever forget.

"I believe I will take a look at your horse if you have no objections", I said, getting on my feet. "Green says you have two of the best mounts in the army."

"I like him very much myself, but this fellow is not in show condition just now. A little soap and water would help his appearance, as well as his master's", he said, patting the neck of the animal as he turned him around for an inspection. He was a black gelding, scant fifteen hands, two white ankles behind and a little snip of white on his nose. His back and quarters were stout, and his girth immense for a horse of his size; the bones in his legs were broad and flat, the tendons large and stood out like cords; his neck was well set in deep sloping shoulders and the width of my hand could not more than cover the great throttle between his wide and clean-cut jaws, He turned his bony head towards me, with his shapely pointed ears thrown forward, gave me a look of almost human intelligence, and when I extended my hand he gave it a sniff then rubbed it with his soft velvety muzzle.

"What do you think of him?" said Green, as I stepped back to admire him.

"I never saw a better one, or one so good for this special service. If he has the courage, his lung capacity, powerful muscles, stout legs and feet ought to carry him over a lot of ground in a day."

He is a half thoroughbred, Captain", said the little scout, and after a moment's hesitation, added, "he has covered ninety miles in ten hours without food, and only four stops for water, with a hundred and fifty-two pounds on his back."

Green smiled at the look of astonishment I gave him.

"I would not have thought you weighed so much", he said.

"I do not", said the boy, "but he carried forty pounds extra weight."

"He has another, sorrel even better than this one", said Green, hoping to draw the boy out to tell us some of his scouting adventures, but he was not of the communicative kind.

"Not better, Captain, but I think equally as good", was the limit to his answer.

"I notice you don't use either our cavalry bridle or saddle, I remarked, pointing to the bit, "if I am not mistaken it a smooth jointed English Phelham with curb strap; but your saddle is beyond me. I've never seen one like it."

"The bit is a Phelham as you say. I prefer it because it is not as severe on the mouth as a cavalry bit. The saddle is Mexican and the tree is made entirely of rawhides. They are a little heavier than wood, but when stripped of the useless leather trimmings and metal ornaments always put on by the Mexicans, there is but little difference in the weight. The leathers actually necessary may wear out, but the trees will last a lifetime."

To the casual observer the saddle was quite an ordinary looking affair. It had a low flat pommel, probably three inches across the top, studded around with a row of brass tacks with large oval shaped heads, evidently intended for ornament, but there was no other metal of any kind, not even a buckle, about it. All the fastenings were made of leather thongs. The girth was of hair and fastened with a cinch knot. A stout piece of leather covered the seat, with fenders for the legs and feet of the same quality. Around the low flat pommel was fastened a pair of well protected holsters and tied behind the cantle a light rain coat. A very plain looking little saddle certainly, but I was to learn later that it often carried secreted about it papers that would have hung the little scout in twenty minutes if found on him by the enemy. He had tightened his girth while talking to me, and as he finished, swung himself with easy grace on his horse, and said, as he saluted. "I hope to see you gentlemen tomorrow", and galloped away towards Cotton Plant.

"What do you think of him?" inquired Green.

"A boy with a history, either behind him or before him, it is our guess which."

"Right: but it is time we were moving. Let the men fall in, orderly."

An hour later, we joined our comrades in camp across the bridge.

CHAPTER XIII

LITTLE WALKER AND HIS BRIGADE.

The conscripts, followed by the infantry, were on the march to Little Rock early next morning, and we were informed by our Colonel that the regiment had been detached from the brigade and was to re-cross the Cashé and follow the enemy into Helena, keeping in touch with their rear guard to help prevent the pillage and destruction of property of citizens by small marauding parties. We located the enemy marching on three roads that converged at Helena, and soon came up with his rear guards. For the following four days, they were not out of our sight, with running fights, until we struck their permanently established posts five miles out of Helena.

The country was rich in supplies, and the Federal commander having established his headquarters in the town, began to gather them in, first along the main roads, then out through the country. This gave us nearly twenty miles of territory to protect, and to do this most effectively the Colonel stationed the companies a mile or two apart, but in supporting distance of each other, where he could assemble the regiment if necessary to oppose a larger force than one or two companies could handle. His headquarters were about at the center of the line, and it was his custom to visit each company every day looking after the men and horses.

My troop had just been moved to the extreme right of our line to relieve a company that had been actively engaged for the past week, the Colonel had ridden down to see that our camp was properly located. He was just mounting his horse to return, when looking up the road, he exclaimed. "Yonder comes little Walker. He has his brigade with him, which means he is going to stop with us for a time."

Looking in the direction he indicated, I saw the little scout coming around a bend in the road mounted on the black gelding with a nondescript object following at his heels. As they came nearer I discovered the head and long ears of a little Mexican burro protruding out one end and four little twinkling legs beneath the bundle of blankets, buckets, pans and other camp utensils. Close behind the donkey came a magnificent chestnut gelding carrying another almost nondescript person the shape of a shriveled, old servant with two beady black eyes that shone with the cunning intelligence of a fox.

"Glad to see you", said the Colonel in response to the lad's smiling salute.

"Two of us are glad" I added as he bent in his saddle to shake hands.

"You may not be so glad, gentlemen, when you learn I come to trespass upon your hospitality for an indefinite time."

"Then I claim the privilege of extending the hospitalities, colonel, for the service he rendered us at Cotton Plant."

"He is a 'free lance' and generally selects his own company," said the Colonel.

"Then on this occasion, Colonel, I will put myself under Captain Hord's protecting wings for a while", replied the boy.

"As long as you like. My camp is only a short distance down the road. The Yankees have not yet pillaged the place, so you will find plenty of feed for you horses."

The colonel watched him as the scout rode away, followed by his donkey and servant. He remarked, "There goes the puzzle of the army." "Who is he", I asked. I can tell you a little about him, he replied, and began as they passed out of sight.

"You remember when Price made that raid up in Missouri, you were not with us, but our regiment was attached to Shelby's brigade, and he led the advance of Price's army. We camped one night within ten miles of St. Louis. About midnight that boy rode up to our picket, said he was just out of St. Louis and asked to be taken to the commanding officer. One of the men took him back to Shelby. He repeated his story to Shelby and in evidence gave him the evening papers from St. Louis. He also told Shelby that three thousand cavalry had left St. Louis that evening to get in his rear. He then asked Shelby to give him an escort to General Price's headquarters, two or three miles back, that he had some important papers for him, and in evidence of this statement produced a letter addressed to Price. The circumstances were so unusual that Shelby went with him. General Price was half dressed and half asleep when they were usered in, but woke up quickly as he listened to Shelby's statement. 'And this is the boy?' asked Price at the end, when the lad handed him the letter.

I am telling it as Shelby told me the day after. He said it was a flimsy little note, not more than a half dozen lines, and as he was holding a piece of candle for Price to read by, he saw it was written in cipher, every word of it, that Price jumped to his feet when he saw the writing, and after reading it, turned to the boy and asked if he knew the contents of the note. He said he did. 'Then answer this question', said Price and turning the paper over he wrote a line in cipher and handed the boy the pencil. Evidently to astonishment of the old General, the lad wrote the answer in the same cipher. Turning to Shelby he said, "General, you can trust this boy with your life, as I would trust him with mine. There are but three persons living that can read that cipher he is one, I am one, and the third is a prominent friend of mine of the Confederacy who lives in St. Louis. He is the head of our Secret Service Department in that city. Walker is the lad's name. He will be special scout for me and you will issue orders to your troops that he is to pass in and out of our lines at all times, and any assistance he may call for must be given him".

"Shelby hurried back to his command; in two hours we were mounted and going back over the road we had advanced on the evening before, to strike the troops the boy had reported to be in our rear. We found them, followed their pickets in and struck their camp before they were awake, capturing more than half and scattering the others in every direction. This was the first valuable service the boy rendered us. The next was two days later.

"Price had started on his retreat and Shelby was covering his rear. We had been hard pressed by superior forces for two days; in the afternoon of the second day the little scout made his appearance for the first time since he joined us. Shelby was looking through his field glasses at a large body of the enemy's cavalry about five hundred yards away evidently forming to attack us. I was sitting on my horse near by and heard the boy, who had also been observing the enemy through his glasses, say to Shelby he thought he could disable the Federal General on the white horse who seemed to be in command.

" 'What with?' said Shelby. 'I've nothing but a cannon that would carry that distance.'

" 'With my rifle', the boy replied.

" 'Then for the Lord's sake use it', said Shelby.

"I watched the boy as he dismounted, drew his little gun out of the case and adjusted the sights. He looked a little pale I thought, but steady as a clock as he stepped a pace or two in front and asked Shelby to keep his glasses on the group of Federal officers. He waited until, Shelby had adjusted them, threw the gun to his shoulder, and apparently without taking aim fired, and without taking the gun from his shoulder fired again. A waste of ammunition I thought until I heard Shelby call out, 'By the lord Harry, he has knocked two of them out of the saddle'. The boy had returned the little rifle to its case, mounted his horse and was turning to ride away when Shelby stopped him to shake hands and compliment him by saying he was worth a whole brigade, and since that day he, his servant, and donkey have been known as Walker's brigade.

Now you know as much about him as any one, unless it is General Holmes, who has succeeded Price in command of our troops and who seems to rely upon the boy more than Price did, but I doubt if either of them know more than the rest of us, and all we know is that he is the best scout, the best shot, the best rider, and the most perfect little gentleman in the army."

"He gave me a sample of his rifle shooting at our Cotton Plant fight, but I've never seen him use a 'pistol'".

"Then you have a wonder yet to see. With his pistol he is simply marvelous", said the Colonel as he rode away.

I had established my camp on an abandoned plantation. My men occupied a number of cabins formerly used by the negroes who had followed the Yankee army into Helena, the owners having left some weeks before. When I returned late that afternoon from visiting my outpost, I noticed a little brown "Syble" tent some two hundred yards from the nearest cabin. The little scout was engaged with a hatchet digging a water trench around it, his two horses and the donkey stripped of bridles and saddles were browsing on the young cane that fringed the bayou just beyond, and his old servant was cooking supper.

"Do you prefer your tent to a cabin?" I asked as I rode up.

"Yes, I am more accustomed to it and certainly sleep better."

"But how do you manage to pack it with you? I didn't see it when you came in this evening."

"You didn't recognize it, as it was packed on my little burro. Get down and come in and I will show you how easy it is to make a small , light page of a tent. I am rather proud of my tent, as it is my own invention." He pushed aside the flap and beehoved me to enter. As

I did so, I passed my hand over the cloth, it was soft, smooth, and as flexible as a kid glove.

"What is it made of?"

"The best quality of heavy Irish linen soaked in a waterproof solution and treated with a coat of linseed oil on the under side."

I soon saw the little scout's claims for his tent were correct. The center pole was a hollow steel rod of three joints each about two feet long, that telescoped into each other like a jointed fishing rod. The end of the lower joint was pointed and driven into the ground three or four inches. The top was fashioned like an umbrella, but not attached to the jointed center pole. It had six small hollow steel ribs about two feet long, hinged to a hollow steel rod upon the same principle as an umbrella, and when the top was spread the rod that supported it fitted down in the hollow of the top joint of the center pole. A stout cotton cord fastened to the end of each rib of the umbrella top was stitched to the cloth down to the lower edge and then fastened to a steel tent peg. When these were securely driven in the ground and the canvas properly stretched, it made the tent impervious to wind, rain, heat or cold. The furnishings were in keeping with the tent, an eye for durability and lightness in everything.

"How do you like my dwelling?" he asked with a smile in his big blue eyes as he noted my surprise.

"Excellent, could not be improved.

"Not quite that, Captain", he said with a soft little laugh, "but if you will take supper with me I think I can spring a surprise you will appreciate more than the tent. Do you drink coffee?"

"Stop! stop right there. Your invitation is accepted. Only name the time and place." When I returned half an hour later, he called out.

"Just in time! Mater had announced dinner and, like all good cooks, grumbles if the soup is allowed to cool before serving." Our dinner consisted of half a squirrel each, and a cup of delicious coffee. I asked my host if he liked coffee too. "Not at all," he said. I never drink it. Sometimes I have a cup of tea if I am unusually tired, but Mater there", smiling at his old servant, "had two vices I am entirely free of, coffee and tobacco; unless I keep him supplied with both, he is liable to run off to the Yankees some night and leave me".

I looked at the old man; there was the shadow of a smile on his wrinkled face and I caught a glimpse of affection in his eyes. It was only a flash, for the next instant the wrinkles had assumed their proper places and he had resumed his usual quiet, immobile expression.

"How do you manage to keep him supplied? Coffee is a great luxury to the rest of us."

"Oh, I frequently visit your Yankee friends, in a quiet way, to get the news and such other information as may be useful at headquarters, and while inside their lines, make purchases of any articles I want."

"And get hung as a spy if they should find you out." I protested.

"Oh, yes, but you know the old saying, 'catching before hanging'."

"But the dreadful risk you run every moment you are inside their lines", I exclaimed.

"Not much as you think, Captain. Of course, I do not go in as a Confederate soldier spying around for information, but as a citizen usually a country boy and not an overly intelligent one. In this way I can gather quite a lot of useful information by simply keeping sharp eyes, keen ears, and steady nerves. Sometimes I get nothing for my venture, but perhaps a curse from a drunken soldier for my stupidity and a pound of tobacco for Mater."

I looked with astonishment and admiration at the boy, a mere child in appearance, who would voluntarily stick his head in the loop of a gallows simply to get a pound of tobacco for his servant, and think no more of the risk and danger than most men would of catching a cold. I tried to draw him out in conversation to tell some of the adventures I knew he must have had, but he was not inclined to speak of them. However, he was enthusiastic about his horses. From horses the conversation naturally drifted to dogs and field sports, all of which I soon discovered he knew decidedly more than I did, although I was proud of my knowledge of all of those topics.

"If your field shooting is only half as good as I saw you do with your rifle at our Cotton Plant battle, you rarely miss," I offered.

"Oh, yes, I frequently do, but owing mostly to my carelessness. I think I shoot better with my pistols than I do with my rifle, for I've had more practice with them."

"I hope to see you shoot tomorrow. The colonel sent me a supply of fresh ammunition today, and gave me permission to let the men use up the old stuff in pistol practice."

I thanked my host for my supper, and as I turned to go, offered the old man servant a five-dollar Confederate bill for a tip, saying I wanted to make good my offer for a good cup of coffee. The old fellow refused to take it, lifting up both hands in protest and speaking a French jargon I could not understand.

"The old man understands English, but cannot speak it any better than you can understand his dialect," the scout said. He wishes to thank you and say he cannot accept tips from his master's guests and hopes you will do us the honor of repeating your visit, to which his master adds his invitation."

As I walked back to my quarters thinking of our conversation and incidents that took place during our light supper. I had the same opinion as the Colonel, that Walker and his brigade were the "army puzzle". That the boy was well educated, no one could doubt after five minutes' conversation with him.

Next morning walking over to where the men were engaged in pistol practice, I passed the little scout's tent and invited him to go with me. We stopped with the first group shooting at a target fifty yards away. Every man had a style of his own, most of them shooting from a rest, but all carefully and deliberately sighting their pistols before pulling trigger. The tree was covered with bullet marks, but none had hit the target.

"Try your hand, Captain. You're a good shot", a soldier said.

"That may be so, but here's the best pistol shot in the army", I said placing my hand on the scout's shoulder. "Ask him to try one at your target."

All of them remembered his rifle shooting when he was with us at Cotton Plant and all had heard of his skill with a pistol, so they gathered around to persuade him.

"Any of you men, I dare say, could shoot as accurately if you had practiced as much. I will try a couple of shots at your target", and drawing his pistol he fired two shots so quick it was almost like one report. "Dead center, both of 'm", called out the scorer, "one right on top of the other."

The men gathered around and were lavish in their praise, which seemed really to embarrass the little fellow.

"On, it's nothing but practice", he said, "beside shooting at a stationary target is not much evidence of skill." We were standing under a walnut tree. One of the men had picked up a half grown nut and was smelling it. "Now if my friend there will toss up that walnut fifteen or twenty feet, I think I can show you a better shot."

"You don't mean to say you can hit it?" said the astonished trooper.

"I can try."

"Which way shall I throw it?"

"Any way you choose, so you toss it up above the bushes."

"Well, get ready", said the trooper stepping out in front.

"I'm ready", replied the boy standing with his left hand resting on his hip and his right arm swinging naturally by his side over his pistol.

"But you haven't drawn your pistol", said the man with the walnut.

"That would be taking advantage of the walnut", replied the boy with a smile, " 'getting the drop on it' as you say. Toss it up, I'll take the chance.

I noticed he had tucked the flap of his holster inside of his belt leaving the handle of his pistol exposed and ready for his grasp. All eyes, except my own, followed the walnut as the man tossed it up, but

I was watching the little scout and he was watching the man with the walnut. As it left his hand, the scout with a motion as quick as any juggler ever made to deceive the sight, drew his pistol, fired, and shattered the walnut before it began to descend. For a moment the men stood in mute astonishment, then gave a loud cheer for "Little Walker and his brigade".

"Do it again." "Try it once more." "Get another walnut", came from all parts of the crowd, which now included the entire company. No more walnuts, however, could be found on the ground.

"Wait a minute, boys, I will knock some down", said one of the men preparing to throw a large stick up in the tree.

"I think I can save you that trouble", said the scout as the man drew back to throw. "Do you see those two nuts hanging together on that twig out to the right? I think I can cut them down for you."

Waiting until all the men had located the nuts, he fired. The twig was cut as clean as if with a knife, and the nuts fell to the ground without even breaking apart.

"I hope there is no bullet mark on either of them", said the lad to the trooper as he brought them to him. Not a scratch. You couldn't have done it neater with your pocket knife. Now say when", he added preparing to toss one up.

"I've only two shots left", the boy said twirling the cylinder of his pistol around a time or two, "and I believe I will try a double, if you will toss up both nuts at the same time.

The trooper turned and looked at him to see if he was in earnest.

"Do you mean to say" and stopped.

"Yes I mean to say if you will toss up both nuts at the same time I will try to break them before they touch the ground. But you must give me a skyline to shoot by."

"By thunder, he's going to shoot the stars out of the sky", said one.

"He kin do it if he tries", said another. "Or hit a gnat's heel at fifty yards."

"What I mean by a skyline", said the scout smiling at the comments, "is that the nuts must be tossed up so there will be nothing back of them but the sky; this will give me a clear sight of them from the time they leave your hand. A few steps to the right will do it."

The man took the desired position, and when the scout said "toss", let them go. There were two distinct reports but only a few seconds between them. The loud shouts of the men announced the boy's success in shattering both.

"Your shooting is simply astonishing" I said, as we were walking back into camp. "Had I not see it, I would have thought it impossible for any one to acquire such skill with a pistol."

"I think I shoot well", he said with unaffected modesty, "but I think any one with a really quick eye at measuring distances and steady nerves could do equally well with practice."

"How long have you been shooting a pistol?"

"Ever since I've been strong enough to hold one at arm's length."

"But I notice you do not hold it at arm's length when you shoot.

"No one can shoot a pistol quickly and accurately who depends on sighting his pistol at the target, because no one can hold a pistol absolutely steady. All shots are made on a wave motion, the accuracy depending on the quickness of the shooter in firing when the pistol covers the target. Where it is a case of life or death, one cannot wait to look through the sights of his pistol, he must shoot quick and accurately. At first my efforts were to hold it steady. Then I began shooting without attempting to look through the sight, and have kept it up ever since. This with constant practice accounts for my skill."

We walked a short distance in silence when he stopped and, placing his hand lightly on my arm, looked up in my face with his big blue serious eyes and said:

"I hope you will not think me 'chicken-hearted', as the men would, but I have a perfect horror of killing any one with whom I have no personal quarrel. Do not misunderstand me or think I'm a worthless soldier in a fight. In our Missouri campaign I was with Shelby's brigade and engaged in half a dozen little fights with the enemy in pistol shot and saber distance, and I shot thirty-three times and every shot put one of the enemy out of commission, not only for that fight, but for all future service as a field soldier. You have just seen a specimen of my shooting, Captain, and can readily understand that I can hit any part of a man's body I choose.."

"Even to a button on his coat", I asked.

"My target is larger than that. It is his shoulder, and as most men shoot from the right shoulder, that is invariably my mark. I may sometimes miss the joint but never the shoulder. Either shot is sufficient to retire him from service. And now, Captain", he said as we stopped in front of his tent. "You know more of my 'shooting to kill' than any man in the army except your colonel. All others think I am a bloodthirsty little fiend. Let them think so. It will do me no harm. I hope you will respect my confidence, and in return I wish to ask a favor.

"My 'brigade' " he said with a smile, "is as familiar to the army as the old General's, but as this is the first time we ever camped with you, your men will naturally be curious about my old servant, and have some sport with his speech and manners -- also to investigate my tent. I will be grateful if you will issue strict orders that no one may annoy him, and keep away from my quarters during my absence. I will leave tomorrow and be away several days, and he has all supplies he will need until I return."

Assuring him that his wishes would be observed I returned to my quarters, agreeing in my thoughts this time with General Shelby when he said the boy was worth a whole brigade - thirty men put out of commission with thirty shots and by a smooth face boy - what could a brigade trained like him do?

CHAPTER XIV.

SCOUTING SERVICE.

I had just finished washing my face the next morning when the little scout rode up to my quarters.

"You are a late riser", he said.

"Rather you are in early one, I retorted. The bugle hasn't blown reveille yet."

"I have a sixty mile ride before me today, as most of it is through the swamp and necessarily slow, I am making an early start."

"Where are you going?"

He raised a hand in smiling protest. "Now, Captain, you are stepping on forbidden ground. No one but General Holmes and myself know that, and even he does not know when I am going. You have the advantage of him in that respect, for I am starting now and only rode by to extend an invitation from Mater and myself. Should you want a cup of coffee in my absence, call on the old man and he will be glad to make it for you."

"I am not stepping on forbidden ground when I ask you how long you will be away, am I?"

"Not at all, but I cannot answer because I do not know myself; two and perhaps three days.

It was a pretty sight, the boy and his horse, and one I long remembered. He had on his usual picturesque dress of buckskin, his gray sombrero and high boots with the tops turned up and tied above his knees. His easy graceful seat in the saddle, his light body swaying with the motion of his horse, proved his skill as a rider, and the magnificent black gelding he rode was worthy of its master. I put out my hand to stroke his glossy neck, when he snorted and jumped violently aside.

"He doesn't like strangers? It is a trick I've taught both of my horses. Sometimes I have occasion to leave them and it would be a difficult matter for anyone to catch either, and still more difficult to ride them after they are caught."

Tied behind the cantle of his saddle, covered with a gum cloth, was a bundle I supposed were his blankets. In front tied up under the broad flat horn was his "slicker". The violent jump of the horse had slightly displaced the large bundle, and as the boy turned in his saddle to arrange it, I saw in the folds a pair of boy's rough brogan shoes. Having adjusted the bundle, he extended his hand to say good-bye. I held it a moment and smiled, as I remarked, if his boots got wet to be sure and put on the dry shoes he had in his bundle. His eyes opened wide with surprise, then he blushed like a girl. He knew I had seen part of his disguise.

"I caught a glimpse of them as you were re-tying it", I explained.

"Now you see, Captain, how very important it is not to overlook the minutest detail in taking a hazardous risk. This was very careless in me. Such a blunder might cost me my life. I thought I tied that knot securely. I ought to have been certain. How do you like your coffee?" he asked, abruptly changing the subject, "green, parched, or ready ground?

If I use those shoes you saw, the probabilities are that I will trade some with 'Uncle Sam's people before I return."

"Anyway I can get it, but for God's sake don't take such a risk for me."

"It's not your risk, Captain. I get my orders from headquarters. Have you instructed your men to pass me in and out of our lines?"

I assured him I had. Touching his hat in salute, he lifted the bit in his horse's mouth and the gelding broke into a canter that soon carried them out of sight. Gone again to stick his head in a hangman's noose, I thought, as they disappeared.

His cool indifference to the dangers of his service aroused my sympathy as well as admiration. I felt that it was almost brutal that orders from headquarters should constantly send a youth like this to risk the ignominious death of a spy.

It was in the afternoon of the third day since he left. In my restless anxiety for his safety, I rode out to my picket thinking perhaps they could give me some information. A mile or more out I saw him coming, a man walking by the side of his horse.

"Who's your friend" I shouted? I see you have put your mark on him", indicated the dirty, bloody, villainous looking creature walking, his right arm and hand hanging limp by his side covered with blood from the shattered shoulder joint above.

"It is one of the Ferguson gang of bushwhackers."

"I thought, between the Yankees and ourselves, we had hung or killed all of the villians. How did you get this one?"

"It's a bit of a story, Captain, with a tinge of romance in it."

"Then fire away, we've a mile or more to ride before we get back to camp."

"When I was in Duval Bluff amongst our Yankee friends a day and night, I secured the information wanted at headquarters, and was on my way out, when I had rather a close call with some drunken soldiers; but that has nothing to do with the bushwhackers. After reaching my horse I started through the woods on a direct course for our lines, avoiding the public roads as much as possible. I had to cross the road that leads from Helena to the Bluff, and as I was still inside the enemy's lines, I approached it very cautiously. When I saw I was close to it, I stopped in a clump of bushes to listen before riding out. Just then one of those big swamp owls hooted almost in front of me across the road and the next instant a turkey yelped just below me on my side of the road.

Now Captain, you may not be as familiar with woodcraft as I, but my suspicions were at once aroused. Those big owls rarely hoot in daytime, and never on a big public road, and a turkey hen never yelps in response. A gobbler might respond, but a hen never, and when the sounds were repeated in a moment later, I knew they were signals, and waited for developments. I had only a few minutes to wait, there was a low whistle from my side answered by another on the opposite side, then four murderous looking scoundrels, two from each side, stepped out in the road not fifty feet from where I was concealed. I knew as soon as I saw them they were a remnant of Ferguson's bushwhackers. Three of them had shotguns, one a carbine, and all had pistols. I was yet ten miles inside the Yankee lines, and was hesitating what I should do, when I heard the jingling of harness and rattle of wheels coming from the opposite direction on the road. The bushwhackers evidently heard it too for they immediately slunk back in the brush, and the next moment a Yankee ambulance drawn by two mules passed within twenty feet of me, driven by an old gray-head Yankee sergeant with two passengers, an old lady and gentleman.

"When the ambulance came opposite to where the bushwhackers were concealed, they sprang out, two of them caught the mules by the bits, while the others covered the driver with pistols shouting "hands up"! Expecting something of this kind, I prepared for it, and the wheels had scarcely stopped turning, before my horse jumped into the road, and as the fellow in front of the wheel on my side raised his pistol to cover the driver, I fired. He fell, and I rode over him. His companion was holding the mule with his left hand and had his shotgun in his right. Before he could use it, I fired. He dropped the gun and turned to run, and to make sure of him, I broke his other shoulder with another shot. As I fired the second time, I heard the report of a pistol on the other side and the agonized scream of a woman. I wheeled my horse around in front of the mules and his shoulder struck the back of the fellow who evidently had been holding them, but was now leveling his shotgun at the people in the ambulance. The shock from my horse knocked him down, discharging his gun, and sending the pellets up in the air; he was under my horse's feet so that I could not shoot, but with the discharge of his gun came the report of a pistol in front of me which was fired by the fellow who was standing at the wheel on that side. He was in a stooping position with his back to me preparing

- 234 -

to take another shot when I fired. I did not have time to note the result, for I had passed over the shotgun fellow and wheeled my horse just in time to catch him on his knees drawing his pistol. I fired first, and added another shattered shoulder to my score. Two shots in quick succession were fired behind me. Again I wheeled my horse around and saw it was the old Yankee sergeant pumping lead into the prostrate body of the fellow who had been shooting at him.

" It is all over, sergeant", I said as I rode up.

" "Who are you?' he asked.

"I told him I was his friend.

"I noticed the blood was trickling down through the stubby gray beard from a wound on his cheek and asked if he was badly wounded. He said it was slight, but was afraid they had killed the old gentleman, and would I please look after him. The screaming had subsided into pitiful moans as I stepped from my saddle into the ambulance, and it was indeed a pitiful sight. An elegant and refined looking old lady, the tears streaming down her pale cheeks, was holding the grayhead of the old gentleman in her lap.

" 'You have killed my husband' she said, as I lifted my hat and stood before her.

"I explained the situation, but it really looked as if the old gentleman had been killed, for when I picked up his high silk hat I noticed a bullet hole in the front and back, but as I saw no blood on his gray head and pallid face I told her I hoped not, and on examination found the bullet had only grazed his skull knocking him insensible for a few moments. Assuring her he would soon be alright, I brought my canteen of water and a little flask of brandy I always carry in my saddle bags. Bathing his face with her wet handkerchief, she soon had the satisfaction of seeing him open his eyes, and, after I have him a good stout drink of brandy, expressed himself as all right.

" 'Now, sergeant, let me look after your scratch" I said, after the old gentleman had recovered. It was more disfiguring than painful. The ball had simply seared the flesh up to the cheek bone and there cut it leaving a wound an inch or two long. I washed and bound it up in some bandage I had. He seemed very grateful, so I told him I was a Confederate scout, ten miles inside of his lines, so it would be a favor if he would not start any troops after me for an hour or more. He assured me that not a man in his regiment would harm a hair of my head.

"I noticed the old couple were engaged in a whispered conversation while I was dressing the sergeant's wound, so when I finished, he called me to him and asked my name. I gave it. He replied, "Mine is Teague and this is my wife. He told me that they lived near St. Louis and come down to Helena, Arkansas by boat to visit their son, who was a Major in the 80th Missouri Cavalry in the Federal army. He had sent the ambulance to meet them at Helena and bring them over to Duval's Bluff, where his regiment was stationed. He had heard me say I was a Confederate soldier. He could see that I had undoubtedly saved their lives and he wanted to express his gratitude in a way more substantial than words. He owned that he was comparatively rich, but had only 4 or 500 or dollars with him -- would I accept them until he could send 500 more through his son by flag of truce? Of course, I declined. Told him I was sure his son was a gallant soldier and would have done as I did under the circumstances. But the old lady was insistent.

"You must take some token of our gratitude. Wear this for our sake. It was given to me by my soldier boy, who had saved the lives of his mother and father, to have it. She had taken off a ring, as she spoke, and slipped it on my finger. I could not refuse the tender, beseeching look in her pretty old face with tears in her eyes."

"What do you think of it?" he said drawing off his gauntlet and holding out his hand for me to inspect the ring.

"A magnificent ruby. The largest and handsomest I ever saw!" I exclaimed.

"Given with gratitude thrown in for good measure", said the lad, smiling as he replaced his glove.

"What became of the others?"

"The sergeant shot one and wanted to shoot the others to save time, he said, but I persuaded him to tie them one on each side to the collars of the mules, drive them in to the Bluff and then hang them. This fellow seemed to be live enough to cause trouble so I brought him with me."

"Perhaps I was tedious in telling your story, Captain, but the action was quick."

"But that wasn't in the plan was it", I said.

We rode some distance in silence before he spoke.

"You know about me coming out from St. Louis to General Shelby with dispatches for General Price. Well, sometime before I left the city someone had pointed out to me a handsome Federal officer mounted on a magnificent horse: he said his name was Teague.

I believe I mentioned that I had rather a close call in getting out of the Yankee lines last night. It was this way. I had purchased some coffee, tobacco, and sugar and had them in an old sack across my shoulder, when three half-drunken soldiers stopped me and wanted to see the contents of my sack. I declined and they were preparing to take it by force when an officer called in a commanding tone to "stop worrying that boy". I was disguised as a country boy. I looked up and at once recognized the handsome man and horse, for he was riding the same animal, I had seen in St. Louis.

"What have you in the sack, boy? he asked after taking the names of the ruffians and ordering them to leave. I emptied the contents on the ground before him. "Not much to fight over." he said with a smile. "Put them back and get out of the lines before dark", which I did."

He paused a moment and then asked, "Do you think such trivial actions are directed by chance or Providence?"

"I believe it was, for in sending, as he thought, a simple boy out of his lines, he could not in his wildest dreams have fancied he was sending that boy out who, in less than twelve hours, would save the lives of his father and mother."

We rode into camp as the scout finished his story. I called the orderly to take charge of the prisoner, telling him that he was one of the Ferguson gang and we would postpone hanging him until morning.

"You will have to excuse me from the hanging, Captain", said the scout as he untied the rope that bound the bushwhacker to his stirrup. I've been in the saddle since eight o'clock last night.

An hour later, I found him asleep on his cot. My step roused him, for as I turned back, he called, "Come right in, Captain, I was only cat-napping. I am ashamed to say I was too tired to take the food from my saddle. Just wait a moment and Mater will get your package of coffee."

The tent was lit by a tin oil lantern suspended from a ring on the center pole. In looking around at the snug, comfortable quarters, a bright object on a small mahogany box just beneath the cot in which the boy had been resting attracted my attention, and I picked it up.

"A Spanish stiletto" I exclaimed, examining it under the light of the lantern, and drawing from its silver scabbard the little sharp-pointed, three-edged blade not more than three inches long. Attached to the pearl handle was a small gold chain sufficiently long to be worn around the neck. "It looks like a child's toy."

"But a deadly one in a desperate hand, Captain", said the boy standing by my side.

"I wonder if they make them all alike?"

"I should think not, I've never seen any but this one, why do you think they do?"

"I never saw but one other, and that, with the exception of the chain, was exactly the same as this. It belonged to a very dear friend of mine. We were in college together at Chapel Hill, North Carolina. He was from Texas, and had a perfect arsenal of all kinds of weapons, amongst them a little stiletto like this.

There was a muffled sound and something fell on my foot". I looked down and saw the boy had dropped my package of coffee, and the precious grains were scattered all over the ground. I turned quickly toward him and saw he was about to faint; his face was pale, a vacant stare in his blue eyes, and he was supporting himself by clinging to the tent pole, I laid him on the cot and called to Mater to come quick. I was supporting the boy's head when he rushed in, his little eyes flashing like a mad cat's.

"Water quick, your master has fainted".

Instead of obeying, he seized me with a strength no one would have thought the old man possessed, tore me away, and took his master's head in his arms. It was no time to exchange civilities. Looking around, I found a canteen of water, and after bathing the boy's face, he opened his eyes and looked bewilderingly around.

"Don't you know me, Walker?" I said stepping to the side of the cot where he could get a good view. He stared at me nearly a minute, then color began to come back in his face, though he continued to look steadily at me.

"Certainly, Captain, I know you, but I believe I fainted."

"Yes, but you are alright now. You have simply overtaxed your strength for the past three days."

"I am sure you are right, sir, for I am very tired."

"But don't you get up. You need two days sleep at least before you are fit for service". I said as I bade him good night.

The next morning before breakfast his servant came to me with the coffee. "Evy grain uv it" he said as he gave it to me. He apologized profusely for his conduct the evening before, told me his master had a good night and was still asleep.

I walked down that evening to see how the lad was getting along, and found him writing, using the little mahogany box in his lap for a table. I started to turn back when he hailed me.

"Come right along, Captain, I'll promise not to 'throw another fit' as I did last night. It's not a chronic disease", he said laughing more heartily than I'd ever heard him.

"You are busy writing. I don't wish to disturb you."

"Not at all. Just jotting down a few notes for headquarters, and they can wait", he said, turning the paper over with the blank side up. "Wasn't it disgraceful in me keeling over as I did last night?"

"Not at all. I only wonder you had not passed out sooner."

"I think I am weaker in my head than body. I tried to understand what you were telling me last night, but it was only a jumble of disconnected words of stiletto, fried, college, etc. Now if you will be kind enough to repeat it, I promise you all attention. Never having attended college myself, I've always had a desire to learn something of a boy's college life."

Beginning with my hazing experience and first acquaintance with Nick Hardeman I told of our warm friendship and incidents of our college life until he graduated.

"And what became of him afterwards?" asked the lad as I finished.

"We corresponded, of course, but I never saw him but once afterwards. I spent the night before the battle of Pea Ridge with him; we slept under the same blanket and next day I was by his side when, leading his regiment in a charge, he was killed, his heroic blood spouting on me as I tried to save him. It was the death he would have preferred to all others, but I know there was one last wish in his heart."

I paused to recover; it was tearing open the wound in my heart as I recalled the bloody charge and the falling figure of Nick. The lad evidently saw I was moved, for it was a moment or two before he said:

"What was that wish?"

"To kill the brute that murdered his father and sister, and as long as I live there is at least one chance that his wish will be accomplished, for it is my life's work to find that fiend and kill him. It is my only reason for serving in this western army away from all my friends, because Nick told me he thought the man was in the Federal army west of the Mississippi."

"Perhaps I can help you, Captain. You know I am in and out of the Yankee's lines quite often, I may be able to locate him."

"A splendid idea. I had not thought of that. Find him for me, Walker, and anything I can give you is yours for the asking."

"I will begin my search in a day or two, for I have to go back to Duval's Bluff as I failed to get all the information needed at headquarters."

"Don't start, until you are thoroughly rested", I said, "and don't take any unnecessary risk. Fate or premonition tell me I am destined to catch this fellow some day."

It was in the afternoon of two days later, the scout mounted on his sorrel passed my quarters.

"You are mounted on a fresh horse, but how about the man?"

"Fresh as the horse, Captain. I'm off again and probably will be absent several days. Please have an eye on my servant and traps."

I had no time to think of the scout, for we were almost constantly engaged fighting the enemy's foraging parties for the next few days, and my troop had just returned from one of these affairs when the boy came riding up marching a tall slender old negro in front of him.

"Who's your friend, this time?" I asked.

"Say yours and you will be nearer the mark, and if you appreciate him in proportion to the trouble I had in catching him you ought to give him a royal welcome. I rode up on him in the woods between the lines. He had heard the fighting, and was as wild-eyed as a deer and dodged me like a rabbit. When I finally caught him, it required my most persuasive eloquence to convince him I was a Confederate soldier. He then admitted he was trying to get inside the Confederate lines to see Captain Ben McCulloch Hord.

The old negro stood just within the light of my campfire and his rusty old Prince Albert coat made him look unusually tall. He wore a pair of blue Yankee trousers and gaiters that had seen better days, but there was no mistaking the old family servant in his appearance as he stood before me, his shabby old silk hat in his hand showing a gray fringe of hair around his bald head.

"What can I do for you?" I asked.

"Is you Captain Ben McCulloch Hord?"

"Yes."

"Do you live in Tennessee?"

"Yes, that's my native state."

"Did you go to school in No'th Ca'lina?"

"Yes, I did", hope risng up in me.

" 'Scuse me, boss, but I've got a letter and was told to be shore 'n give it to the right man.' "

"If you let me see it and if it's not for me, I'll give it back to you."

He unbuttoned his Prince Albert, then a sweater, then a vest, and from the inside pocket drew out a package wrapped in a red bandana handkerchief. He unfolded it and gave me the letter. It was properly addressed to me by a lady's hand, and I opened it with considerable curiosity, but was astonished beyond expression when I saw the signature, 'Catherine Hardeman, the young sister of Nick'. The letter was written at her home in Texas and dated May 15, 1863. She wrote she had just learned from reading an account in a Texas paper of our combat at Cotten Plant in which my troop was mentioned. It said that I had finally joined the western army. The last letter she had received from her brother written the night before he was killed at Pea Ridge, stated that I had not arrived, and they had given up all hope of me doing so. She asked me where I had joined, and if I knew any of the particulars of Nick's death. She felt almost sure Carrier was with the Federal Army in the West. She asked if I would deal with him as he deserved, should I ever meet him, and concluded by saying the mails were so uncertain, and she was so anxious for me to get her letter, that she was sending it by her father's old coachman.

I was deeply moved, and questioned the old man about how everything was getting along at home. I told him that I would have an answer to his letter by morning, then turned him over to Andy's hospitality for the night. The little scout was standing by talking to some of the men and as I finished I motioned him to join me and gave him the letter to read, explaining it was from the sister of my friend we were speaking of a few nights before.

"Poor friendless little girl", he remarked as he returned the letter.

"Not friendless. She has one, loyal and true, as long as I live, knowing how she loved Nick my heart bleeds for her."

I was engaged in answering Miss Catherine's letter when a cheery voice outside asked if a weary traveler could stay for the night. The next moment young Holmes, a son of our commanding General, stepped inside. He was serving as an aide-de-camp on his father's staff. We had been classmates at Chapel Hill.

"You don't even wait for permission" I said, affecting a cold stare. "What on earth brought a member of the staff so near the fighting?"

"Orders, nothing by orders, my boy, could induce any of us to risk getting our precious hides punctured. The old gentleman had some orders for the Colonel, also some for Walker, and I persuaded him to let me bring them. I have delivered the Colonel's, and he told me I would find the scout with you."

"He was here about an hour ago. You will likely find him at his tent."

I finished my letter and gave it to the coachman, who was as careful in secreting it as the one he brought. Advising him to get a good night's rest before starting back, I bade him goodbye.

"What's the news from headquarters?" I asked Holmes when he returned.

"Nothing. Your regiment are the only troops actively engaged just now, and you know what you are doing better than headquarters."

"Could you get nothing from the scout?"

"Not a word. The little rascal is as close as an oyster. I watched his face as he read his dispatches, which were in cipher, and might as well have been looking in the face of a sphinx, but from the few French words I caught when he spoke to his servant, I think he is going to move, where or when only he and the General know."

Neither Holmes nor myself were left in doubt long. Next morning, before we had breakfast, the boy rode up followed by the little burro carrying all of his camp equipment, with Mater on the sorrel gelding bringing up the rear. "Little Walker's Brigade" was on the march.

"I am leaving you, Captain", he said stopping in front of my cabin, to bid you goodbye and thank you for the kindness you and your men have shown me. I'll always remember it with pleasure."

"Don't mention it; I sincerely wish you could stay longer, and I hope wherever you are going you will have good, if not better, treatment. Where are you --" I started to say "going", but checked myself, remembering our former conversation. He smiled when I hesitated.

"You are not stepping on forbidden ground this time, Captain. I'm going to Little Rock to report to headquarters, but I hope we will meet again soon." And giving me a hearty handshake, the "brigade" resumed its march.

CHAPTER XV.

COMBAT INTENSIFIED.

As the supplies were soon consumed around Helena, the enemy pushed their foraging parties further into the country, causing greater activity on our part against increased numbers. Fighting along some part of our line occurred almost daily in a very rich section. My troop was getting more than its share of attention from the enemy. After three weeks of more of almost daily fighting we were five or six miles behind our original position, with a troop of worn out men and horses. We were relieved by a troop who had not been so constantly engaged and sent to the extreme left of our line, where the enemy was not so active.

There was an abundance of supplies there, but inaccessible to the enemy, except by boat steaming up the St. Francis River. As yet they had not tried this route, but late in the afternoon of the second day, after reaching our "rest camp" a courier from the Colonel informed me that the Yankees would send a boat up the St. Francis next day to get some corn from the Neely farm on the river, and for me to be on the lookout for them.

It was only five miles away, and I waited until the early morning before the enemy landed. We rode up through the woods and thick underbrush to the fence that separated the woodland from the dwelling with its garden of vegetables, flowers, and shrubbery. A short distance down the fence and not more than thirty steps from it was the back of the long granary filled with sacks of corn.

Neely had two sons in the Confederate army, and no one was there except himself, his wife and two or three family servants, none of them up yet. The ground sloped gradually from the dwelling down to the river some two hundred yards away. Its location was marked by a fringe of cottonwood trees on the banks, and was as open as a parade ground. I concealed the men in the brush just behind the granary so they could cover either side and stationed myself as lookout.

It was an hour before I looked down the river and saw the smoke of the steamer. Shortly after, she whistled for the landing, which was a well known shipping point to the surrounding country. Normally the cabin and upper deck of the boat could have been seen from our position, but the river was quite low, and we could only see the smoke stacks and the top of the pilot house.

A moment after the boat had touched the landing, an orderly sergeant, followed by a bugler and half dozen men came up the bank towards the granary. I had expected to see infantry, as they are usually detailed for such duty, but much to my surprise these men carried carbines and wore cavalry uniforms.

This gave me confidence. I had forty-five men under cover, which had ninety shots in our double-barreled shot guns, besides our pistols. My troopers were not to fire until ordered, and then only one barrel; so the orderly with his little squad passed around the building unmolested, coming within ten steps of us. Then he ordered his men to break open the door and his bugler to blow a note to signal to the others on the boat. In response they came swarming up the bank scampering about like schoolboys. We waited for them all to come up and collect around the barn door before ordering my men to fire. I saw an officer followed by an orderly, walking towards the house from the landing and decided to capture him. Moving quietly back through the dense foliage I beckoned my orderly sergeant to me telling him to take a couple of men, slip through the garden into the house unobserved, and when he heard our fire, rush in and capture the officer and his orderly.

Now there were two continuous lines of the enemy between the landing and the granary, one going with sacks of corn on their shoulders, others coming for more, and old man Neely and his wife standing silently to one side watching the robbery they were powerless to prevent.

Having given the orderly ample time to carry out my instructions and waiting for a bunch of the plunderers to bunch together, I gave the order to fire. Of course, it threw them into great confusion, as all such attacks will do with the best disciplined troops. When I ordered the second valley, and jumped over the fence to complete the work with their six shooters, we found nothing to complete.

Sacks of corn were scattered over the ground from the granary to the boat dropped by the Yankees now fleeing to the river, while Neely and his wife were making equal speed towards the house. At such short range, it was necessarily a bloody fight. Five men had been killed outright, and twice as many so severely wounded they could not get away. We found three sound ones in the granary, who chose capture rather than risk being killed if they came out. I told my lieutenant to secure the uninjured prisoners, break up their carbines, fire off the ammunition, parole the wounded, leave the dead, as their friends would doubtless come for them, and prepare to move at once. Then I went up to the house to learn what success the sergeant had had, and, if possible, rustle up a cup of coffee.

I found two of my men standing just inside the hall with a little lad between them.

"What luck?" I asked as I stepped in.

"We've caught the colonel and his little courier. The boy thinks we are bushwhackers and are going to kill all of them."

There were tears in boy's eyes, but he gave me a look of defiance that reminded me of our little scout as he looked up; that decided me at once to let him go.

"Well to convince him we are not bushwhackers, take him to the lieutenant and tell him after he gets ready to move, to turn this boy loose so that he can return to the boat and have a burying squad sent up to look after their dead."

Telling, the other solider to follow me I sent to the room where the colonel was being guarded by my orderly sergeant.

"He is a cool one, Captain", he said as I walked up. "Had ordered his breakfast, but jumped to the door when the firing commenced. I met him, stuck my six-shooter in his face and backed him into this room. He made no fight, for I don't think, from the way he cussed himself for a fool, that he even had as much as a pocket knife with him, and when he saw that he was trapped, he quietly sat down at the table, which was set with plate, knife and fork, and said he believe he would wait for his breakfast."

I opened the door and stepped inside followed by my two men. One glance at the prisoner and my heart gave a leap that for an instant made me speechless. Mingled feelings of vengeance, pleasure murder, and triumph swept over me. It was none other than the cruel, handsome face of Carrier I was looking at. For the flash of a second there was a look of surprise, the next instant his face wore its habitual, cruel reckless look in the face of danger, for he evidently read in my looks the feelings of my heart, and was the first to speak.

"Upon my word" he exclaimed, assuming a surprised tone. "It is the little cub I thought I killed at Pea Ridge. What fools these doctors are! they said the least jar would kill you and I gave you a kick that would have jolted a mule and yet here you are, still good food for powder."

"Which is something better than you are. Your filthy carcass is only good for the buzzards. I'm going to hang you, Carrier."

"Certainly, do so by all means, and it will give our government a good cause to hang one of you dirty rebels for every hair on my head, but let me tell you something, after the hanging, you can think of your friend, Nick Hardeman, ironed, in solitary confinement in a loathsome dungeon, praying for a death denied him until he becomes a gibbering idiot finally to rot and die in prison."

"Only such brutal imagination as yours could draw a picture like that, Carrier, and you would, beyond doubt, make it real if you could, but thank God he is out of your power. He was killed at Pea Ridge and I was right by his side when he fell. He died a gallant soldier's death."

"So you thought. Now listen to the rest of my story and then go on with your hanging, that's over in a minute, the other is a life-time job. It was my regiment that struck your flank at the battery. Riding amongst the guns after the fight I found Hardeman desperately wounded but not dead. My first impulse was to finish him with another shot, but I thought of a more exquisite way of gratifying my intense dislike for my brother-in-law, so I decided to save him for future punishment.

I told the surgeon to save his life at all cost, that he was a very dear friend of mine, but under no circumstances ever mention my name to him. When Hardeman was sufficiently well to be moved from the hospital, I got permission to move my "friend" to the house of a friend in St. Louis who would be responsible for his safe keeping. My St. Louis friend was a bachelor, a man I knew I could depend upon in a private affair of this kind, and who also had a good dark cellar under his house. I met the ambulance there, had my friend give the driver my receipt for the prisoner and bring him in. It was then that Hardeman knew who was his unknown friend.

I confess he did not, on recognizing me, seem to appreciate my kindness in saving his life. On the contrary he became so violent that my friend, with my permission, knocked him down twice, the last time sufficiently hard to stun him, and before he recovered, we had him tied hand and foot, for he seemed to be unusually strong from a convalescent just out of the hospital."

Though I believed every word a lie, my imagination pictured poor Nick as weak and emaciated, knocked about like a child by two ruffians and it made the blood surge to my face with suppressed rage. He evidently enjoyed it, for with a cruel smile he continued.

"When recovered sufficiently to understand, I enjoyed his wrath as I recounted some of our past history. When I thought it time for invalids to retire, we carried him down to the cellar. As I was leaving, I asked if he wished for anything. He said he only wanted to live long enough to kill me. I told him he would be my prisoner the rest of his life.

"Shortly afterwards I went to headquarters, represented my friend, the prisoner to be well enough to send home. My urgent solicitation was approved, now I hastened back to my friend in St. Louis, who was keeping Hardeman for me. I instructed him in the answers he must make, carried him before the proper officials, introduced him as Hardeman, secured the parole, and thus disposed of my friend Hardeman forever so far as the United States Army is concerned. Quite clever, wasn't it? he asked with the cruelty of a devil in his face. "Quite an implausible lie, Carrier, from start to finish", I said."

"You will think more so when you hear the finish. Having disposed of Hardeman, I re-named my prisoner, call him Smith.

"Unfortunately, my friend who had charge of him was taken sick three months ago, and for fear outsiders might get an inkling of our affairs, I preferred serious charges against Smith so as to have him sent to a regular United States prison and be placed in solitary confinement until I could produce specifications of my charges before a court-martial. There he is now, fretting his life away, without friends and without a name. I will not give you the name of the prison and Smith is not the name he is know by. Now if you can find any clue to release him after you hang me, you are welcome to it."

My men had become interested in the villiain story and were standing by me near the table.

"Now Carrier", I said as he finished and was toying with the table knife, "I've listened to your story drawn from your imagination. Now listen to me, if Nick was situated as you describe and could speak to me, he would tell me to kill you rather than relieve him, and I'm going to do it. You are unworthy to die the death of a soldier. I am going to hang you before sundown. I am going to leave you hanging stripped of the uniform you have disgraced, so the buzzards will have a fair chance at your rotten flesh."

Like a flash Carrier jumped from his seat. I felt a blow and stinging sensation on my cheek. The same instant he fell across the table and rolled to the floor, with the blood spouting from a gash on his head. The sergeant had delivered the blow with his pistol as Carrier struck me, and now stood over him ready to shoot when I caught his arm.

"Don't kill him, I want to hang him alive. Feel and see if his skull is broken."

Carrier was lying unconscious on the floor bleeding freely.

"He is alright, sir, or will be in a little while, no bones broken."

There were rapid footsteps in the hall, and as the sergeant rose from his examination, he looked towards the door and exclaimed, "What's up, Jimmie?"

"The Devil's to pay and no pitch hot", was the answer.

I turned round and saw the colonel's courier splashed with mud, his face flushed and eyes shining with excitement.

"I beg your pardon, Captain, he said, touching his hat as he handed me a note, "but these are urgent orders from the Colonel."

I saw at a glance the importance of prompt action. The Colonel advised me the enemy were coming out in strong force on every road leading out of Helena. I was ordered to abandon our boat expedition, and join him as soon as possible, with every man able to sit in his saddle. He would hold the road open for me as far as LaGrange, and to join him there. Writing a line or two reporting our success with the boating party and that I would be with him as soon as possible, I sent the courier back to him.

The men were standing by eager to know the cause for such haste. I told them the situation, sent orders to the lieutenant, by the sergeant, with instruction to get the troop on the road quickly, and that I would be detained a few moments, but would catch up with him."

"Tell him", I said as the sergeant turned to go, "to have the old mule grazing out on the lot caught, and to send it here with corporal Jones, an extra man, and the prisoners."

"Now we'll see if we can bring more life into this filthy carcass", I said, pointing to Carrier's still unconscious form. Bring some water and pour it on his head, but first take off his sash and tie his hands behind him."

"It's a fine one", he said, unwinding it and handing it to me. It was a knit sash made of the finest silk, and I little thought as I drew the soft folds through my hands what a tragedy it would help to play in a few hours. He tied Carrier's hands, rolled him over on his back and brought in a bucket of water.

"You had better wash the blood off your jaw first sir," he said holding the water up.

In the excitement I had forgotten the little stinging sensation on my cheek where Carrier struck me. Withdrawing my hand, I saw that my fingers were stained with blood.

"How did he do it?" I asked.

"If that point had been sharp and he'd struck an inch lower, it would have been all over with you but the funeral", the soldier answered pointing to the broken blade of the table knife I had seen in Carrier's hands.

The corporal reported with the mule and prisoners just as Carrier was reviving. I explained the situation to him, and told him I had selected him especially for this important trust. I said I would rather lose half my troop than for this one man to escape, that I wanted him carried through alive if he had to kill all the others, but to kill him, of course, if there was no other way to get him to our reserve camp twelve miles back.

"I can only spare one man to go with you, corporal, and you must let him guard the three prisoners, march them in front of him and you follow with your prisoner on the mule, keep his hands tied behind him and the reins of his bridle looped over the horn of your saddle." And once more cautioning him of the desperate character of his prisoner, I watched the little squad move off before mounting my horse, and followed by my trooper galloped out to catch up with my company.

We joined the regiment just in time to meet the shock of a heavy column of the enemy that forced us back. Savagely our colonel held us up to the work and we fought for every foot of ground, but the odds were overwhelming, and mile after mile we were pushed back until the enemy gave up the pursuit, turned back to Helena and left our battered but unbeaten regiment to rest for the night within two or three miles of our reserve camp.

Tire and slightly wounded as I was, my anxiety concerning Carrier overcame my fatigue and after a little rest I rode over to the camp. As soon as I looked into the face of the trooper who was with the corporal I knew some disaster had happened. He told me that he and his prisoners had stopped at a house by the roadside to get water. The corporal and his prisoner rode up shortly after they left also stopping for water, he supposed, for when he heard a shot and looked back the Yankee was on Corporal Jones' horse jumping the fence into the woods. While looking back, his prisoners made a break also. He shot one but held onto the other two. Hearing fighting on both sides of him and knowing the woods were full of Yankees he had driven his two prisoners double-quick to camp, but didn't know whether Jones was dead or not.

After taking in this awful news, I sent the driver to get his ambulance ready, and find a few convalescents and the surgeon to accompany me. I also took the man who was in charge of the prisoners as our guide and started for the scent of the tragedy.

When we reached the house we found poor Jones dead on the porch.

We found the ball had gone in on the right side, passed up through his heart and out the left breast.

"The man must have been bending over when he received this shot", said the surgeon after probing the wound.

"He was, sir, He was bending over to dip the Yankee a drink of water out of the bucket I was holding, when he shot him, pushed him out of his saddle on top of me, jumped on his horse and was over the fence and in the woods before I could get up."

"That's about all there is to tell, sir. The mule broke loose and run down the road, this fell off just outside the gate", he said handing me Carrier's silk sash.

"This is what he was tied with, doctor." I gave him the sash. "And that is why he freed his hands", he said, examining it. "Don't you know you can untie a silk knot as easy as you can a yarn thread; beside knitted silk like this will stretch like rubber."

Jones' belt was still around him, and when I saw the empty pistol scabbard had no flap to cover the handle of his pistol, I saw at once the easy and simple manner of Carrier's escape. Having freed his hands, he only waited for an opportunity to use them effectively. This came when Jones bent over to get the water. Riding on the side next to the pistol, he caught the uncovered handle and shot the unsuspecting corporal, pushed him out of his saddle, and in less than an hour was reunited with his army.

My anger at Carrier's escape was softened by sorrow for my unfortunate Corporal. We carried his body back with us to give it decent burial. The pressing demands of combat gave me little time to think of the tragedy.

It was the first of July when we heard that General Holmes had left Little Rock with his entire army, crossed the White River, and was about to attack the Federal army at Helena. He was advancing over the same roads as the Federals had traveled. As our regiment was familiar with the country, we were sent in advance to brush away their pickets.

On the afternoon of July 3rd, I was ordered to drive in a picket of the enemy twelve miles outside Helena, then follow them three or four miles, go into bivouac, and wait for orders. I had but little trouble in performing this duty. The enemy knowing our army was advancing, made but slight resistance, and as the sun went down I went into bivouac just across the road from a little farmhouse. There was a well in the yard and a long water trough just outside the fence. The men had stripped their horses and were watering them, some inside drawing water and pouring it into the trough, others holding the horses. I was sitting on the stile that led into the yard, when a woman rode up from the direction of Helena.

"Kin I git a drink uv water an' a drink fur my critters?" she asked as she stopped.

"You shorely 'kin', miss, whether you have any kin here or not, provided you 'kin' drink out of a canteen", replied on of the men drawing water, mimicking her.

"I recon I kin ef you kin, providin' the aint nothing' ketchin' 'bout it like the itch or sore mouth."

"Nothing about it, fair lady, to stain your ruby lips", he said, handing the canteen over the fence with a profound bow. She squirted out a stream of tobacco juice and rinsed out her mouth before drinking. There was an audible chuckle from the men.

"Would you mind giving me a chew of your tobacco, my fair queen of hearts?" asked the trooper.

Now, look here, mister, I aint any more your queen uv hearts 'n you is my jack uv spades, and what's more, I haint got any tobacco to give away. You kin buy all you want when you git to Helena if you ever git thar but the Yankees say you'll never git in 'n I believe what they say and more 'n that, they say Vicksburg is surrendered 'n I believe that too."

"Fair lady --"

"Oh, shet up your blarney" she said, turning her horse around to leave.

I had listened with amusement to the banter between the trooper and the woman, but her statement that Vicksburg had surrendered startled me, for it was generally known that our attack on Helena was made to relieve Grant's pressure on Vicksburg and give Pemberton a chance to fight his way out with his little half-starved army. But if Vicksburg had fallen, it would be throwing away lives for us to attack Helena. General Holmes must know this, and as the woman rode up I stopped her. She had on an old split sunbonnet, the strings tied under her chin, a calico waist not particularly clean, half-fingered black woolen mits, and a soiled well worn riding skirt that left her foot exposed encased in a patched and rusty old gaiter. Her face was in keeping with her custume.

She looked to be thirty or thirty-five years old, but the innumerable freckles on her face and nose might have made her look older than she really was. Her horse was a wretchedly poor old gray.

"Now what do you want?" she asked in an irritable tone with emphasis on the *you* as I caught her bridle rein.

"To know your name and where you live."

"My name is Sallie Soot and I live three miles beyant her but Pap --"

"I don't want to hear anything about your Pap.

What were you doing in Helena and how did you happen to hear about the surrender of Vicksburg?"

She replied, "I carried in a little truck to barter fer sugar and coffee fer Pap 'n was comin' outen the store when a officer come runnin' up wavin' a little yellow paper at two officers standing by the door saying it was a copy of despatch General Grant had sent to Washington saying Vicksburg had surrendered and he would march in and take possession tomorrow 'n that's all I know 'bout it. Now I reckon I kin go, cain't I?"

General Holmes must know this at once, and would doubtless want to question this woman, so I decided to send her to him.

"I must ask you to go by General Holmes' headquarters. He will want to ask you some questions."

"Well, I jes wont do it. It's nigh dark now and I'm going home."

"It's but little out of your way. I will send a man with you and the General will send one home with you."

"I shant do it --"

"Then, miss, I'll have to send you under guard", and I called to the orderly to send me a man to take her to headquarters.

"Who are you and what right have you got to stop a poor lone woman on the big road?"

I told her this was my picket post and my duty to investigate every one who passed. She put her hands to her face as if to cry, and as the guard came up she said, "Well if I must, I must, and if you will show me the way instead of this man, I will go."

Knowing that the importance of the information she had might materially change our plans, I dismissed the trooper, ordered my horse and accompanied her. Riding two miles to the rear brought us to headquarters. A short distance from the General's tent, I spied by the light of the fire the scout's little brown tent, and rode up to where old Mater was busily engaged in getting his supper.

"Hello, Mater!" I exclaimed, as we rode within the circle of light is your master at home?"

The old man looked up at me, with one of his spasmodic grins as he recognized me, gave a quick sharp glance at the woman, and shook his head.

"Where is he?"

"Dunno."

"Do you have any coffee?"

"Dunno."

"On, come on, I aint got no time for you to waste talking to that old man", and without waiting, the woman rode towards the General's tent and I followed. Young Holmes was just coming out as she rode up. He stopped with astonishment seeing it was a woman, but catching a glimpse of me just behind, lifted his hat as he passed by and asked me in a low tone.

"Who's your friend?"

Miss Sallie Soot and pretty as a peach. Do the decent thing, boy, run and help her down."

He turned to do so, but Miss Sallie needed no help. She rode up to a log and threw her bridle over a limb, took an old carper sack off the horn of her saddle, dismounted, and was properly adjusting her skirts before Holmes had made two steps.

With the carpet bag in her hand she followed me into the General's tent. No one was present except the old man and Colonel Lindsy, his adjutant general. To each of them Miss Sallie curtsied gracefully, brushed her old riding skirt with her hand, adjusted her sunbonnet and stood at "attention". Having told the General all I knew concerning Miss Sallie and why I brought her to him, I stood aside to let him question her. He looked at her critically before speaking, then asked her name, where she lived and a hundred other questions I had not thought of. He reflected a moment and then said:

"Miss, I will have to detain you for the night". She threw up her hands in protest, but he continued. "If this information is correct, you will be released in the morning, if not, we will consider the matter later. Colonel Lindsy, I wish you would see that this lady is properly cared for tonight. You can see a room for her up at the house with the family and place a guard at the door."

As the Colonel rose to obey, Miss Sallie dropped her carpet bag on the floor whining most piteously to Lindsy and me, for the general was so deaf, he could not hear that she wanted to go to Pap, at the same time taking off her bonnet showing a little wad of hair twisted in a knot on the back of her head about the size of a walnut and tied with a shoe string.

"Wait!, I want to appeal to the general", she said as the colonel started for the entrance of the tent.

Not having heard any of this conversation, the old general was looking from one to the other with amazement. When she untied the string the little wad of hair fell about her neck; catching a broad gold ring as it dropped, she placed it on the table before the old man. He put on his glasses and examined it carefully, and to the amazement of Linsy and myself, began to laugh immoderately. Miss Sallie, unmoved, still stood at "attention".

"Never mind that order, Colonel, but move the sentinel out of ear shot and tell him to let no one in on any pretext."

The old man continued to look at Miss Sallie and laugh and Miss Sallie continued to stand at "attention" until I began to fear the news and she brought was so startling that it had thrown him into hysterics.

"Gentlemen", he said when the colonel returned, "let me introduce you to my little scout Walker."

Had he exploded a bomb-shell at our feet we could not have been more surprised.

"You will pardon, me gentlemen", he said with a smile, turning to Lindsy and me, "but I never drop my disguise when on duty, and had not the Captain arrested Miss Sallie Soot, a poor lone woman on the road, I would have changed my costume before reporting to the General, but he guarded me so carefully there was no chance to escape. This is the first time the General ever saw me in disguise."

There was a merry, devilish little twinkle in his eyes as he spoke. I could say nothing, but I heard Lindsy mutter, "Well I'll be damned". The boy picked up the old carpet sack, touched a secret spring and part of the bottom opened. Taking out some folded papers he gave them to the General.

"There are the drawings of the fortifications around Helena, General", he said handing him the papers. "I was a day longer than I expected making them, and tried to get out yesterday, but they have put out a double guard around the place, and I could not get through. Sir if you will furnish me a blanket to throw around me, I will go to my tent, change my costume, return and explain them to you.

"It is not safe to let anyone know your disguises, Colonel", he said to Lindsy when he was handing him the blanket, Lindsy had asked what on earth Walker wanted with it. Gathering it close around him and inviting me to go with him, we left the tent.

"You infernal little rascal", I said when we were past the sentinel, "I don't know which tempts me most - to break your jaw or hug you."

"Now if it was Miss Sallie you could decide at once, couldn't you?" The scamp was shaking with suppressed laughter.

"There it is again -- I've been looking upon you as a paragon of virtues and free from the vices of boys of your age; now I find that you chew tobacco like a teamster." With his mouth smothered in the folds of the blanket he struggled to hold a straight face. As soon as he could speak, he said, "Now, Captain, you chew a little yourself. Let's compromise by you taking a chew of mine, and you may keep it if you wish."

He handed me a little round stick that in the dark I thought was a small twist of tobacco, but biting it I found to be licorice.

"Look here, Walker, if you don't stop making a monkey of me with your shams, I'll cut your acquaintance and betray you to the enemy the first chance I have", I said as I threw the stuff away.

"Then I'm done. I might take a chance about the betrayal, but not in losing your acquaintance and I hope friendship. But really, Captain, isn't it a fine advertisement for tobacco when used by a Miss Sallie?"

"Please go and see what Mater is going to give us for supper while I change my costume", he said entering his tent and dropping the flap behind him.

In a few minutes he joined me divested of all signs of his disguise.

"How do you do it?" I asked.

"Oh, I have a solution that will remove the simple and harmless little stains I use almost as quick as water."

But where do you get them?"

"I make some myself of barks, berries, and leaves, but mostly depend upon ready made colors. That little mahogany box you saw has material in it that in skillful hands can make a boy of twenty look like a man of forty."

"Or a boy of eighteen like a Miss Sallie Scoot of thirty-five. I wonder if Mater knew who you were when we rode up tonight?"

"Of course, he did. He helped me make up my face, and it was all the old fellow could do to suppress his surprise and amusement when he saw the situation."

We had but a limited time to talk, as the scout had to go to the General and explain the drawing he had made of the fortifications we were to attack the next day. I told Walker of my experience with Carrier, and that I learned from one of the prisoners that he was Colonel of the 80th Missouri Cavalry. It was the same regiment in which his friend Teague of Duval's Bluff was a major.

"An unfortunate disaster, but not as great as will befall us tomorrow if we attack Helena. We can and will catch Carrier again, but we cannot recall the lives of the gallant men we will lose in a fruitless offensive. There is no possible doubt in my mind about the surrender of Vicksburg, but if we take Helena, we cannot hold it any longer than it will take the Federal gunboats to come up and shell us out. One is already lying out in the river opposite the town ready to give valuable assistance to their army. Goodnight and I hope you will come through safe tomorrow."

Squeezing my hand he entered the General's tent.

CHAPTER XVI

THE LITTLE SCOUT'S LAST FIGHT.

General Holmes had not changed his mind, he could not, for his orders from Richmond were imperative, and while Grant's victorious army was marching into Vicksburg, the signal rocket went up from Holmes' headquarters ordering the assault on the enemy's works at Helena.

Our cavalry were on the left of our line, Walker's brigade on the extreme left, Shelby next, and Marmaduke next. There was little to do in front of Walker. Consequently he did little; had it been Forrest he would have swept down the river until he found something to do, but this was a fight according to West Point rules, and Walker was content to keep his alignment with Shelby, who with his old "Iron Brigade" struck the enemy with his usual vigor and drove them over the ridge down into the valley. Marmaduke had advanced with Shelby, but struck fortifications that drove him back. He re-formed and charged again, but again failed to carry the works. Shelby continued his drive, but having broken loose from Marmaduke his right was in the air. Seeing this and having repulsed Marmaduke's last charge, the enemy turned their guns and began an infilade fire of artillery on Shelby that necessitated his withdrawal, which he did with a shattered arm, tears in his eyes and curses on his lips.

But the most difficult work of the day was assigned to Price. It was a fortified position, decidedly the strongest on the enemy's line, known as Graveyard Hill. He was ordered to take it and most gallantly did the brave Missourians obey. With wild cheers and reckless courage they rushed at the works in the face of withering showers of grape and cannister that cut great gaps in their lines, but that could not stop them until they planted their battle flags over the captured, but dearly won, position. However they, like Shelby, were soon forced to withdraw for lack of support. This marked the ending of the farce.

The unnecessary and unfortunate battle of Helena had been fought and lost because of the ignorance of Western affairs at Richmond and some inability on the field.

Shortly after noon Holme's beaten army was on its way back to Little Rock with the cavalry covering its rear. Soon after, the old General asked to be relieved and Price was given command. It was like "swapping the devil for the witch" so far as benefitting the Western army was concerned, for while Price was a brave soldier, a good brigade commander, he did not have the ability to command a corps, certainly not a Department.

Federal troops at Helena and Duval's Bluff, strongly reinforced by recruits from Grant's army soon began to move on Little Rock, their splendid cavalry out in front. They were supplied with light batteries of field artillery, in which we were very deficient, and as much of the fighting was on open ground, they used them most effectively. It was understood the decisive battle would be fought at Little Rock as the place had been well fortified, having big siege guns mounted, and all that the engineers' skill for the past two years could do to make the place impregnable. Our infantry were concentrated there under Price so we fell back leisurely, avoiding any general engagement until we reached Bayou Metre about eight miles out, where we made a stand to test the strength of their cavalry.

Not since we parted at General Holmes' tent the night before the battle of Helena had I seen the little scout, until the enemy had crossed White River on their way to Little Rock, but now he was with me almost daily. His "brigade" was in camp with us on the Bayou close to my troop. The little fellow seemed to be in his element. With his long range gun and his fleet horses, he was a thorn in the side of the enemy, and not a day passed that one or more of their officers did not go back to the hospital with a broken shoulder, or some straggler in the rear, cut off from his command, who rushed at the muzzle of the boy's pistol into our lines.

The element of danger attending his daring ventures counted as nothing compared to the pleasurable excitement it gave him. In this way he had tested the speed of nearly every fast horse in the enemy's cavalry. Sometimes when too closely pressed, he would cripple the prisoner or shoot his horse, then waving his hat to his pursuers, dash away at a speed that made them stop with amazement.

We went into bivouac on the shady banks of the bayou, and next morning made such disposition necessary to resist the attack which we knew would soon come, and by noon had formed our line of battle. In our front, an open prairie with its undulating swells extended as far as we could see. The regiment was sent out in front of our line to get first sight of the enemy and see where they would strike us. I rode out a short distance in front of the regiment and was scanning the prairie to the right where our scouts had reported the enemy's advance, when the Colonel rode up.

"See anything of them" he asked.

"No sir, not a sign, but we will have a short wait, judging from the report of our scouts."

"If it had been little Walker who made the report, I'd have more confidence in it. By the way, where is the boy. I've not seen him today". Adjusting his glasses, he looked over the vast plain of waving grass.

"Not a living soul in sight, the Colonel said, but I thought I saw a dark object disappear, just as I caught sight of it on that far rise directly in front of us. Turn your glass in that direction, it will come in view on the next swell and see what you can make of it."

I had scarcely fixed my glasses oh the place indicated when two dark spots came in view. They were nearly two miles away, but I had no trouble in recognizing the little scout on his sorrel gelding driving a Yankee trooper at full speed directly towards us.

"Well, what is it?"

"Little Walker with another Yankee prisoner."

"The little rascal! He'll be caught or killed some day in his dare-devil ventures and the army will lose the most valuable individual member in it. Lord, how he is making the Yankee ride!" he said with a laugh as he turned his glasses to take another look for the enemy, but instantly exclaimed, "By heaven, the yankees are going to cut him off, and will either catch or kill him! Captain, look to the right!"

A mile or more to our right a regiment of Federal cavalry, protected by a swell of the prairie from our view up to this time, were marching on a line that would cross the scout's path. They evidently saw him about the time we did, for a troop broke from the regiment and started at full speed to intercept him. I saw that if the boy did not deviate from the straight line he was coming on it would be a close call if he got by.

"For God's sake, Colonel, don't let us see him caught without lifting a hand to help him. Let me take my troop and make a dash at 'm, it will draw their attention from the boy."

The old man shook his head sorrowfully, for he loved the boy as did every man in the army.

"It's against orders. We must wait for them to attack, besides the boy seems to have lost his head. Why don't he shoot the Yankee and take to the open prairie, they couldn't catch him unless they had wings."

"Lost his head! Did you see that?"

Word had passed down the line about the scout, and the entire regiment was watching the race, which could now be distinctly seen without glasses.

My exclamation was caused by the tactics of the little scout. He evidently had just noticed the troop racing to cut him off for pulling up his horse, he let his prisoner pass him, then came up on the opposite side of him thus placing the Yankee between him and his pursuit thus protecting himself from their fire. The men saw and understood the move for they gave a loud ringing cheer. To me it meant the lad intended to come straight to us and bring his prisoner with him at all costs. The race was desperately uncertain and time was precious.

"Can I take my troop and simply make a demonstration? It will save him, Colonel."

The old man shook his head, he was afraid to trust his voice.

"Then, sir, please accept my resignation. I'm going alone." Wheeling my horse facing my troop, I called to them, "All who would save little Walker, follow me." In an instant every man was in his saddle. "Forward! Form fours! Trot! Gallop!", were the quick commands obeyed almost before they were given, and we went at full speed towards the gallant fellow. The scout won the race by a narrow margin, and not a shot was fired at him for he kept himself covered by the body of his prisoner, who did not stop his flight until he ran into the arms of our regiment a half mile behind us. But it was a different scout who wheeled his chestnut gelding by my side. His face was pale, but not with fear, for in his big blue eyes there was a deadly gleam I had never seen before.

"It is Carrier, Captain, Carrier! Now's your chance, forward!" he shouted.

I had accomplished my purpose, and knew I should return to the command, but the boy's wild enthusiasm was infections and the mention of Carrier's name stimulated me like a bee sting.

"There is the murderer of Corporal Jones, let's get him, men", I said pointing to the Federal troop.

"Lead on, we follow", they shouted, and the next moment we were on them.

A cavalry fight, when hand to hand, is quick, short and bloody, but the brain and every nerve and muscle in a man's body is drawn to the highest tension while it lasts. We received the fire from their carbines and delivered ours from our shotguns so close it cut an opening, and the impetus of our charge carried us far into their lines. Then it was pistol against saber. The little scout was by my side, the blood gushing from his horse's neck.

In the bloody fight that surged around me there was nothing to think of except to kill or be killed, but through it all the desire to meet Carrier possessed me, and twice, when for an instant my look for him wandered from my own safety, the little scout saved my head from a saber by an accurate shot. An officer not twenty feet in front of me, who with powerful sweeps of his saber, was hewing his way through our lines. He caught sight of me just as I leveled my pistol and he jerked his horse's head up as I pressed the trigger. The ball must have entered the animal's brain, for he fell crushing his rider beneath him. As he fell, Carrier filled the vacant space, but before I could make a move, the scout's sorrel leaped a length in front of me and I heard the boy say "at last" as he fired.

It was no broken shoulder shot this time, for Carrier fell backward as if struck in the face, his saber flying over his head; but as the boy fired a big trooper was whirling a saber above his own head. The little fellow instinctively threw up his arm for protection. I saw the fire flash along the barrel of his pistol as the steel blade struck it but it did not stop the cruel stroke that came down on his head. The pistol fell from his nerveless grasp, and with arms outstretched, he fell over the head of his dying horse, almost on the body of the officer pinned beneath his horse. I shoved my pistol against the body of the trooper and fired, but it was too late to save my friend.

We were completely enveloped. Carrier had brought up his entire regiment and it was twenty to one against us now. We must get away or surrender. Calling to the men to stick together, we made for the thinnest part of their line and finally succeeded in getting through, leaving some dead, wounded and prisoners in their hands.

"You've played Hell", said the old colonel as I rode up with my battered troop, and his wrath was not modified when I told him of the little scout's death.

"Go back and report yourself under arrest for disobedience of orders."

"But, Colonel, I've resigned."

"Not by a damned sight, sir. Who accepted your resignation? Go back, but keep out of General Price's sight until this blows over."

I followed his order and rode to where little Walker had his tent. Everything was ready to move at a moment's notice. The little burro stood half asleep under his load, the black gelding was saddled and old Mater was sitting in the sun nearby. When I told him of his master's death, he was in the saddle instantly, and simply asking which way, darted to the front. He rushed through the army's lines without halting for a challenge, and the last the men saw of him and his horse, the man and his burro looked like a black streak across the prairie.

Price had concentrated his army at Little Rock. The situation was very serious, and required the ability of a general far superior to Price, who was undecided whether to run or fight. He chose the wisest course and ran, for excepting Shelby's brigade, his army had lost all cohesion. Discipline was slack, bickerings and quarrels between minor officers were taken up by the generals, resulting in a duel between Marmaduke and Walker, in which the latter was mortally wounded, and died in a few days. With Walker dead, Marmaduke under arrest, and Shelby still unfit for duty from his Helena wound, the command devolved upon our colonel who, while a gallant and efficient colonel, was as little capable of commanding a division as Price was an army.

We held the Federals for two days at the Bayou, then withdrew and crossed the river below town to meet their cavalry crossing below us. Fortunately, next morning as the fight opened, Shelby galloped onto the field with his broken arm in a sling and took command. We put up a sharp little fight to give Price a good running start, after he had destroyed such property he thought would be of service to the enemy, and as we went out Steel's cavalry came in. Again the duty of covering the rear of our retreating army devolved upon us.

And thus fell our strongest fortified position in the West north of the Red River, without firing a gun, except the little fight below town. The battle was doomed from the beginning. Not for lack of skills in fighting, for no braver or better soldiers ever stood under the battle flags of any nation than those furnished by Missouri, Arkansas and Texas. It was the vacillating policy of the generals and politicians in dealing with General Price before his state seceded. He was dealing with the United States, and at the same time with our officials at Richmond through his political emissaries, until the United States was ready to strike. They they drove Lyon and his disorganized militia out of the state. The second blunder at Richmond followed quickly when they sent Van Dorn out to take command of our Western army. Whatever his ability might have been, he failed to show any in planning or execution at the battle of Pea Ridge. It was his first fight with us, and the first battle lost by the Western army up to that time.

The enemy did not immediately follow us with much force beyond Little Rock, and it gave us time to look over our depleted condition. Our men were scattered from Helena to Little Rock on expired furloughs, from sickness, wounds, and desertion. It was decided to send small squads back into the enemy's lines and bring out as many soldiers as would come. The work was to be done quietly and with no fighting. Being familiar with the country, I was sent back east of White River, but before getting there, I rode into an ambush of Federal cavalry who were out hunting our bushwhackers. They gave me the pleasing assurance after my capture that only the sight of my uniform as a Confederate officer kept them from shooting me without challenge. They had with them a number of citizens arrested as "suspects" of disloyalty to the United States giving assistance to the Confederate soldiers. I knew their suspicions were perfectly correct, but of course did not recognize them. The scouting party continued their search for bushwhackers, but the prisoners were escorted back to Little Rock under guard by an old gray-head sergeant. I rode by his side, the other prisoners following under guard. "You've seen quite a lot of service, sergeant", I said.

"What makes you think so?" "Well your gray head and beard for one thing, but mostly your firm seat in the saddle; for a man of your age, it shows you are no stranger to it."

"You are right, Captain. I served all through the Mexican War under both Generals Taylor and Scott."

"I had a kinsman who served the same way, only he began fighting under Houston, and made his first reputation as a soldier at San Jacinto. You may have heard of him, General Ben McCulloch?"

"What! Do you men Ben McCulloch of the Texas Rangers? Major Ben, as we called him in the old army?"

"The same. He was a general in our army and was killed at Pea Ridge. I was a member of his staff at that time."

The old fellow was regarding me with a look of pleasant surprise and interest in his Irish blue-gray eyes.

"I know, I know, and it brought sorrow to me heart when I heard it." "Were you there?" "Yes, but we were on our left. It was our regiment that broke up your charge on the battery." "Then you belong to the 80th Missouri, Carrier's regiment?" "Not Carrier's regiment anymore, sir. He was killed a month ago in a little fight near Bayou Metre." "I saw the hand that fired the shot." "Was it your hand, sir?" he asked looking at me sharply and adding quickly, "I bear no malice and not a man in the regiment does against the man who fired the shot."

"No, not mine, but the hand of the best pistol shot in the world and the best and bravest little scout in the Confederate army. He was killed the next instant by a saber stroke from one of your men. I would have given my life to have saved him."

The old sergeant was leaning forward looking eagerly in my face as I spoke. "You love him much", he said when I finished. "As if he had been my own brother." "Then it's joy I give ye, Captain, when I tell you the lad's not dead but, barrin' an ugly cut on his scalp, is as well as you are this minnit, and much better cared for."

For a moment I was speechless with surprise, then I caught his arm. "Don't trifle with me, sergeant. I saw this boy cut out of his saddle and fall over the head of his horse. Are you sure we are speaking of the same boy?"

"I don't know who you are speaking of, Captain, but I'm talking about the little scout who saved the lives of our Major's mother and father from bushwhackers the time the dirty villains made this mark on me", he said pointing to a scar on his cheek.

"It is the same boy, sergeant, unquestionably, but tell me about it. How did it happen?" It appeared to please him as much as to talk about the little scout as it did me to listen, and he started to tell about his experience, but as I had heard the story from the scout, I asked him to tell me what happened to the boy after falling into their hands.

"You see, sir, it was this way. The Major was riding in front with a troop, because he despised the colonel as all of us did, and never associated with him except on duty. You see, sir, he was not our choice. The government sent him to us after the regiment was formed. He had the reputation of being a good fighter, but he was not with us a month before the Major began to shun him and the men to despise him. His brutal treatment of the men frequently brought on hot words from the Major and he said to me not long since. "Uncle Tim, I would exchange into another regiment if it was not for the men". Timothy Sullivan is my name, sir, and the Major calls me Uncle Tim when not on duty and I call him Tommie. You see, sir, his father and I were chums when we were little, though he was a rich man's son and my father was poor, but we growed up friends, and when I come back from Mexico, he was a lawyer, owned a big building, and made me the janitor. Tommie was just six years old and the little rascal took to me like a young duck to water. His father used to say to me, "Tim, if that kid ever comes to any good, it won't be lack of spoiling on your part", and so it is, sir, you see --"

"Yes, I understand, sergeant", I said interrupting him, for fear the old fellwo would wander in his reminiscent mood from what I wished to learn about the scout. "But you started to tell me about the little scout and what became of him. You said the Major was in front with a troop."

"So he was, sir, so he was, and the regiment was following half a mile or more behind when we heard the firing and started for it. And a beautiful little fight you were making when we came up. The boys tell me they had their hands full, but when we struck you with the rest of the regiment, it was all over. I saw the Colonel fall, and as soon as I had time, looked around for Major Tommie. I found him lying under his dead horse.

" 'I'm afraid my thigh is broken, Uncle Tim', he said as I knelt down by him. "But look at that hand there.'
"The lad had fallen on his face with outstretched arms and one of his hands was within a foot of the Major's face. There was a ring with a big red jewel on one of his fingers.

"That's the ring my mother gave the little scout who saved her life. Don't let the men trample on him. We must give him a decent burial." the Major said.

"I looked at the boy and at once recognized the buckskin uniform.

Telling the men who had gathered around to lift the horse off the Major, I turned to straighten out the lad's body. He was lying on his face, showing a bloody saber cut on the back of his head, but, the blessed Virgin be praised, I found it was only a scalp wound made by a glancing blow that didn't reach the skull. When I told the men who it was, and that he was not dead, they were almost as glad as myself, for it had been a campfire story of how the scout had saved our lives from the bushwhackers. The men moved the horse, and spread a couple of blankets on the ground. They made the Major as comfortable as possible as I finished binding up the boy's head.

" 'Spread a blanket here, some of you, by me. Lay him here, Sergeant, until the ambulance comes and put him in with me, said the Major. As I did so I heard screaming, curses and laughing on the outside, the next moment an old negro came squirming and dodging through the men who tried to stop him.

He threw himself down by the boy, crying or praying, we couldn't tell which, for all we could understand were the words, 'my little Marster, my baby, my child', and kissing him all the time.

"I had laid the boy on his side to keep from hurting his wound, and when the old servant lifted his head and put one of the lad's arms around his neck, I started to take him away, but the Major told me to let him stay. He gave his handkerchief to the servant and told him to bind it around his master's head. He said that it was nothing but a scalp wound, that he was going to take him to the hospital wit him, and his master would soon be well. The old man could not speak out language, but he certainly could understand for he bowed his head to the ground and kissed the sleeve of the Major's coat.

"When the boy opened his eyes a few moments later the first thing he saw was the black face close to his; he gave a bewildered look, then put his arm and fingers around the black neck.

"Tell him he is in the hands of friends", said the Major. "I am Major Teague. I recognized my mother's ring, so I know who he is and will take good care of him."

"The old man delivered his message, putting his mouth close to his master's ear. They spoke a few words to each other in the old man's lingo, then the lad spoke for the first time, feebly but distinctly.

"I thank you, Major. I hope your parents are well. Where are they now?"

"Both well and still at the Post, where we are going as soon as the ambulances arrive."

" 'Here they come now sir', I said, 'two of them', and following his orders, I put the lad and his servant in one with the Major and started back. I saw a group of cavalry streaking over the prairie, trying to catch a black horse that was unbridled and had an empty saddle on his back. I recognized it as the one our scout was riding on the day we had our fight with the bushwhackers. I call the Major's attention to the chase and told him they might as well try to catch the wind and he had better shoot him.

"The old servant watched the chase, and from time to time said something to his master. As I finished speaking to the Major, there was a little groan from the boy, the first sign of pain that had escaped his lips. In a quivering tone he said, "Oh, please don't have him shot, sir. If you will stop the men from chasing him, I can make him follow us to the Post and you can have him yourself, for I saw one of our troopers kill yours."

"It was the pathetic appeal in the boy's tone, I'm sure, not a desire to get the horse back, that made the Major say to me sharply, 'Stop the men'. They were some distance away, the black horse standing watching them. The scout's servant slipped out of the rear of the ambulance and blew a dog whistle. The horse threw up his head and galloped up to the old man, rubbed his nose on him, and you may believe it or not, sir, trotted like a dog behind the ambulance all the way. About five miles out we met the Major's father and mother; a courier had been sent in with a report of the fight, and as soon as they heard it, secured an ambulance, and came to meet us. After satisfying themselves that their son was as comfortable as possible the Major said,

"There, there, mother, I'm alright. A broken thigh is not half as bad as a broken head. There is some one who needs your sympathy and attention more than I", motioning to the lad.

"She saw at a glance who it was and dropped on her knees, slipping her arm under his neck as the old servant moved aside."

The sergeant rode in silence for a time, and I grew impatient.

"Well, what became of the boy?" I asked.

"I've never married, Captain, and don't know much about such things, but was just thinking what a wonderful thing a woman' sympathy must be. When Mrs. Teague dropped down by the side of the lad and slipped her arm under his neck, he just naturally put his arm up around her neck and drew her face down to his and there they were so long that the old Judge says, 'Don't be so distressed, wife, son tells me it's only a scalp wound and the little fellow will soon be well.'

"Yes, but a very bad one', she says getting up, and I am going to take him and his servant back in my ambulance. You and Tim can ride with Tommie. Now Husband, she said placing her hand on the Judge's sleeve, 'I want you to do me a favor, I want you to see the commander of the Post, explain to him what this boy did for us and get him to let me take the lad to our boarding house and nurse him myself. I know it is out of line, but you must get his consent. You and I and Tommie and Time will be responsible for him. Won't we, son?'

" 'I, indeed we will, mother', said the Major."

"And so it was, Sir. We put the lad and his servant in the ambulance with the madam and moved on, but they were nearly an hour behind us in reaching the hospital.

"When the orderly reported their arrival, the General, who had come down to see the Major, told him to have the ambulance carry the boy wherever Mrs. Teague directed. I went out and bid the little fellow goodbye, and that's the last I saw of him, for I had to rejoin my regiment the next day. Fortunately one of our men who was in the hospital at the time, reported for duty about a month ago, and told me that Mrs. Teague had gone home taking the boy, servant, and his horse with her. The quartermaster had pronounced the horse too small for our services, so the Judge had bought him from the government for his wife. We also learned that the Major was up on crutches and expected to leave in a few days for home on furlough until he was fit for service.

"But here we are, sir, at the guard house and it's sorry I am that I have to turn you over as a prisoner."

"Don't mention it, sergeant. Knowing my friend is alive and well, cared for, and the kindness you showed him telling me of his safety, more than compensate for being captured. It's a risk every soldier must take. If you have a chance, tell the scout I'm alright, and tell the Major I am the man responsible for his broken thigh, but I thank God I killed the horse instead of him", I gave the sergeant, a warm handshake and turned to the officer of the guard to let him know I was ready to follow him.

I was kept in prison a few days at Little Rock, then I was sent to St. Louis and confined in McDowell's old medical college building that had been converted into a prison for Confederate soldiers. I found several hundred prisoners there, some had been confined more than a year. We were quartered in two large rooms on the ground floor separated by a hall in which there was a stairway leading to rooms above. A door from each of our prison rooms opened into this hall and a guard stood just outside the door. There were none of the horrors of prison life at that time, especially in St. Louis, as I experienced later in Rock Island, Illinois.

I was allowed to keep the blankets I had on my saddle when captured, and in looking around for a bedfellow, found a young man from my state with the same name and same initials, only his was M.B. Hord and mine B.M. We traced up a distant relationship, became warm friends, and soon began to discuss the ever present thought in our minds of how to escape.

Separated from our prison room by a thick wall was a school room, or chapel. We decided to pick a hole through this wall some night and make our escape. I heard footsteps frequently at night, after the prisoners were asleep and everything quiet in the room above us. It was near midnight, Howard and I were lying in our bunk discussing in whispers our plans to escape, intending to make it on the following night, when I called his attention to the footsteps above, and suggested it might be an extra guard put on at night, as I never heard them in the day.

"That's because of the noise, for I imagine he walks day and night, poor devil."

"Who is he?"

If you were not a fresh arrival, you would know. That's our 'Prisoner of Chillon', the men call him, but who he is, where he came from, whether Federal or Confederate, General or private, no one knows. I've been here eight months, and he was here when I came and the men here before told me he was here when they came. He evidently is in solitary confinement, as no one ever sees him except the guard who carries up his rations and water once every morning. I am certain he has on chains, for occasionally I've heard the clink of the irons as they strike in his walking. Now you know as much about him as any of us, turn over and go to sleep, for you'll need to be fresh tomorrow night."

I turned over and pretended to sleep, it was only pretense. For the first time since I heard it, Carrier's fiendish and improbable lie concerning Nick came to memory, and it was hours before I dozed off into a restless sleep with dreams of Nick, the scout, and a life and death struggle with Carrier, from which I was aroused by a sound punch from my companion asking what in the devil I meant by trying to choke him.

The following night we were half way through the wall when we were detected by the guard, and before sunset my companion and I were on our way to Rock Island Prison.

It was a new prison, the barracks built of green, upright boards that had shrunk leaving large cracks between, affording but slight protection against zero degree weather that came on that winter. Had it not been for the bountiful supply of coal furnished us many of the poorly clad prisoners would have frozen. But to counterbalance the plentiful coal was the scanty food given us. The more coal we burned the greater the profit to the contractor who furnished it, and the less rations given us the greater the profit to the post quartermaster who first took his share out of the supplies the Government had issued to us.

Smallpox broke out soon after our arrival, and no provision having been made to care for the patients, it spread so rapidly that there were twenty-nine deaths in one day out of a total of four thousand prisoners. An unused barrack in the prison enclosure of ten acres was finally set apart as a hospital until they could build one. My bunk mate, Howard, caught the dreadful disease, was removed to the hospital barrack, and died two days later.

After fourteen months in prison, I was exchanged at the mouth of the Red River late in February, '65, and reported to General Kirby

Smith for duty at Shreveport, Louisiana as I was unable to reach my own command, far up in Arkansas near the end of the struggle. I was assigned to General Tappan's brigade for duty, surrendered with him in May, and returned to my home in Tennessee.

x x x x

It was late in June before I reached home. I came up the back way from the little railroad station, whre Uncle Andy was the first to greet me. He was sorrowfully eyeing the wretched conditions of an old gray mare and equally poor roan horse, both branded "U.S." and "I.C.", which signified they once belonged to the United States army and later had been condemned unfit for service. I was some distance away when he looked up and saw me.

"Mr. Ben! Mr. Ben! Bless d' Lord, it's him." And with outstretched arms he came running to meet me.

"How is my father and all the folks, Uncle Andy?" I asked after our embrace.

"Old Marster is powerfully bad off, Mars Ben, and all d' young servants is gone. D' ole house is marked up scanderlous and so is d' plantation. After d' big fight 'round Murfreesboro, General Rosencranz's folks used d' big house fer er hospital. Every floor in d' house is kivered wid spots uv blood 'n dey cut off arms 'n legs and flung ' in d' cistern whar ole Marster wus diggin' and kivered 'm up wid dirt, so d' negros tells me when I got home. But lord, lord, Mars Ben, we wus havin' er time uv it ourselves then in Arkansas, wusn't we?

The old man and I exchanged news of what we had experienced since we were separated. He pointed to a large hole in the west wall of the "big house". A solid twenty-four pound shot had landed in one of the rooms on the second story where my young sister had stored cotton that she and Cary our coachman, had picked to sell for provisions.

"That was done by our folks. Two Yankee cannon was on d' front pavement shootin' at our folks' cannon over on Mr. Anderson's place 'n when d' ball went through d' wall Miss Alice feared it might set her cotton on fire and run into d' room grabbed up d' ball and flung it outen d' front window whar d' Yankee guns shootin' 'n one uv d' Yankees look up at her 'n said 'bully fer d' gal', and Miss Alice she made er mouth at him 'n run down stairs to her Pa."

It was many years after the war that I learned from a Captain Chaleron of New Orleans, at that time commanding a battery of the Washington Artillery, that it was one of his guns that fired the shot when trying to get the range of the two Federal guns in action on the pavement not thirty feet from the door.

x x x x

The brutal days of "reconstruction" quickly followed the surrender. The Confederate soldier was disfranchised, and the social and political destiny of the South partly placed in the hands of her former slaves.

Rarely in the history of the Americas has there been such a vile and vicious attempt to prostrate and humiliate a proud, intelligent people. The Confederate soldier had won the respect of the nation for his courage and endurance in fighting overwhelming odds for the past four years, but the true heroism of the man was shown in these dark days. He was not allowed to vote; consequently many public offices were filled by a villainous set of scoundrels that followed the Federal army in as ever carried a carpet bag or pillaged a house. It was under guidance from these rascals that the former slaves were cajoled into passing laws that absolutely deprived the Confederate soldier of the little remnant of his property, and he was obliged to stand by helpless.

CHAPTER XVII

I AM ENTERTAINED
BY MY OLD ANTAGONIST.

Ten years had passed since the close of the war and the South was coming into its own again.

Bellemeade, the famous breeding establishment for thoroughbred race horses, near Nashville, Tennessee, was the mecca of all turfmen when the annual sales of its yearling colts took place. The cream of the offerings were usually bought by wealthy eastern sportsmen, for as yet the southern racing clubs had little money to gratify their love for the sport.

"I notice you have a new buyer General, I said to the beloved proprietor, General W.G. Harding, at the close of a successful sale.

"Yes, a good one, and if I am not mistaken an experienced judge of pedigree as he is of a horse. Did you notice he bought two of the best colts and the best filly in the catalog?"

"I certainly did, and I also noticed William Johnson's look of astonishment when the auctioneer knocked them off to the Texas man. I wonder who he is and if he intends raising them or start a breeding farm in Texas?"

"Billy was certainly astonished", said the General, "Yes, Billy was certainly surprised. It is the first time anyone ever stopped him in buying what he wanted. I would like to know what the Texan intends

doing with them. Suppose you go and ask him. "I will, what's his name",
I asked.

"I didn't catch it from the auctioneer, but Cheatham will introduce
you."

The stranger was standing with his back to me as I walked up. I
approached General Cheatham, and as he said "Captain, let me --", the
stranger turned. No further in introduction was necessary. I would have
known the black eyes of Nick Hardeman if they had been dimmed
by death. For an instant we gazed in speechless amazement at each
other, then without a word we embraced, stronger and warmer with
age. He had arrived that morning and came directly to the sale. Nick
was comfortably housed under my own roof that night, for I had been
living in Nashville since the end of the war.

"Alright Nick, fire away and give an account of yourself. You should
speak first", I said as we seated ourselves in my den after supper.

"You tell me first, why you didn't answer my letters? I wrote you twice
soon after I returned home. One letter came back marked 'uncalled for'
and I never heard anything from the other. Both were addressed to you
at Murfreesboro."

"So that's the reason, I said. I've not lived there since the war."

"Then why in blazes didn't you write to me?"

"Because I saw you struck down at Pea Ridge."

"Better if I had been, Freshie, much better", he said sadly, "and I will
tell you why."

The he repeated the horrible story of his captivity almost word for
word as Carrier told me the day I captured him, which I had thought

was an impossible lie, told simply to enrage me to shoot him instead of hanging him.

"When Carrier ceased to visit me, I suspected that he had been killed. Aside from this thought it brought me no comfort. My conditions and surroundings were unchanged. He had laid his plans well to have me die in prison in irons. There were other prisoners in the building. I could hear them in the room below me, but had no way to communicate with them, or the world outside. For there were only two openings in my small room, the door, and a window in the rear well, grated with heavy iron bars. A solid brick wall of the building, not two feet from the window, shut out all sunshine and shed but little light."

"You were confined in McDowell's Medical College in St. Louis, Nick!", I explained as I recalled the tramp, and clanking fetters of the prisoner I had heard above me in prison. "How did you know, Ben? I told him of my short stay in that jail before being sent to Rock Island. I had slept in the room just beneath, and at night could hear him walking and the rattle of his fetters.

"I knew I was in St. Louis, but that was all, for I saw no one but the guard who came very morning to push my rations and canteen of water through an opening in the door. They evidently had been instructed not to talk to me. They were Germans mostly; sometimes I would speak courteously to them in their language, but they would place a finger on their lips and leave me. I could not bribe them, for Carrier had relieved me of everything I had when he put me in prison."

"Well, to make a long story short, one morning soon after the guard had brought my rations, the wicket to the door opened and much to my surprise a voice called out. Well, Harris what are you in here for? I told him my name was not Harris and that I had no idea why I was in there except by order of Colonel Carrier. He unlocked the door and walked in. I must have presented a pitiable sight, emaciated, hair and beard of three years growth, tattered clothes and heavy fetters. After listening to my story, which I concluded by begging him to take me to the Post commander, he ordered one of the men with him to remove my irons, and rode with me to headquarters, where I repeated my story to the General and his staff. They listened with astonishment, and as I concluded the old gentleman got up and walked across the room a time or two, and I heard him mutter the damned scoundrel, the damned brute. Then turning to me said, 'I knew Carrier well, served on the border with him before the war. He was thoroughly capable of doing just what you say. But it will take some days to straighten this matter out, red tape from the Department of Washington, but right now I think you need a bath, a shave, and a hair cut. I suggested, all of which required some money. Said a member of the staff behind me,"Winston is my name, Major Hardeman, Captain Winston of the staff. We have made up a little purse of Fifty Dollars which we beg you to accept to supply your immediate wants." "Fifty Dollars! Just think, my boy, what it meant to a man who had suffered as I had for three years, and when the General said. "You have conspired against your superior officer, young gentleman, and are subject to court-martial. I propose to add Twenty-five dollars to that purse myself."

"That unnerved me completely. I was weaker than I thought. I placed my hand on the corner of the table to steady my legs as I rose to thank them and paused a moment to steady my voice, and -- Freshy, tears rolled out of my eyes and fell on the table.

"There, there, Major, don't try to say it, we all know how you feel, said the General placing his hand on my shoulder after I gulped a few times while trying to speak. These young gentlemen will look after your comfort. You will be our guest until we hear from Washington, and I'll ask you to say nothing about this matter, as it will do no good to have it made public."

"Two of the staff rode with me down to a barber-shop with Turkish bath attached. They had anticipated my wants, for after the attendant had finished bathing me, he brought in fresh new clothing.

"At the mess table that night it was my time to listen, for I knew literally nothing of what had happened. They told me the Confederate armies had surrendered in May, it was now September, that all prisoners had been paroled and sent home months past, and that General Grant was in command. I expressed my pleasure at learning of Grant's appointment, as I had heard my father speak of him as a friend in the Mexican war.

"Then you are in luck, Major, for I considered that your case demanded immediate attention, so I wired General Grant giving your name, and an outline of the case, and asked for orders."

"Next morning when at breakfast a messenger came in and gave the General a dispatch. He read it, smiled, and passed it over to me, remarking as he did so that I was again in luck. The message only said:

"Send the prisoner to me. Furnish first-class transportation, U.S. Grant, General."

"I left St. Louis that night and next day presented myself at General Grant's headquarters in Washington, and sent in my name. I was soon admitted. He listened without speaking a word as I told my story, and ordered me paroled immediately remarking at the time, if he ever caught the fellow Carrier had substituted for me, he would hang him. He ordered first-class transportation furnished me to New Orleans, and four hours later I was going as fast as an express train could carry me."

"Of course you wired Miss Catherine?"

"No, I did not. I didn't know either the physical or mental condition of the poor child, and the shock might do her harm, so I wired Mr. Walker, our banker, that I was on my way home and would he please inform Catherine as he thought best."

Nick smoked a moment in silence, then placing his hand on mine continued: "I've told you of suffering and torture that would break a man's courage. Now I'll tell you something that will break his heart. When I walked into Mr. Walker's office, although expecting me, the old man turned white as a sheet, but the next instant had me folded in his arms.

"Where is Catherine? How is she?" I asked soon as I could catch my breath.

"He closed and locked the door and then asked me to sit down, taking a seat himself and looking at me without speaking. His action and silence foreboded sorrow and chilled my heart.

"Where is she?" I whispered, not dead? Surely not dead?"

"Oh, no, he said, but she is in Europe."

Though greatly relieved, I was disappointed at not being able to see her, and upon asking when had he heard from her, and when she expected to return, he told me that when the news of my death and that of Colonel DeJean reached her the shock seemed to daze her. For weeks she went about pale as a ghost, tearless and apparently only half-conscious.

At last tears came to her relief, and in a few weeks she recovered and began to take such interest in her father's and Colonel DeJean's affairs as to astonish Walker. She began by asking him to read and explain both wills to her. She had him consult a lawyer and let her know for certain if she was the rightful heir to father's, Uncle's, and my estates, and being assured she was, took legal steps to have it confirmed. Then she made him her trustee. At the same time, she asked him to give her an inventory of the property. Mr. Walker said she amazed him by how quickly she adapted, and at the industry she applied to learning the details of the business.

"Then she and her old nurse, who followed her like a shadow, went up to the ranches, and Tommie Gibson, the superintendant, reported that she was more like herself since her father's death. She had taken up riding and shooting again, and showed strong interest in the affairs of the two ranches.

Some days she would ride fifty miles with him visiting different herds of cattle and horses, or enquiring about the tenants and crops, until the old man was almost ready to fall out of his saddle, while she appeared as fresh as when they started. She had him make an inventory of everything on the two ranches, then returned to New Orleans.

The very next morning, she stepped into Mr. Walker's private office at the bank, gave him the inventory, and told him she was starting for Europe the next day on the English steamship *Prince Albert*.

She said she would be gone an indefinite time, asked him to manage her affairs as he would his own, and to give her letters of identification to his Liverpool cotton brokers. These would authorize her to dispose of the cotton they held. At the same time she handed him a sealed envelope labeled "Not to be opened until two years after the war closes", signed, Catherine Hardeman.

"You can imagine the old gentleman's astonishment, Freshy", said Nick smiling, "when the little Kitten asked for the letter with power to dispose of the cotton in Liverpool at that time, was worth seventy-five cents a pound and rapidly advancing in price.

" 'But, Miss Catherine, that's big sum of money for a young lady in a foreign country', protested the old banker. But she said: "Yes, a good bit. Mr. Walker, nearly a million and a half at present prices. I may use it or I may not, but I'll thank you for the letter."

"I cannot help but smile when I think of the old gentleman's expression when he was telling me this. "Why, Nick, my son, he said, I know it was out of all business sense and judgment to put such a sum of money in a young girl's hands with no one by to advise her, but what could I do? There she stood, only a little strip of a girl, but she had that determined glint in her big blue eyes your father had when nothing could stop him."

"Well she got the letters, sailed the following day, and reached Liverpool safely. She sold the cotton, placed the proceeds amounting to $1,480,000 to her credit in the Bank of England. This much we learned from the brokers and that is the last we have ever heard of her.

"Of course I opened the sealed letter. It was her will disposing of her estates in event of her death, or if she did not return within two years after the war closed. Including my father's, Colonel DeJean's and my own estate, it amounted to something over two million dollars, all of which she went to charity except two hundred thousand dollars in bank stock, which she gave outright to their old partner, Mr. Walker.

Nick continued "As soon as I recovered sufficient strength, I went to London to begin my search for her. Now you would think it an easy task to locate a young lady passably good-looking with a million and a half dollars in the bank and followed about by an old negro maid. I thought so, but I could not trace her a foot beyond the doors of the bank. The most remarkable thing is that she had drawn out the entire amount within ninety days after her deposit on checks payable to herself in gold. I scoured Europe for six months, but could not get even a trace of her and returned home heartsick. The next year I went again and spent nearly a year, visited every city in Europe and came home this time convinced I would never see her again.

It would be some comfort if I only knew she was dead, but when I think what a horrible fate may be hers, robbed of her money and in the hands of villainous men, it nearly drives me crazy. "When did she leave for Europe, Nick?" "The 15th of June, 1862." "You mean '63." "No, '62"

"You are simply mistaken in the year, Nick, for I had a letter from her the latter part of May or first of June, 1863, dated at the Ranch."

"What!" he exclaimed. "A letter from her in June, '63? But you are mistaken in the date yourself."

"Now listen to me and I'll convince you I'm not, for the man who brought the letter told me he was your father's coachman and had lived with him many years.

Then I filled him in on my own experience at Pea Ridge, and how it happened afterwards that I remained in the Western army including my capture of Carrier, our conversation concerning Nick, (which I thought was a lie) my acquaintance and friendship with the little scout, his fight with the bushwhackers, his capture a few days later of the old man with the letter from Miss Catherine, and seeing the scout kill Carrier later, in the fight on the prairie.

"Describe the man that brought you the letter and what was his name?" Nick asked after listening to my story. I did not remember the name, but I did the old man's appearance. "Your description is right, but your dates are all wrong." he said, after I finished. "Now let me prove it to you.

Five or six months after my sister left for Europe, Uncle Jo, born and raised in our family had been my father's servant in the Mexican War and afterwards was his coachman. We all loved and trusted him. But he stole two of the best horses on the ranch one night and ran off to the Yankees, and we've never heard of the old rascal since. Mind you now, this was five or six months after Catherine sailed for Europe, consequently it would have been impossible for her to have sent a letter by him, for old Jo's desertion caused more astonishment at the ranch than Catherine's departure to Europe."

"Yet, Nick, I will swear to getting the letter. I do not remember the exact date, but know it was only five or six weeks before the battle of Helena, and that was fought on the 4th of July, '63."

We smoked in silence for a few moments. There evidently was some mystery about this letter, and each of us were trying to reconcile the dates with the events.

"Do you know Catherine's writing?" Nick asked me.

I told him I did not, and after another pause he said,

"Freshie, that letter was a forgery."

"Then it was by some one quite familiar with our past, for she spoke of the last letter you wrote her the evening before the Pea Ridge fight, and that you did not mention my arrival out West, and she only found it out from an old paper giving an account of the part my troop took in the Cotton Plant affair; otherwise she would have written sooner. She wrote that she thought Carrier was in the Western Federal army. You remember, Nick, you told me the same thing that night we slept together before the battle, and she hoped if I met him I would deal with him as deserved, and it was a lady's handwriting."

"Nevertheless it was a forgery. Old Jo could have furnished sufficient information for any one to write such a letter, but for the life of me I can't see the purpose of anyone writing it."

"Except your sister."

"Oh, that's out of the question. She never wrote it. It might have been Carrier setting some trap for you, but then old Jo would never have gone to him for he hated him worse than he did the Devil and was mortally afraid of him."

"But Carrier did not know I was living then. It was some weeks after I received the letter that I caught him, but we'll sleep on the matter tonight and talk it over tomorrow. Are you going to spend a week with me, right?"

"Wish I could, but must leave tomorrow night for New Orleans. But if you'll invite me, I'll not be years in accepting it as you've been laggardly in accepting the one I gave you the morning I left Chapel Hill", he said, slapping my shoulder as we passed into his room.

The next night we parted at the depot with the assurance that he would be back next year to attend the annual sale of Bellmeade. Business called me to St. Louis the same night, and while Nick was speeding towards New Orleans another train was carrying me in the opposite direction.

I finished my business the following day in St. Louis, and was returning to my hotel when a magnificient pair of closely matched horses hitched to a light carriage waiting in front of an office building, attracted my attention.

"A handsome team, and I venture to say a good driver", I remarked to the coachman. "Whose are they?"

"Colonel Teague's, sir", he replied, smiling, evidently pleased with my compliment.

"Is this his building?" I asked, noticing "The Teague building" cut in the marble slab over the main entrance.

"Yes sir and his office is on the fourth floor."

Teague -- the name was unusual, but yet it had a familiar sound to me. The next instant the little scout, the bushwhackers and the Major with the broken thigh flashed in my memory. It might be possible. Anyway, I would take a chance. The elevator boy put me out on the fourth floor, and a grizzly bearded, gray-headed old man with "Janitor" in gilt letters on his cap, and a slight Irish brogue, directed me to the Colonel's office. "Come in" was the response to my knock, and the moment I entered I knew I had found the right man. Handsome, broad shouldered he stood leaning on a cane, a light top coat thrown across his left arm, with a silk hat in his hand.

"It is after business hours and I was just starting home."

"I beg you will pardon me for detaining you a moment, but I am satisfied we are in a way old acquaintances, yet I haven't seen you since you were Major of the 80th Missouri Cavalry."

He was at once interested.

"Take a seat, sir, but I cannot recall your name just now - it has been so long."

"I am afraid if I tell you, Colonel, you might be tempted to use your cane on me as I am the man that made it a necessity for you, but I'll chance it. Hord is my name. I was a Captain in the Confederate army."

He caught my extended hand with a bewildered look on his face as he asked, "Not Captain Ben McCulloch Hord of the First Arkansas Cavalry?"

"The very same, Colonel."

"Why, man, the records show you died of smallpox in Rock Island Prison."

"It was my kinsman and bunkmate, M.B. Hord, who died of smallpox. There were so many dying at that time, I suppose they got the initials of our names mixed."

He clasped my hand now and shook it heartily.

"Well, well, well, Captain, I certainly am glad to see you. When we heard of your capture, we made every effort to reach you."

"Not to hang me, I hope, Colonel", I said, smiling and pointing to his stick.

"No indeed, but to supply you with every comfort the government would allow a prisoner. We traced you form Little Rock to this city and from here to Rock Island, where we were informed of your death."

"It is not too late yet to thank you sincerely for your kind intentions, Colonel. When you say we, I suppose it was you and the little scout! I thought he had been killed until I was informed by the sergeant who escorted me to prison. He told me of your and your mother's kindness to the boy, for which you have my sincerest thanks, for I loved the lad as tenderly as if he had been my brother, and there never was a braver soldier or more perfect thoroughbred gentleman in any army." I was speaking very earnestly, and he was looking at me the same way.

"You were very fond of him, I dare say and so he was of you, for I've heard him speak of you often."

"Do you know what became of him, Colonel? Is he still living?"

"Oh, yes he is living and sound as a mint dollar."

"Where?"

"Near the city."

"All the saints be praised! I intended going home tonight, but I'll stay a month to see the lad."

"Certainly you will, and be our guest, between us I think we can interest you. To start with, you could take dinner with me tomorrow eveing. After that we will hunt up the scout."

"No denial", he said as I hesitated. "Remember you owe me some compenstation for this broken thigh, and I'm going to demand it this way."

"Tell Mr. Sullivan I want to see him", he said to the boy who answered the tap of his bell.

"I want to see if Uncle Tim will remember you, for when he and the scout get together you are sure to come up sooner or later for discussion."

There was a knock on the door and the janitor I had seen in the hall stood at "attention" in the door.

"Come in, Uncle Tim, I want to see if you remember this gentleman. He's one of your heroes, you ought to."

The old fellow looked me over carefully.

"I've seen him somewhere I'm sure, sir, but can't place him this minute."

"I have a better reason to remember Sergeant Tim Sullivan than he has me" I said smiling at the perplexed look on his face.

"Thin it must have been in the old days, sir, when ye knew me as Sergeant Tim Sullivan?"

"Yes, some years past, Sergeant. But don't you remember you carried a kinsman of General Ben McCulloch to prison. Captain --" Hord by the blessed Virgin! 'exclaimed the old man catching both of my hands. "And is it yeself or your ghost, for it's these tin years or more since ye've been dead.

"The scout, the little scout, Tim", interrupted the Colonel. "Won't he be glad to see the Captain?"

"Certainly sir, the little scout", continued the old sergeant hesitating a moment. Won't he fairly shout? You'll be stopping some time with us, I hope?

"A day or two, sergeant, I must see the lad before I go."

The Colonel insisted on taking me in his carriage to my hotel.

"Tomorrow afternoon at 4:00 sharp", he said as he set me down at my hotel."

The next evening, I was waiting in the lobby when a footman came in and handed a card to the clerk at the desk, who directed him to me.

"The Colonel is waiting for you, sir", he said touching his hat.

"Like an old soldier, Captain, punctual to the minute!"

"Like two old soldiers", I said glancing at my watch.

He was seated in a high English dog-cart holding the lines over a handsome tandem team, a large gray in the shafts and a seal brown, something lighter, in the lead. How would you like to take a look at the place where your prison, McDowell's old medical college, stood?" We swung around the corner into Gratiot Street, and in a few moments stopped in front of a handsome block of businesses.

"This is the spot. It has changed some since you saw it."

"It has indeed, but I will carry the memory of the old building with me as long as I live. It was only there three weeks, but the best friend I have in the world suffered the tortures of hell there in solitary confinement and in irons for more than three years, for he was not released until months after the war ended."

"Tell me about it", he asked with much interest. I own that block of buildings, and when I was having the old college torn down, some ex-Confederate soldier who had been confined there, but now living here, started some kind of ghost story about a solitary prisoner in irons dying in there. What do you know about it?"

"A great deal sadly enough, and will tell you some time, but if I'm not mistaken that's your team and carriage coming."

"So it is. Stop a moment, Uncle Jo", he said, lifting his hand to the old coachman as he drove up.

The carriage stopped within a few feet of the cart and a sweet, bright, smiling face of a woman looked over the door.

"My dear, this is Captain Hord, I spoke of to you, our guest for dinner", said the Colonel introducing me.

"I am very, very glad to see you, Captain."

It was a soft, low, almost tremulous voice, but one that impressed you with sincerity and truth in every word.

"Thank you, madam. It gives me an opportunity to thank you for the kindness your husband tells me you have shown my friend, Walker."

"Oh, you mean the little Confederate scout? Yes, I've often heard him speak of you. He and my husband tried very hard to find you in prison in order to lighten the hardships of prison life as much as possible for you."

"It was exceedingly kind, especially in your husband after we had tried to kill him and succeeded in breaking his leg, for which hope you hear no malice."

"On the contrary, she said, "I'm rather glad of it, as I could catch him more easily. You know a cripple cannot run from danger, matrimonial or otherwise, as quickly as one not afflicted", she said giving the Colonel a loving glance out of her soft gray eyes.

"He certainly would not have tried to escape from you, madam, I'm sure."

"Now you have it at last, Madam. Hord, she has been fishing for a compliment since she first stuck her pretty face over the door.

She laughed happily, admonished us not to be late for dinner, and dropped back into her seat. "Mrs. Teague is a Southern lady, is she not, Colonel?" I asked as we resumed our drive. "Yes, and as much a little rebel as ever you or your scout were" he answered, "Don't class me with the Yankees' he said laughing, "I'm much Southern as either of you. My mother was born and reared in Virginia, my father in North Carolina, and I'm a 'Tar Heel', by birthright. My parents moved to this state when I was only five years old."

We were now driving through a wealthy suburban part of the city, judging from the handsome residences.

We soon turned into one of them, and followed a broad driveway that wound through the beautiful grounds and stopped in front of a colonial dwelling with its wide porches and massive pillars.

"What a beautiful place, Colonel."

"Father built it soon after we moved here, but it's mother's design. It is almost a duplicate of her old girlhood home in Virginia."

Mrs. Teague was waiting for us on the porch and extended both hands to me as I came up the steps, saying as I caught them, "Welcome, doubly welcome to our home."

"I told your husband after meeting you this evening, I knew you to be a Southerner, your cordial hospitality convinces me." "And what did he say?" "Oh, he admitted you were most readily, and immediately claimed he was a Southerner himself, by birth. "I might also say he called you a little rebel." "Did he? He dare not do that to my face", she said as she tiptoed to meet his kiss.

"I might substitute tyrant for rebel, Captain, for I feel compelled to kiss her whenever I see her." The reply brought a blush, a laugh and little slap on his cheek from her, a hearty laugh from him and a stupid grin from me, as we passed into the hall.

"You are certainly in the house of your friends, Captain. There are two more little rebels", he said as a little five-year old girl with outstretched arms came running to meet him, followed by a handsome boy of ten or twelve. "Captain Howard, let me introduce my mother."

She was a handsome old lady, sixty years of age, with culture and refinement marked in every feature of her face to the slender shapely hand she extended.

"Now you are acquainted with all of the garrison Captain" said my host.

"When we rose from dinner, the colonel said if the ladies would excuse us, we would adjourn to the smoking room.

"I go with you", said his wife, "I'm not going to risk you two old soldiers fighting your battles over again without having someone to separate you if you come to blows. Shall I have your coffee served in there?" "Not for me, thank you", I answered. "You are not as fond of coffee as you once were, are you?"

"Yes indeed, why do you think I'm not?"

"Because I heard your scout say that you once offered his old servant five dollars for a cup of genuine Yankee coffee."

"I don't remember the circumstance, but if the scout said I did, I did."

"You had great confidence in the lad?" asked Mrs. Teague. "I did indeed, madam, second only to my friendship and admiration for him."

The room the Colonel had led us into was an ideal smoking and lounging room, not large but furnished with every luxury required.

"We have heard the scout tell some interesting stories of his adventures, but as you know he is a modest little chap, I dare say you can tell us of some he did not mention", said the Colonel.

"It is a subject I love to dwell on, Colonel, and if I get a little tiresome, you and Mrs. Teague must bring me down.' I began my first experience with the scout in the Cotton Plant fight up to the time I saw him fall, as I thought, by the fatal saber stroke in combat on the prairie. I did not fail in my praise of the lad, his courage, his intelligence and nobility of character.

"Your friendship for him must have been very strong."

"It was and is, Madam, for your husband tells me he is yet living, and

- 310 -

I am only waiting to see him before I return home".

She rose from her chair as I finished. I heard a rustling noise behind me, and a tremulous voice ask,

"How will this do?"

I stood up and looked around. The shade had been run up and instead of the French window there was a full length portrait of the little scout standing in his picturesque costume, one arm hanging by his side, the other resting on the bowed neck of his black gelding. The likeness was so strikingly lifelike that I involuntarily extended my hands towards it.

"What do you think of it"? asked the Colonel. "I am astonished."

"Perfect, absolutely perfect, even to the ring on his finger that your mother gave him."

"Was it like this?" asked his wife placing one hand on my sleeve and lifting the other before me.

"It was exactly. I've never see two finer stones.

"And do you recognize this?" Her voice was almost inaudible, her face pale and tears trickling down her cheeks. I saw she was making a brave effort to suppress her emotions as she held a little Spanish stiletto before me.

"Certainly, I do. It belonged to the little scout," I said.

"Both ring and stiletto are mine -- were mine - I - I - I'm your little scout. I am Catherine Hardeman, the sister of your dear dead friend, Nick Hardeman", she sobbed, burying her face in her hands resting on my arm.

Her husband sprang forward and caught her as she was sinking to the floor and placed her on a lounge. I started to ring the bell for assistance.

"Don't do that" he said, She will be all right in a few moments. She has been in such a state of nervous excitement between joy and fear since I told her you were alive; joy to know you were living, but fearful that you would condemn her for what she did.

I was so dumbfounded, I could only stand and stare stupidly from one to the other. Thoughts of the little scout, the death of Carrier, Nick's lost sister, and neither knew the other was alive, raced through my befuddled brain for a moment before I could realize the situation. My first impulse was to tell her Nick was alive, but he had told me himself he was afraid to write the startling news to her. She certainly could not stand the shock joyful as it might be. No, I must first tell her husband and let him break the glad news to her.

"It's all over", said the Colonel as she opened her eyes.

"What does he say?"

Her blue eyes full of tears looked at me. Her husband was kneeling by the side of the lounge with one of her arms around his neck. I caught her hand and told her I thought she was the bravest, noblest and most heroic woman I ever heard of, and worthy to be the sister of such a man as Nick Hardeman. She pressed my hand and gave me a look of unspeakable gratitude.

"Now I am happy. my husband approved of my conduct long ago, and now the best friend of my dear brother does the same."

"But, Madam, I hoped I was going to stay to see the little scout. Well, I've seen him, but I'm not going home until I give him a fair chance to explain some of his experiences in the army; not tonight, but maybe tomorrow at your convenience."

"Then bring him early, husband, and we'll make a day of it. Can you come before lunch, Captain, and husband can join us later."

"I would be happy to do that, and Colonel, would you be willing to ride back to town with me. Your coachman knows the way and I'm selfish enough to need your company."

CHAPTER XVIII.

ALL'S WELL THAT ENDS WELL.

"Your wife is the most remarkable woman I've ever known or heard of Colonel. Of course you know her story." "I do, all of it from the time she was born, up to this minute", said Teague. "I've known of her only since her brother and I met at college. "But she knew who you were when you were scouting together", he said, laughing. "Knew me!" I exclaimed, you must be mistaken, Colonel."

"I have her word for it, and can tell you excactly when she first discovered who you were. Do you remember the night you went down to her tent to get some coffee, saw the little stiletto and said a college friend of yours at Chapel Hill owned one exactly like it?"

"Yes, I remember that the scout fainted; I thought, from fatigue."

"It was not fatigue. It was the sudden shock of joy discovering that you were her brother's friend, for the dagger was his, and the dread of your disapproval of what she was doing caused her to conceal her identity from you just as it did tonight, but she was determined to kill Carrier, and nothing on earth could deter her unless someone else killed him, or she was killed."

"But, Colonel, I had a letter from her no more than a week after this incident, brought by her father's coachman and dated at the Ranch nearly a month before, and I know the scout was in the army with us at that time. How do you explain that?" He was silent a moment before he spoke: "Ben, she thinks you are the closest friend she has on earth, outside of my immediate family, for you know how her father and sister were murdered by Carrier. If you care to hear it, I will tell you her story after she left her home in Texas to search for him. Before she agreed to marry me, she had me investigate her family. You doubtless know her history up to the time of her brother's death," Teague said.

Then related the same story Nick had told up to the time he had lost track of her after she had drawn her gold bank of London. He continued.

"When she drew her money out of the bank she carried it to Paris and deposited it inthe Bank of France in the name of Catherine Walker."

I saw at once why Nick could not trace her beyond the doors of the London Bank.

"She remained in Paris until all of her arrangements were completed, then she had her tent made to her own design. She bought her specially designed rifle; and had the bank insure the delivery of her gold to its agent in New York; under the name of "Catherine Walker." Then she sailed home in the same vessel. Assured her gold was safe and subject to her order, she came directly to St. Louis, where her only friend in the world lived in whom she could confide, Judge Rodgers, who was a wise and wealthy man.

"He had lived in New Orleans many years before moving to St. Louis, and knew her father well. She described her preparations and what she intended to do asking him to protect her under her assumed

- 315 -

name, Catherine Walker. The judge tried in vain to dissuade her, but promised to help her any way he could.

St. Louis was quite a gay place in those days, Teague said. My father and Judge Rodgers were warm friends, but differed entirely in politics. Father was a staunch and uncompromising Union man, and the Judge was intensely Southern. Both kept open house where the upper crust of the city met, regardless of politics, to wine, dine and dance.

At one of these balls I met a Southern girl just returned from abroad. She was as so entirely different from the average society girl I at once became interested. She was so self poised, so intelligent and well informed on any subject that came up for discussion that I was undecided whether she had been educated to be a college professor or a lady-in-waiting for some court in Europe. I could not say I thought her pretty, but she had the most wonderfully beautiful blue eyes I ever saw.

"My leave of absence expired a week later, and when I called to bid her good-bye, the maid who answered the bell told me Miss Walker had left the city. She did not know when she would be back, but supposed soon, as she did not take her trunks.

"A month later our regiment was ordered to St. Louis on garrison duty. I lost no time in calling to see if Miss Walker had returned. She had, and I was flattered by her most cordial reception. I was delightfully entertained, and when I rose to leave she walked out on the front porch with me.

" 'Oh, what a beautiful horse you have, Major!" she exclaimed, as her eyes rested on my chestnut gelding hitched just outside the front gate.

I'm going to have a look at him if you'll permit. I do love a good horse', she said smiling sweetly up at me.

"Nothing could have pleased me more unless she had said she loved the owner, so taking her hand I assisted her down the steps. We were looking over the gate at the gelding when a lanky old negro in a battered silk hat and blue Federal pants, came lounging up the street, apparently without seeing us, he stopped and with evident delight and admiration began to look at the animal and mutter to himself.

" 'You shorely is a beauty n' not a blemish on you, honey 'cept jest er little splint on de fore leg what any man wid any' horse sense could rub off in er week.'

"He had not yet seen us. Miss Walker put her finger on her lips, looked up at me and smiled and shook her head for silence. After walking around the horse a time or two he looked up, pulled off his hat, and asked if it was my horse. He said it was the best one he had seen since he left "Virginy. He suggested that I ought to have the splint removed, etc. It happened that I needed a servant and was only waiting to find one who knew a lot about horses. I mentioned the fact to Miss Walker as we were walking to the gate. " 'Why not hire him if you need a groom? He seems to know all about horses," she said.

"The suggestion was most timely, so after asking him a few questions, I gave him my card. I wrote on it an order to the guard to pass him, told him where to find the regiment, and reluctantly bade Miss Catherine good-by. "The old man reported for duty next morning, and has been with me ever since. Now, can you guess who the old man was, Captain?" Teague asked. "I really can't," I replied.

"He was her father's old coachman and husband of her nurse who went to Europe with her. She disguised as a man, like her mistress, had gone with her through her scouting days and is with us now. Uncle Jo drives my wife's carriage every day, but I was ignorant of all this, until she told me just before we were married."

"But how did the old man get there and happen to be at the right place at the right time?"

He laughed before he replied.

"The smoothest put-up job you ever heard of. You see I had mentioned incidentally during our conversations that Carrier was our Colonel, never dreaming she had ever heard of him. In order to carry out her plans she wanted a friend upon whom she could risk her life inside of our lines, and two good horses. She knew she could find both at her old home on the Ranch. She and her nurse left St. Louis by boat and made a secret trip to the Ranch. They succeeded in seeing Uncle Jo without any one else knowing they were on the ranch. She had him bring her two good horses the following night to a designated place.

Two weeks later, she landed here with her two servants and two horses. She kept these in Judge Rodgers' stable. She thoroughly coached old Jo as to what she wanted him to do. She had her trap set, and was just waiting on a opportunity to spring it, when I gave her the opportunity within a week after she returned to St. Louis. Jo was evidently watching for me, and when I came out with his mistress he began examining the horse. Of course, it was a put-up job between them and I bit like a sucker.

x x x x

"You know of her adventures after that! General Price was advancing into Missouri in command of the Confederate army. Our regiment was sent out to meet him. I did not see her again until I was sent home to recuperate from that broken thigh you gave me." "I still deeply regret that injury Colonel." "I don't see how she concealed her sex from your mother."

"She didn't try. When I called mother's attention to the wounded lad in the ambulance as the boy who had saved her life, she dropped down by his side to console him. She put an arm around mother's neck, drew her ear to her lips, and told my mother that she was a girl. She begged her to take her in her ambulance, which she did; then told mother everything, and when they reached the post she had her carried directly to the house where she and father were boarding. She and a nurse waited on her exclusively, mother accounting for her interest in a wounded Confederate soldier by saying he was the one who had saved her life.

Of course, mother told father, but did not breathe a word to me or anyone else. Father succeeded in getting Walker paroled a few days later, and in a week, mother, the scout, his servant, and the black horse left by boat for St. Louis.

Mother had wired home to have a room prepared for a young lady friend of hers who had met with an accident.. Wearing one of mother's dresses, and in the crowd and confusion when the boat landed, they passed through followed by her maid in a wrap mother had prepared for the occasion. The carriage was ready, and the invalid young lady was soon resting under the same roof that shelters her tonight.

"Father remained with me at the post until I was able to be moved and brought me home on furlough and a promotion to the rank of Colonel. He at once began investigating Miss Hardeman's statement and found it was correct in every particular. Not until this was thoroughly established through his friend, Jude Rodgers, and other sources in New Orleans, was I informed who was the invalid girl that mother had brought home. To this day, since father and Judge Rodgers are both dead, there are only six people in the world who know that the elegant, wealthy Mrs. Teague was once the famous Confederate scout."

"And who are they, Colonel?"

"Mother, the two servants, Jo and his wife, the union sergeant (Tim Sullivan) you, and me. Tim was the only one that discovered who she was without being told."

"When and how did that happen? Surely not when we were in the army?"

"Not when she was, but you and I were still battling away at each other. When I had recovered sufficiently for duty, I took command of the regiment. Tim got quite an ugly chest wound in a little fight down in Arkansas. I sent him home and wrote mother to please look after his comfort. Catherine insisted on going to the hospital with her. Tim gave her a bewildered stare as she bent over him and pulled the cover down to see where he was wounded. She made the bandages more comfortable, he watching her intently, and when she passed her hand a time or two over his forehead he half rose from the cot exclaiming, 'be the holy saints, I've felt that touch before. She put her hand over his mouth, smiled and told him to keep quiet. She would tell him all when he got well. Today, next to the 'Hold Virgin' I believe he loves my wife the best.

You can guess the rest, a wounded soldier, a charming, most fascinating young girl gowned in the best Paris could offer, could only end in marriage; especially as they had first admired and then loved each other before either would admit it even to themselves. Catherine told me, before she consented to be my wife, that she had given away a fortune, she said she had made her will and deposited it with her trustee, Mr. Walker, in New Orleans, and under no circumstances would she ever go back there. We were married here at home. Judge Rodgers gave the bride away and father gave us a $10,000 check as a bridal present, and the Judge gave me two little bank pass-books and an official looking envelope, which he said was a present from the bride to her husband. Now, what do you think they were, my friend?"

I told him I had not the slightest idea unless it was the purpose of having him deposit the $10,000 check to her credit.

"Not a bit of it. The check books showed that she had a million and a quarter dollars to her credit in New York banks, and the official envelope made me her trustee with full power to act for her. If a bomb shell exploded in our midst we could not have been more astonished, except the old Judge and my wife. He was chuckling, and she was looking at me with a smile on her lips and tears of happiness in her eyes.

"The good man died a few weeks later. My father died a few years afterwards. So you see, as I told you, the little scout's history is known to only six living people."

Wonderful, Colonel", I said as he concluded, "Now let me tell you one to match it in some ways. It's that ghost story you spoke of this morning in connection with the old prison on Gratio Street in St. Louis.

"Yes, I remember you promised to tell about a prisoner kept there in irons and solitary confinement."

Assuring him I knew the man and had seen him only a few days past, and that the story was true, I told him the hard story of Nick Hardeman's imprisonment from the time he was captured up to the time he was released. Occasionally, when telling of Carrier's most brutal treatment, he would express his horror and indignation.

"And now, Colonel, who do you think the prisoner was and who was the brutal officer was who held him captive?" I asked after I finished my story. I've no idea who the poor fellow was, but I will say this, if the officer is still living, I'll spend a fortune to have him brought to justice and cashiered if he is in the army.

Fortunately the prisoner is living, but his oppressor is dead. I saw the shot fired that killed him. It was fired by a steadier hand than yours or mine. It was the little scout who did it."

He was silent a moment, then the truth came to him. "Then it was Carrier! For she told me you were by her side when she fired the shot. I gathered the villain was capable of any kind of cruelty, but this is almost beyond belief. It was a miraculous escape for your friend. Such treatment is apt to wreck a man physically and mentally. You wont take offense, Captain, if I say as an old soldier, that if your friend needs any financial assistance it would be great pleasure for me to render it, simply to show him that the men of my old regiment are not of Carrier's stripe, besides we owe it to him."

"I can take the liberty of thanking you, Colonel, in his name, for he is the best friend I have, but he's worth a million or more, has everything on earth he wants except one, and he's going to get that within the next few weeks, for Catherine Hardeman Teague is his lost sister and his name is Nick Hardeman."

"My God, man! Do you know what you are saying? Can it true?"
"Every word of it, and if you will drive me by the office, I will send him a wire that could bring him here by tomorrow night. I don't want him to know I've found his sister until he gets here, and in the meantime you can gradually break the news to Catherine. I came very near telling her tonight, but was afraid the shock would be too much for her."

It was only after the message had gone that Teague was thoroughly convinced of my story. When he dropped me at my hotel half an hour later, I told him to tell his wife the story of Nick's imprisonment just as I had told him, but to mention no names, neither the time nor place where my friend was wounded, and that possibly Nick might yet be living, as she had never heard from New Orleans since the war ended. Saying he would send the carriage for me next morning and would join us at lunch, he said good night.

Mrs. Teague and her two children were on the porch as I drove up.

"How old are you Walter?" I asked the boy after bidding them good morning.

"Walker, if you please sir, my name is Walker after my uncle, who was a Major in your army and was killed at the battle of Pea Ridge. Mother has told us what a brave soldier he was."

"I'm going to be a soldier like my father and uncle, for father is going to send me to West Point soon as I am big enough."

"Now you children go and play with the dogs, the Captain and I are going to have a chat to ourselves, said their mother. Finding a comfortable bench on the lawn, we were soon going over our soldier days. She was a fine mimic and was laughing heartily over some of my army expressions.

"But you had the advantage of me. You knew who I was, and I only knew you as a reckless daredevil scout."

"Not until the night you recognized the little stiletto. I often wondered what use you thought I had for such a trifle of a weapon, but I wore it to save me from hanging if caught as a spy or worse, if captured and my sex was discovered; in either case I would have killed myself.

"But what about that story my husband told me last evening?" Catherine asked. Did it really happen? It seems incredible."

"Not at all, and by no means unusual. I was right by his side when he fell and would almost have taken on oath he was dead, yet ten years later I meet him. Then take your own case. I saw the saber stroke I thought had split your head open, and here you are a happy wife and mother; or take my case, you and your husband felt sure I had died of

- 324 -

smallpox in prison and you had, as you thought, an official record of the fact, but I feel very much alive."

She did not speak for a moment, she was in a deep study, then looking up with a white face, she said,

"You saw my brother killed?"

"Indeed I did, or thought I did. I also saw you killed or thought I did, but if Nick hadn't been killed, you would have heard from him long ago through some of your friends in New Orleans."

She gave me a quick glance, then with averted looks, she told me why she left and never expected to return, just as her husband had told me the night before.

"And why should I return?" she asked as she concluded her story. "My happiness here is as complete as mortal woman's can be, my husband, my children, my home, and wealthy that is sometimes hard to that dispose of fairly to charity. You know my purpose in leaving home. The chances were a hundred to one that I would get killed myself, and I made my plans accordingly, by disposing of my estate. I hope and believe that beneficiaries are happy and love my memory. I do not have any kin to quarrel over the estate."

"May I ask how long it will be before lunch?" said her husband as he joined us. "I didn't know you had arrived. Let me go and see."

"Well, how are you progressing?" Teague asked when we were alone.

"Fairly well, I think. I have got her to the point of defending herself for hiding from the world, so in the event her brother was living he would not know where to find her. She didn't say so, but I could see she had caught the idea, and doubtless would soon ask her banker in New Orleans, but it will be too late. Read this!"

I handed him a telegram I had received that morning from Nick, saying he would leave on the first train for St. Louis.

"You can see that the despatch is dated ten o'clock last night. I've consulted a schedule, and the first train left at twelve. If he caught this, and I bet he did, it will put him here at eight o'clock this evening. I will bring him to your office at nine o'clock tomorrow."

"All right, I'll send the carriage for you. Meantime I'll encourage the idea you gave Catherine that her brother may be alive. But here she comes.

The Colonel and I were in the smoking room after lunch when Mrs. Teague entered followed by her two old servants.

"Here are two friends who wish to speak to you, Captain," she said smiling.

"Why Jo, I said, you deceitful rascal, I don't know that I ought to speak to you. You came spying into my camp pretending to have walked all the way from Texas to deliver a letter from your mistress."

"I did come from Texas, sir, but not all the way that day", said the old fellow grinning as we shook hands.

"And I wrote a letter to her in reply and gave it to you to deliver."

"She got it in ten minutes after your give it to me, sir." Jo was chuckling with laughter.

"How do I know she did?"

"I'll have to testify in Uncle Jo's behalf", said Catherine taking a bundle of old letters from a desk. Here is the letter, tied up with those my brother wrote after he left home, some from Chapel Hill, and he writes about a certain freshman who is his friend. These dear letters went with me to Europe in my trunk."

"Well it was the quickest mail delivery I ever heard of for nearly a thousand miles and I don't think I paid the postage, so I'll pay it now."

I offered him a bundle of dollars, he hesitated, looked at hi mistress. She nodded assent, and he thanked me with is eyes brimming.

"And this is Nan. Do you remember Nan?" she said as the old woman with her red turban curtsied. "No, I don't remember her." "Oh yes you do. She was with us, my servant. Remember you offered her five dollars once for a cup of genuine Yankee coffee."

"I remember a dried up old man you called "Mater", to whom I offered five dollars, but he could not possibly have been this good looking, middle-aged woman who looks as if she might be Uncle Jo's youngest daughter." That sparked a hearty laugh, adding a thousand more wrinkles to the old woman's face.

"Nan, this is a token of friendship in remembrance of our campaigning days, giving her a five dollar gold coin.

I watched them pass out of the room, and knew the little scout's hidden identity was as safe in the loyal hearts of these two servants as in her husband's or her own.

It was nearly eight o'clock when I returned to my hotel a few minutes after Nick entered. I had reserved rooms for us, and as soon as the door closed behind us, he said:

"Well, old boy, what is it? A fuss, fight, or finance, that caused such an urgent command? "Thought maybe you might borrow enough money to buy you a berth in a sleeper." "Happened to have money in my pocket. But what's the row?" "No row at all, neither fuss, fight, nor finance. Have you had supper? "No, I am hungry as a wolf. Let's go and get it." "I've already had mine." "The mischief you have. Why didn't you wait for me?"

"If you don't show me the way to the supper room inside three minutes, I'll turn you across one of these knees. Now move."

It was not until after supper that Nick again asked what I wanted with him.

"Now fire away, Freshie, tell me what you want and where I come in."

"Have you heard anything further from Catherine since I saw you last?""

"Not a word", he said shaking his head. "Why do you ask?"

"Because I have."

He jumped from his chair and caught my shoulder with a crushing grip.

"Are you sure? When? How? Where? He almost shouted.

"Please sit down just a moment, and I will tell you, and to remove any anxiety, first of all, if I was called on to name the happiest woman I know, with good reason, I would name your sister. She is the mother of two beautiful children, the wife of a gallant soldier and true gentleman, and their combined wealth exceeds yours, Nick!"

He stood speechless for a moment, then tears filled his eyes and throwing himself across the bed, his powerful body shaking like a child's with sobs and his big brave tender heart melting with tears of joy. Waiting until his emotions subsided, I gave him an account of his sister's adventures from the time he lost her in London up to the present. Then I told him that I had dined with her that very evening.

"Then let's go to her at once", he said, jumping to his feet and preparing to leave. I explained the situation, that she did not yet know he was living, why I had not told her, and that her husband would tell us in the morning how matters stood. "She is not sick or an invalid?" he asked anxiously. Neither. Sound as a mint dollar, I venture to say she can beat you right now either at riding or shooting. On the other hand, your folks have such a funny way of standing up and laughing in the face of death, but when great happiness comes you keel over like sick puppies. She wilted when she saw me. What do you suppose she will do when she sees you? To bed and sleep. You'll see her tomorrow."

"You blithering idiot! Do you expect me to sleep now when every night for the past ten years thoughts of her, living or dead, have been racing through my brain and pressing the sorest spot in my heart?" And I heard him mutter to himself as he entered his room, "The little Kitten, the blessed little Kitten."

A few minutes before nine o'clock next morning, Colonel Teague's carriage was announced. As we stepped out on the pavement I saw Nick give a quick glance at the turnout, then linger in admiration of the horses. They had just been groomed and their glossy hair was shining in the morning sun like satin. "My brother-in-law certainly has a good eye for a horse", he said as we drove away. "They are not his selection. He told me himself that they were his wife's, that she is the better judge of a horse." "The little Kitten! Still true to her instincts."

Nick, it was this team of horses that led to her discovery. I told him how the team had attracted my attention, so that I stopped and inquired from the driver whose they were. Also Teagues' name had sparked old memories, so out of curiosity, I had gone to his office to see if he was the same Teague I had met in the bushwhackers' assault and if so, make enquiries about the scout he had captured.

"The hand of Providence is in it all, Freshy", he said after a moment's silence.

"Just what your sister said when she saved the lives of her future husband's parents and showed me the ring that later saved her own."

As we stepped out of the carriage in front of the Teague Building, Nick remarked what a handsome place it was.

"Only a small wad of your sister's pin-money." I said laughing.

He gave a low whistle of surprise, then grasping my arm he asked earnestly if I thought Teague had married her for her money.

"Not on your life, Nick. In the first place, he is not that kind of man, and he is very wealthy himself. When he married her he did not think she had a dime except for the $10,000 check his father gave her as a bridal present, Here we are at his rooms, and you can judge him for yourself.

We were shown into his private office. He came forward with both hands stretched out to meet us. I introduced Nick, and with clasped hands they looked searchingly into each other's eyes. Each saw, and knew by instinct, they were looking into the eyes of a man they could esteem.

"You have added another to your list of former ghosts, Major", Teague said smiling.

"I hope I do not have a ghostly appearance, Colonel."

"Not more than the Captain there who, according to official reports, died of small pox in Rock Island Prison, and saw you killed at Pea Ridge. Again he saw our scout killed."

"I hope she is well this morning, Colonel, and if you will pardon me, I should like to see her as soon as it is convenient for you."

"Certainly", Teague said, I told her last night that you were alive and well. "How long would it take for a note to reach her?" "Half an hour perhaps.

"The may I write the note?", asked Nick. Taking a sheet of paper and scrawling on it, for his hand trembled so he could scarcely hold the pen. He wrote, "Sister, I will be with you soon, Nick." "I'll see she gets it" said their host, and he left the room to send it on its way.

Within an hour, their carriage drove up to the front of the Colonel's residence. "You will find her in there, Major", Teague said, pointing to the little room I remembered so well. "The Captain and I will join you, or you can join us whenever you wish."

Then I recognized the thoughtful delicacy of this man for screening the almost sacred happiness of these loving hearts from all eyes.

It was a happy party that met at lunch. The children were a bit shy with their new uncle, but Nick's namesake was soon his friend and admirer. And Nick could scarcely keep his hand off the boy.

"Mother", he said, "You say I'm named for Uncle Nick, then why don't you call me Nick?"

"Well said, my son, if your uncle doesn't object, Nick it shall be", replied his father, "but you must try and live up to it."

Nick gave the Colonel a grateful look and the lad, jumping down from his uncle's knee, hurried to inform the servants that they must hereafter call him Nick.

I left for home that night after we agreed to meet again soon at the Hardeman Ranch in Texas. Nick had satisfied Catherine that the story of her stay in Europe followed by her marriage, would account for her long absence, and that no one would ever know that Catherine Hardeman had avenged the murder of her father and sister, or that she was once a famous Confederate scout in the Western Army.

The End.